CLOCK WI'

GERALD KERSH was born in Te
1911. He left school and took on
and-chips cook, nightclub bouncer, freelance newspaper reporter – and at the same time was writing his first two novels. His career began inauspiciously with the release of his first novel, *Jews Without Jehovah*, published when Kersh was 23: the book was withdrawn after only 80 copies were sold when Kersh's relatives brought a libel suit against him and his publisher. He gained notice with his third novel, *Night and the City* (1938) and for the next thirty years published numerous novels and short story collections, including the comic masterpiece *Fowlers End* (1957), which some critics, including Harlan Ellison, believe to be his best.

Kersh fought in the Second World War as a member of the Coldstream Guards before being discharged in 1943 after having both his legs broken in a bombing raid. He traveled widely before moving to the United States and becoming an American citizen, because "the Welfare State and confiscatory taxation make it impossible to work [in Great Britain], if you're a writer."

Kersh was a larger than life figure, a big, heavy-set man with piercing black eyes and a fierce black beard, which led him to describe himself proudly as "villainous-looking." His obituary recounts some of his eccentricities, such as tearing telephone books in two, uncapping beer bottles with his fingernails, bending dimes with his teeth, and ordering strange meals, like "anchovies and figs doused in brandy" for breakfast. Kersh lived the last several years of his life in the mountain community of Cragsmoor, in New York, and died at age 57 in 1968 of cancer of the throat.

By Gerald Kersh

NOVELS

Jews Without Jehovah
Men Are So Ardent
Night and the City
The Nine Lives of Bill Nelson
They Die with Their Boots Clean
Brain and Ten Fingers
The Dead Look On
Faces in a Dusty Picture
The Weak and the Strong
An Ape, a Dog and a Serpent
Sergeant Nelson of the Guards
The Song of the Flea
The Thousand Deaths of Mr. Small
Prelude to a Certain Midnight
The Great Wash★
Fowlers End★
The Implacable Hunter
A Long Cool Day in Hell
The Angel and the Cuckoo
Brock

STORY COLLECTIONS

I Got References
The Horrible Dummy and Other Stories
Clean, Bright and Slightly Oiled
Neither Man nor Dog: Short Stories★
Sad Road to the Sea
Clock Without Hands★
The Brighton Monster and Other Stories
The Brazen Bull
Guttersnipe
Men Without Bones
On an Odd Note★
The Ugly Face of Love and Other Stories
More Than Once Upon a Time
The Hospitality of Miss Tolliver
Nightshade and Damnations★

★ Available from Valancourt Books

CLOCK WITHOUT HANDS

BY

GERALD KERSH

With a new introduction by
THOMAS PLUCK

VALANCOURT BOOKS

Dedication: For Helen Pacaud

Clock Without Hands by Gerald Kersh
First published London: Heinemann, 1949
First Valancourt Books edition 2015

Copyright © 1949 by Gerald Kersh
Introduction © 2015 by Thomas Pluck

Published by Valancourt Books, Richmond, Virginia
http://www.valancourtbooks.com

All rights reserved. In accordance with the U.S. Copyright Act of 1976, the copying, scanning, uploading, and/or electronic sharing of any part of this book without the permission of the publisher constitutes unlawful piracy and theft of the author's intellectual property. If you would like to use material from the book (other than for review purposes), prior written permission must be obtained by contacting the publisher.

All Valancourt Books publications are printed on acid free paper that meets all ANSI standards for archival quality paper.

ISBN 978-1-941147-56-6 (*trade paper*)
Also available as an electronic book.

Cover design by Lorenzo Princi/lorenzoprinci.com
Set in Dante MT 10.5/12.6

CONTENTS

INTRODUCTION
page vii

CLOCK WITHOUT HANDS
page 1

FLIGHT TO THE WORLD'S END
page 59

FAIRY GOLD
page 107

INTRODUCTION

Gerald Kersh has been nearly forgotten longer than most writers will ever be remembered, but his work endures, hardier than lichen, the only living thing that actually seems to extract nourishment from stone. Kersh was the kind of writer beloved by other writers, who are always amazed that the rest of the world hasn't caught onto him. With this reprint, that may change. You're reading this through the valiant efforts of Valancourt Books. I first read Kersh thanks to another persistent champion of his work, Harlan Ellison.

Harlan and I had a brief correspondence, back in the days before the Internet, when finding something as simple as the source of a quotation, or even what a Nash Rambler looked like, became an archaeological adventure worthy of Indiana Jones. Searching through libraries, requesting inter-library loans, digging through periodical catalogs, scanning *Bartlett's Familiar Quotations*, re-reading entire texts to find a reference, and yes, writing letters to famous writers, in the hope that they could answer your question and relieve you of the madness consuming you.

The quote was:

". . . there are men whom one hates until a certain moment when one sees, through a chink in their armour, the writhing of something nailed down and in torment."

It had been quoted by Harlan Ellison in one of his Kyben stories; I had found nearly all of his books, and scoured them to find the source, to no avail. So despite Mr. Ellison's pleas to fans not to write him and take time away from his writing, I rolled a sheet in the old typewriter and sent it off. You see, I wanted to collect some Kersh, and back then even the collection Harlan had edited, *Nightshade and Damnations*, had been out of print for over a decade.

As a student, collecting and finding rare old books was quite the luxury; there was no eBay or AbeBooks, with bargains to be had. Instead there were Book Finders, people who made a living or a side job hunting books for you, and charging fifty '80s-era bucks for the service. I couldn't spend my hard-earned ramen money on the wrong book, so I fired off a missive to one of my literary heroes, and got back a letter that has since taken on a life of its own and had its fifteen minutes of fame on the Internet, been enshrined in *Letters of Note* and shared on FlavorWire as "a great literary burn" or some such, when in actuality, Mr. Ellison had been kind enough to give me the answer that I'd sought and also take time to share his admiration for Gerald Kersh's unheralded talents.

The quote comes from the story "Busto is a Ghost, Too Mean to Give Us a Fright," which you can read in *Nightshade and Damnations*, which has thankfully been reprinted by Valancourt and collects some of Kersh's best stories. The quote showcases Kersh's innate humanity, his ability to paint a full-fleshed character's DNA, what makes them who they are, in just a few beautifully crafted words.

Nailed down, and in torment. Behind the angry mask lies a Prometheus, waiting for the carrion bird to take his liver. Those lines have haunted me ever since reading them, and bring a spark of empathy when dealing with people who lash out at everyone around them. It doesn't forgive all their trespasses, but it reminds me that they too, are human, despite all behavior to the contrary.

So I don't regret writing Harlan one bit; I still have the letter, and cherish it. My only regret is that his response sufficiently cowed me into not writing him again, to say thank you. I thanked him online, and after the letter was shared on *Letters of Note*, we had another brief correspondence, and he did remember it. That led to my being asked to write this introduction, and it's quite fitting that this book was chosen, as it contains another of Kersh's greatest characterizations, one where he captures the impossible, the face that fades into a crowd, the everyman who *is* the crowd:

> "He was something less than nondescript – he was blurred, without identity, like a smudged fingerprint. His suit was

of some dim shade between brown and grey. His shirt had grey-blue stripes, his tie was patterned with dots like confetti trodden into the dust, and his oddment of limp brownish moustache resembled a cigarette-butt, disintegrating shred by shred in a tea-saucer."

You'll read that again in the opening pages of *Clock Without Hands*, itself a master class in character, the dark needs of the human heart, the fickle nature of journalism and our own interest in the lives of others, bullies and murder trials, and so much more. Kersh can do more with a story than many can with a novel; with this novella, he does more than others do with a series (and with his masterpiece *Fowlers End*, he packs more humanity than many lauded writers have done in their entire life's work).

His economy of words, his rich but not florid prose, and always, his deep and empathic observation of human nature, have been a great influence to me and many writers before and after. Look into the blank face of a *Clock Without Hands*, and see for yourself. If he is new to you, I envy you the experience of reading Gerald Kersh for the first time.

THOMAS PLUCK
December 2014

THOMAS PLUCK is the author of the World War II action thriller *Blade of Dishonor*, *Steel Heart: 10 Tales of Crime and Suspense*, and the editor of the anthology *Protectors: Stories to Benefit PROTECT*. He hosts Noir at the Bar in Manhattan, and his work has appeared in *The Utne Reader*, *PANK Magazine*, *McSweeney's Internet Tendency*, *Needle*, *Crimespree*, and numerous anthologies, including the upcoming *Dark City Lights*, edited by Lawrence Block. You can find him online at www.thomaspluck.com and on Twitter as @thomaspluck.

Clock Without Hands

Several years ago, when newspapers had space to spare for all kinds of sensational trivialities, John Jacket of the *Sunday Special* went to talk with a certain Mr. Wainewright about the stabbing of a man named Tooth whose wife had been arrested and charged with murder. It was a commonplace, dreary case. The only extraordinary thing about it was that Martha Tooth had not killed her husband ten years earlier. The police had no difficulty in finding her. She was sitting at home, crying and wringing her hands. It was a dull affair; she was not even young, or pretty.

But Jacket had a knack of finding strange and colourful aspects of drab, even squalid affairs. He always approached his subjects from unconventional angles. Now he went out on the trail of Wainewright, the unassuming man who had found Tooth's body, and who owned the house in which Tooth had lived.

Even the Scotland Yard man who took down Wainewright's statement had not been able to describe the appearance of the little householder. He was "just ordinary", the detective said, "sort of like a City clerk". He was like everybody: he was a nobody. At half-past seven every evening Wainewright went out to buy a paper and drink a glass of beer in the saloon bar of the "Firedrake" – always the *Evening Extra*: never more than one glass of beer.

So one evening at half-past seven John Jacket went into the saloon bar of the "Firedrake", and found Mr. Wainewright sitting under an oval mirror that advertised Bach's Light Lager. Jacket had to look twice before he saw the man.

A man has a shape; a crowd has no shape and no colour. The massed faces of a hundred thousand men make one blank pallor; their clothes add up to a shadow; they have no words. This man might have been one hundred-thousandth part of the featureless whiteness, the dull greyness, and the toneless murmuring of a docile multitude. He was something less than nondescript – he was blurred, without identity, like a smudged fingerprint.

His suit was of some dim shade between brown and grey. His shirt had grey-blue stripes, his tie was patterned with dots like confetti trodden into the dust, and his oddment of limp brownish moustache resembled a cigarette-butt, disintegrating shred by shred in a tea-saucer. He was holding a brand-new Anthony Eden hat on his knees, and looking at the clock.

"This must be the man," said Jacket.

He went to the table under the oval mirror, smiled politely, and said: "Mr. Wainewright, I believe?"

The little man stood up. "Yes. Ah, yes. My name *is* Wainewright."

"My name is Jacket; of the *Sunday Special*. How do you do?"

They shook hands. Mr. Wainewright said: "You're the gentleman who writes every week!"

"*'Free For All'* – yes, that's my page. But what'll you drink, Mr. Wainewright?"

"I hardly ever——"

"Come, come," said Jacket. He went to the bar. Mr. Wainewright blinked and said:

"I take the *Sunday Mail*. With all due respect, of course. But I often read your efforts. You have a big following, I think?"

"Enormous, Mr. Wainewright."

"And so this is the famous . . . the famous . . ." He stared at Jacket with a watery mixture of wonder and trepidation in his weak eyes. "With all due respect, Mr. Jacket, I don't know what I can tell you that you don't know already."

"Oh, to hell with the murder," said Jacket, easily. "It isn't about that I want to talk to you, Mr. Wainewright."

"Oh, *not* about the murder?"

"A twopenny-halfpenny murder, whichever way you take it. No, I want to talk about *you*, Mr. Wainewright."

"Me? But Scotland Yard——"

" – Look. You will excuse me, won't you? You may know the sort of things I write about, and in that case you'll understand how this Tooth murder affair fails to interest me very much. What does it amount to, after all? A woman stabs a man." Jacket flapped a hand in a derogatory gesture. "So? So a woman stabs a man. A hackneyed business: an ill-treated wife grabs a pair of scissors and – *pst*! Thousands have done it before; thousands will do it again, and a good job too. If she hadn't stabbed Tooth, somebody else would have, sooner or later. But . . . how shall I put it? . . . you, Mr. Wainewright, you interest me, because you're the . . ."

Jacket paused, groping for a word, and Mr. Wainewright said with a little marsh-light flicker of pride: "The landlord of the house in which the crime was committed, sir?"

"The bystander, the onlooker, the witness. I like to get at the, the *impact* of things – the way people are affected by things. So let's talk about yourself."

Alarmed and gratified, Mr. Wainewright murmured: "I haven't anything to tell about myself. There isn't anything of interest, I mean. Tooth——"

"Let's forget Tooth. It's an open-and-shut case, anyway."

"Er, Mr. Jacket. Will they hang her, do you think?"

"Martha Tooth? No, not in a thousand years."

"But surely, she's a murderess, sir!"

"They can't prove premeditation."

"Well, Mr. Jacket, I don't know about that . . ."

"Tell me, Wainewright; do you think they *ought* to hang Martha Tooth?"

"Well, sir, she did murder her hubby, after all . . ."

"But how d'you *feel* about it? What would you say, if you were a juryman?"

"The wages of sin is . . . ah . . . the penalty for murder is the, ahem, the rope, Mr. Jacket!"

"And tell me, as man to man – do you believe that this woman deserves to swing for Tooth?"

"It's the law, sir, isn't it?"

"Is it? They don't hang people for crimes of passion these days."

At the word "passion", Mr. Wainewright looked away. He drank a little whisky-and-soda, and said: "Perhaps not, sir. She might get away with . . . with penal servitude for life, Mr. Jacket, do you think?"

"Much less than that."

"Not really?" Mr. Wainewright's voice was wistful.

"She might even be acquitted."

"Well, sir . . . that's for the judge and jury to decide. But to take a human life . . ."

"Do you dislike the woman, Mr. Wainewright?"

Jacket blinked at the little man from under half-raised eyebrows.

"Oh good Lord no, sir! Not at all, Mr. Jacket: I don't even know her. I only saw her for an instant."

"Good-looking?"

"Good-looking, Mr. Jacket? No, no she wasn't. A . . . a . . . charwomanish type, almost. As *you* might say, she was bedraggled."

"As *I* might say?"

"Well . . . without offence, Mr. Jacket, you are a writer, aren't you?"

"Ah. Ah, yes. Not a handsome woman, eh?"

"She looked – if you'll excuse me – as if she . . . as if she'd *had children*, sir. And then she was flurried, and crying. Handsome? No, sir, not handsome."

"This Tooth of yours was a bit of a son of a dog, it seems to me. A pig, according to all accounts."

"Not a nice man by any means, sir. I was going to give him notice. Not my kind of tenant – not the sort of tenant I like to have in my house, sir."

"Irregular hours, I suppose: noisy, eh?"

"Yes, and he . . . he drank, too. And worse, sir."

"Women?"

Mr. Wainewright nodded, embarrassed. "Yes. Women all the time."

"That calls for a little drink," said Jacket.

He brought fresh drinks. "Oh no!" cried Mr. Wainewright. "Not for me: I couldn't, thanks all the same."

"Drink it up," said Jacket, "all up, like a good boy."

The little man raised his glass.

"Your good health, Mr. Jacket. Yes, he was not a nice class of man by any means. All the girls seemed to run after him, though: I never could make out why they did. He *was* what you might call charming, sir – lively, always joking. But well; he was a man of about my own age – forty-six, at least – and I never could understand what they could see in Tooth."

He swallowed his whisky like medicine, holding his breath in order not to taste it.

Jacket said: "Judging by his photo, I should say he was no oil-painting. A great big slob, I should have said – loud-mouthed, back-slapping, crooked."

"He was a big, powerful man, of course," said Mr. Wainewright.

"Commercial traveller, I believe?" said Jacket.

"Yes, he was on the road, sir."

"Make a lot of money?"

"Never saved a penny, Mr. Jacket," said Mr. Wainewright, in a shocked voice. "But he could sell things, sir. He wouldn't take no for an answer. Throw him out of the door, and back he comes at the window."

"That's the way to please the ladies," said Jacket. "Appear ruthless; refuse to take no for an answer; make it quite clear that you know what you want and are going to get it. He did all that, eh?"

"Yes, sir, he did. . . . Oh, you really shouldn't've done this: I can't——"

More drinks had been set down.

"Cheers," said Jacket. Wainewright sipped another drink. "Are you a married man, Mr. Wainewright?"

"Married? Me? No, not me, Mr. Jacket."

"Confirmed bachelor, hm?"

Mr. Wainewright giggled; the whisky was bringing a pinkness to his cheeks. "That's it, sir."

"Like your freedom, eh?"

"Never given marriage a thought, sir."

"I shouldn't be surprised if you were a bit of a devil on the sly, yourself, Mr. Wainewright," said Jacket, with a knowing wink.

"I . . . I don't have time to bother with such things."

"Your boarding-house keeps you pretty busy."

"My apartment house? Yes, it does, off and on."

"Been in the business long?"

"Only about eight months, sir, since my auntie died. She left me the house, you see, and I thought it was about time I had a bit of a change. So I kept it on. I was in gents' footwear before that, sir, I was with Exton and Co., Limited, for more than twenty years."

"Making shoes?"

Mr. Wainewright was offended. He said: "Pardon *me*, I was a salesman in one of their biggest branches, sir."

"So sorry," said Jacket. "Did Tooth yell out?"

"Eh? Pardon? Yell out? N-no, no, I can't say he did. He coughed, kind of. But he was always coughing, you see. He was a heavy smoker. A cigarette-smoker. It's a bad habit, cigarettes: he smoked one on the end of another day and night. Give me a pipe any day, Mr. Jacket."

"Have a cigar?"

"Oh . . . that's very kind indeed of you I'm sure. I'll smoke it later on if I may?"

"By all means, do, Mr. Wainewright. Tell me, how d'you find business just now? Slow, I dare say, eh?"

"Steady, sir, steady. But I'm not altogether dependent on the house. I had some money saved of my own, and my auntie left me quite a nice lump sum, so . . ."

"So you're your own master. Lucky fellow!"

"Ah," said Wainewright, "I'd like a job like yours, Mr. Jacket. You must meet so many interesting people."

"I'll show you round a bit, some evening," said Jacket.

"No, really?"

"Why not?" Jacket smiled, and patted the little man's arm. "What's your address?"

"77, Bishop's Square, Belgravia."

"Pimlico . . . the taxi-drivers' nightmare," said Jacket, writing it on the back of an old envelope. "Good. Well, and tell me – how does it feel to be powerful?"

"Who, me? I'm not powerful, sir."

"Wainewright, you know you are."

"Oh, nonsense, Mr. Jacket!"

"Not nonsense. You're the chief witness; it all depends on you. Don't you realise that your word may send a woman to the gallows, or to jail? Just your word, your oath! Why, you've got power over life and death. You're something like a sultan, or a dictator – something like a god, as far as Martha Tooth is concerned. You have terrible power, indeed!"

Mr. Wainewright blinked; and then something strange happened. His eyes became bright and he smiled. But he shook his head. "No, no," he said, with a kind of sickly vivacity. "No, you're joking."

Jacket, looking at him, said: "What an interesting man you are, Wainewright! What a fascinating man you really are!"

"Ah, you only say that. You're an author, and you can make ex-extraordinary things out of nothing."

"Don't you believe it, Wainewright. You can't make anything out of nothing. There's more in men than meets the eye, though; and you are an extremely remarkable man. Why, I could make fifteen million people sit up and gape at you. What's your first name?"

"Eh? Er . . . George Micah."

"I think I'll call you George. We ought to get together more."

"Well, I'm honoured, I'm sure, Mr. Jacket."

"Call me Jack."

"Oh . . . it's friendly of you, but I shouldn't dare to presume. But, Mr. Jacket, you must let *me* offer *you* a little something." Wainewright was leaning toward him, eagerly blinking. "I should be offended. . . . Whisky?"

"Thanks," said Jacket.

The little man reached the bar. It was his destiny to wait unattended; to be elbowed aside by newcomers; to cough politely at counters, to be ignored.

At last he came back with two glasses of whisky. As soon as he was seated again he said:

"Mr. Jacket . . . you were joking about . . . You weren't serious about making fifteen million people . . ."

"Sit up and gape at you? Yes I was, George."

"But Mr. Jacket, I . . . I'm nobody of interest; nobody."

"You are a man of destiny," said Jacket. "In the first place – not taking anything else into account – you are an Ordinary Man. What does that mean? All the genius of the world is hired to please you, and all the power of industry is harnessed in your service. Trains run to meet you; Cabinet Ministers crawl on their bellies to you; press barons woo you, George; archbishops go out of their way to make heaven and hell fit your waistcoat. Your word is Law. The King himself has got to be nice to you. Get it? You are the boss around here. All the prettiest women on earth have only one ambition, George Wainewright – to attract and amuse you, tickle you, excite you, in general take your mind off the harsh business of ruling the world. George, you don't beg; you demand. You are the Public. Let anybody dare lift a finger without keeping an eye on your likes and dislikes: you'll smash him, George! Rockefeller and Woolworth beg and pray you to give them your pennies. And so what do you mean by saying you're nobody? Where do you get that kind of stuff, George? Nobody? You're *everybody*!"

Mr. Wainewright blinked. Jacket drank his health, and said: "So now tell me some more about yourself."

"Well . . ." said Mr. Wainewright. "I don't know what to say, I'm sure. You know everything already. You want my opinion, perhaps?" In Mr. Wainewright's eyes there appeared a queer, marsh-light flicker of self-esteem.

"Perhaps," said Jacket.

"In my humble opinion," Mr. Wainewright said, "the woman deserves to die. Of course, I admit that Tooth was a bad man. He was a drunkard, and a bully, and went in for too many women. He ill-treated them, sir; and he was a married man too. I couldn't bear him."

"Then why did you let him stay in your house?" asked Jacket.

"Well . . . I don't know. I had intended to give Tooth notice to quit more than once, but whenever I began to get around to it . . . somehow or other he managed to put me off. He'd tell me a funny story – never a nice story, but so funny that I couldn't help laughing. You know what I mean? He had a way with him, Mr. Jacket. He must have. He sold Poise Weighing Machines. He told me, once, how he had sold a sixty-guinea weighing-machine to an old lady who had a sweet shop in a little village – it was wicked, but I couldn't help laughing. And then again, his success with the women. . . . But all the same, you didn't ought to be allowed to get away with murder. I mean to say – he was her husband, wasn't he? And a human being, too. And I mean to say – the fact remains, doesn't it? She stabbed her husband to death with a pair of sharp scissors."

"All right," said Jacket. "But can we prove that Martha Tooth *meant* to do it, eh? Can we prove premeditation?"

"I don't know anything about all that, I'm afraid," said Mr. Wainewright.

Jacket said: "They don't hang you for murder without malice aforethought in a case of this sort. And incidentally, there isn't any actual proof that Martha Tooth really did stab her pig of a husband, is there?"

Mr. Wainewright was shocked. "She must have!" he said. "Who else could have, if she didn't?"

"Anyone might have done it, my dear George. I might have done it. You might have done it. The charwoman might have done it. Did anyone *see* her do it?"

"Well, no. I suppose not," said Mr. Wainewright. "But the evidence! The evidence, Mr. Jacket!"

"Call me Jack, George old man."

"Jack," said Wainewright, shyly and with some reluctance.

"But go on, George," said Jacket. "What evidence?"

"*The* evidence, J-Jack. (Jack, sir, since you insist.)"

John Jacket felt a strange, perverse desire to provoke, to irritate this respectable little man. "Evidence," he said, "evidence! I spit on the evidence. A woman comes into a house; a woman goes out of a house. The man she visited is found, stuck like a pig – which he was – with a pair of long, sharp, paper-cutting scissors in his throat near the collarbone. So what? So what, George? He was in the habit of smuggling women into his room. Isn't that so?"

"Yes, that's true."

"Say, for example, this man Tooth had a woman in his room before his wife – this wretched Martha Tooth – turned up unexpectedly. Say, for example, he hides this hypothetical woman in a cupboard. . . . Was there a big cupboard, closet, or wardrobe in Tooth's room?"

"There *is* a big wardrobe," said Mr. Wainewright, meditating.

"Say, then, that Tooth, hearing his wife's voice downstairs, hid his concubine in the wardrobe. The wife comes in. She talks to Tooth. She goes away. As the door closes, the enraged woman in the wardrobe comes out fighting, with a pair of scissors, and – *jab*! An overhand stroke with something like a stiletto, striking the soft part of your throat just where the big artery runs down. A child could do it. What?"

"Possible, I dare say," said Mr. Wainewright, tapping his foot in irritation, "but I don't see the point. Mr. Jacket – I'm sorry, I mean Jack. Jack, since you say I may call you Jack. If there *had* been any other lady in Tooth's room *I* should have known it."

"How could you know?" asked Jacket.

Mr. Wainewright meditated, marking off points with his fingers: he was somewhat drunk. He said, laboriously: "In the first place, I have a respectable house. When my auntie died I converted it into little furnished flatlets. People can do as they like in my place, within reason, Mr. Jacket. I mean to say Jack, Jack. By 'within reason' I mean to say that people can have visitors . . . within reason, visitors. As the person responsible for the house, I was always on the spot – or nearly always. A person can't be sure of anybody, and you don't want your house to get a bad reputation. So I . . . to be frank, I listened to how many footsteps were going up to this floor or that floor. And as it happened my little room was next door to Tooth's. And I can assure you that Mrs. Tooth was the only visitor Tooth had that night. Mrs. Madge, the lady who does the cleaning, let Mrs. Tooth in. I passed her on the stairs – or rather, I stood aside to let her pass on the first-floor landing. I had seen Tooth only about two minutes before. He'd just got home from Bristol."

"Did he say anything?" asked Jacket.

"He . . . he was the same as usual. Full of jokes. He was telling me about some girl he met in Bristol, some girl who worked in a baker's shop. The, ah, the usual thing. Mrs. Madge let Mrs. Tooth in while he was talking to me. He said: 'I wonder what the – the Aitch – *she* wants.' And he said that she had better come on up. He'd been drinking. I went down because, to be quite frank, I'd never seen Tooth's wife, and wondered what kind of a woman she could be."

"And what kind of a woman was she, George?"

"Not what I should have expected, Mr. Jacket – I mean J-Jack. One of the plain, humble-looking kind. You wouldn't have thought she'd have appealed to Tooth at all: he went in for the barmaidish type, sir."

"You never can tell, George, old boy. After that you went up to your room, if I remember right."

"That's right. My room was next door to Tooth's. I mean, my sitting-room: I have a little suite," said Mr. Wainewright, with pride.

"Have a little drink," said Jacket, pushing a freshly-filled glass over to him.

"I couldn't, really."

"No arguments, George. By the by, remind me to let you have some theatre tickets. You and I'll go to the first night of *Greek Scandals* next week. Drink up. Well, go on, George."

"Where was I? Oh yes. I had some accounts to do, you see, so I went to my sitting-room. And I could hear them talking."

"What were they saying, George?"

"I couldn't quite get what they were saying, Mr. Jacket."

"But you tried?"

Mr. Wainewright fidgeted and blushed. "I did try," he admitted. "But I only gathered that they were having a quarrel. Once Tooth shouted. He said 'Go to the devil'. She started crying and he burst out laughing."

"A nice man, your friend Tooth, George."

"Yes, sir. I mean no, Mr. Jacket – not at all nice."

"And then?"

"About a quarter of an hour later, I should say, they stopped talking. They'd been raising their voices quite loud. I knocked on the wall, and they stopped. Then Tooth started coughing."

"Was that unusual?"

"No, not at all unusual. He was a cigarette-smoker. In the morning, and at night, it was painful to listen to him, sir. And then his door opened and closed. I opened my door and looked out, and Mrs. Tooth was going downstairs crying, and there was some blood on her hand. I asked her if she had hurt herself, and if she wanted some iodine or anything, and she said 'No, no', and ran downstairs and out of the house."

"She'd cut herself, it appears."

"That's right, ah . . . J-Jack."

"That's it, George. Call me Jack and I'll call you George," said Jacket. "What made you go into Tooth's room later on?"

Mr. Wainewright said: "He always borrowed my evening paper. I nearly always used to hand it over to him when I'd done with it." He held up a copy of the *Evening Extra*, neatly folded. "When I got back from here – I come here just for one quiet drink every evening, and read the paper here as a rule, you see – I went to his door and knocked."

"And, of course, he didn't say 'Come in'," said Jacket.

"No. So I knocked again. No answer. I knocked again———"

" – And at last you went in without knocking, eh?"

"Exactly. And there he lay across the bed, Mr. Jacket – a horrible sight to see, horrible!"

"Bled a good deal?"

"I never thought even Tooth could have bled so much!"

"That shook you, eh, George?"

"It made me feel faint, I assure you, sir. But I didn't touch anything. I 'phoned the police. They were there in ten minutes."

"Detective Inspector Taylor, wasn't it?"

"Yes, that's right. A nice man."

"He collects stamps for a pastime. Have you any hobbies, George?"

Mr. Wainewright giggled. "It sounds silly," he said. "When I haven't got anything else to do I cut pictures out of magazines."

"And what do you do with them when you've cut them out, George?"

"I stick them in a scrap-book."

"An innocent pastime enough."

"In a way, sort of like collecting stamps – in a way," said Mr. Wainewright.

"Yet you never can tell how that sort of thing may end," said Jacket. "Look at Tooth. He got his by means of a pair of scissors – editorial scissors, paper-cutting scissors. Lord, how often have I wanted to stab the Sub with his own scissors!"

"That's right," said Mr. Wainewright. "Long pointy scissors. They were part of a set – scissors and paper-knife in a leather case. I'd borrowed them myself a few days before. Very sharp scissors."

"Little did you think," said Jacket, "that that pair of scissors would end up in your lodger's throat!"

"Little *did* I, J-Jack," said Mr. Wainewright. "It makes a person think. May I ask . . . are you going to put something in the paper about me?"

"I think so," said Jacket.

Mr. Wainewright giggled. "You wouldn't like a photograph of me?"

"We'll see about that, George. We'll see. What are you doing on Saturday?"

"Next Saturday morning I get my hair cut," said Mr. Wainewright.

"Matter of routine, eh?"

"Yes, sir. But———"

"No, no, never mind. You get your hair cut on Saturday, George, and I'll give you a tinkle some time. Right. And now if I were you I'd go and get some sleep, George, old man. You don't look quite yourself," said Jacket.

"I'm not a drinking man . . . I oughtn't to drink," muttered Mr. Wainewright, putting his hat on back-to-front and rising unsteadily. "I don't feel very well . . ."

Poor little fellow, thought Jacket, having seen Mr. Wainewright safely seated in a taxi. *This Tooth affair has thrown him right out of gear. Bloodshed in Wainewright's life! A revolution! It's almost as if he found himself wearing a bright red tie.*

Jacket, who was on the edge of the haze at the rim of the steady white light of sobriety, began to work out a story about Mr. Wainewright. He thought that he might call it *The Red Thread of Murder*. Never mind the killer, never mind the victim – all that had been dealt with a hundred times before. What about the Ordinary Man, the Man In The Street, who has never seen blood except on his chin after a bad shave with a blunt blade, who opens a door and sees somebody like Tooth lying dead in a thick red puddle? Jacket laughed. In spite of everything Mr. Wainewright had to get his hair cut on Saturday. There was, he decided, something ineffably pathetic about this desperate doggedness with which people like Wainewright clung to the finical tidiness of their fussy everyday lives.

He went to sleep thinking of Mr. Wainewright. Mr. Wainewright lay awake thinking of John Jacket, but went to sleep thinking: To-morrow is Friday: *I put a new blade in my safety-razor.*

So that Saturday, Mr. Wainewright went to his barber. Friday was New Blade Day; Monday was Clean Shirt Day; Sunday morning was Bath morning; and he had his hair cut every third Saturday. This was law and order; a system to be maintained. System; routine – in the life of Wainewright inevitable laws governed collar-studs, rubber heels, sheets of toilet-paper, the knotting of neckties, the lighting of pipes, the cutting of string and the sticking-on of stamps. He ate, drank, walked and combed his hair in immutable rhythm. He was established to run smoothly for ever. Every habit of Wainewright's was a Bastille; his every timed action was housed in a little Kremlin. Therefore, to-day, he had to get his hair cut. But Jowl's display made him stop for a few minutes.

Jowl, who owned the antique shop on the corner, had stripped some bankrupt's walls of a great, gleaming yataganerie of edged and pointed weapons. They hung on sale: double-handed swords, moon-faced battleaxes, mailed fists, stilettos, basket-hilted Italian daggers, Toledo rapiers, needle-pointed Khyber knives, adze-shaped obsidian club-axes, three-bladed knuckle-duster daggers, arquebuses, and a heap of oddments of sixteenth-century body-armour. Wainewright stood, smoking his pipe, looking hard. He stopped and examined some assassin's weapon of the fourteen hundreds – a knife with a spring. You stabbed your man, and – *Knutch!* – it flew open like a pair of scissors.

At the back of the window stood a complete suit of jousting-armour, with a massive helmet shaped like a frog's head. Wainewright looked up and, as it happened, he saw the reflection of his face exactly where his face would have been if he had been wearing the armour.

Then, in his breast, something uncoiled. He gazed, whistling. "Ye Gods!" he said. "Ye Gods!" But even as he looked he was inclined to laugh: his reflection was wearing a bowler hat.

Still, why not? thought Mr. Wainewright. But then he remembered that he was an important person, that the glaring eyes of the world were focused on him. He walked across the court and pushed open the door of Flickenflocker's Select Saloon.

Calm! thought Wainewright. *Calm! Keep calm!* The door of the barber's shop was fitted with a compressed air brake: it hissed behind him and closed with a gentle tap.

As the door hissed, Wainewright stood still, tense. Then he also hissed: he had been holding his breath. When the door closed, he also made a tapping noise: he had been standing on his toes.

Flickenflocker said: "Harpust one! Quarder-nour late! For fifteen years so I never knew you to miss a second! Eh? *Tsu, tsu, tsu!*"

"Am I late?" asked Wainewright.

"Fifteen minutes in fifteen years," said Flickenflocker. "One minute every year. In a hundred-twenty years, so you could save enough time to go to the pictures."

"The usual," said Wainewright, sitting in a chair.

"Nice and clean back and sides," said Flickenflocker.

Wainewright nodded. But as he did so he noticed that a peculiar quietness had come over the people in the shop. They were exchanging hurried words in lowered voices, and looking at him out of the corners of their eyes. Deep in the breast of Mr. Wainewright something broke into a glow which spread through him until he felt that all his veins were burning brilliantly red like neon-tubes. He knew exactly what was being said: *That is Wainewright, the witness for the prosecution in the Tooth murder case.*

In a clear, slightly tremulous voice, he said:

"And I'll have a lavender shampoo."

"Why not?" said Flickenflocker, as his long sharp scissors began to nibble and chatter at the fine, colourless hair of the little man in the chair. "Why not?"

* * * * *

Flickenflocker worked with the concentration and exalted patience of a biologist cutting a section, and as he worked he whistled little tunes. His whistle was a whisper: he drew in the air through his teeth, for he had been taught never to breathe on customers. At all times he seemed to be working out some problem of fabulous complexity – breathlessly following a fine thread through infinite mazes of thought. Occasionally he uttered a word or a mere noise, as if he had found something but was throwing it away . . . *Tss!* . . . *Muhuh!* . . . *Tu-tu-tu!* . . . *Oh dear!* Wainewright liked this strange, calm barber who demonstrated no urge to make conversation; whose shiny yellow hands, soft and light as a pair of blown-up rubber gloves, had touched the faces of so many men whose pictures had filled posters while their names topped bills.

For Flickenflocker's was a theatrical establishment, or had been. A hundred photographs of forgotten and half-remembered actors hung on the walls. As small boys cut their names on desks and trees, actors and sportsmen pin their photographs to the walls of pubs and barber-shops. Thus they leave a little something by means of which somebody may remember them . . . until the flies, in their turn, deface the likenesses which Time has almost wiped away; and the dustbins, which gape around the relics of little men like sharks in a bitter sea, close with a clang. Even in the grave nothing is completely lost as long as somebody can say: *Lottie had a twenty-four-inch thigh;* or *Fruitcake bubble-danced;* or *J. J. Sullivan could have eaten Kid Fathers before breakfast.* We hang about the necks of our to-morrows like hungry harlots about the necks of penniless sailors. So, for twenty-three years, singers, boxers, actors, six-day cyclists, tumblers, soubrettes, jugglers, dancers, wrestlers, clowns, ventriloquists and lion-tamers had given Flickenflocker their photographs – always with a half-shrug and a half-smile of affable indulgence. Flickenflocker hung up every one of them: he knew that the day always came when a man returned, if only to look at the wall and dig some illusion about himself out of the junk-heap of stale publicity.

They always came back to Flickenflocker, whose memory was reliable and unobtrusive as a Yale lock. One sidelong look at a profile opened a flap in his head and let out a name. After ten years he could glance at you, name you with matter-of-fact enthusiasm, and make appropriate casual chatter. As soon as the shop door closed and your heels hit the street he kicked the flap back and waited for the next customer . . . looked up, segregated; silent except for hisses, gulps, and monosyllables.

Yet Flickenflocker could talk. Now, while Pewter's flat French razor chirped in the lather like a sparrow in snow and, on his left, the great hollow-ground blade of Kyropoulos sang *Dzing-dzing!* over the blue chin of a big man in a pearl-grey suit, Flickenflocker talked to Mr. Wainewright.

The barber made conversation with the least distinguished of all his customers.

* * * * *

"You're the man of the moment, Mister Wainewright."

"Nonsense, Mister Flickenflocker."

"I can read the papers, thank God, Mister Wainewright. I'm not *altogedder* blind yet, God forbid. Hm!"

"It's all got nothing to do with me."

"No? Your worster enemies should be where that poor woman is now. In your hands is already a rope. A . . . a . . . a loop you can tie; you can tie a noose round her neck."

"It's the Law, Mister Flickenflocker."

"You're right there, Mister Wainewright. That's what the law is for. That's what we pay rates and taxes for. You want to kill somebody: right, go on. But afterwards don't say: 'Huxcuse me, I forgot myself.' Don't say: 'Once don't count – give me just one more charnsh.' A huxcuse me ain't enough – murder ain't the hee-cups. Murderers get hung: good job too. Poor woman!"

"But if she's guilty?"

"Mmmnyes, you're right. But a woman's got a lot to put up with. With a certain class of man a woman can put up with a lot, Mister Wainewright."

"But murder!"

"Murder. . . . Mnyup. Still, in a temper. . . . I knew a baker, a gentleman. In . . . in . . . in the electric chair he'd of got up to give a lady his seat. So one day in a temper he put his friend in the oven. They found it out by trousers-buttons; by trousers-buttons they found it out. Afterwards, he was sorry. Still, I didn't say it was *right*; only I don't like hanging ladies. N-hah, mmmnyah! Well, you got nerve!"

"Why? Why have I got nerve?"

"Judge, juries: I'd be frightened out of my life."

"But why?"

"They can make black white. White black they can make."

"I've nothing to fear: I can only tell the plain truth."

"And good luck to you! What class of people is a murderer? No class. A man in the prime of life, so she goes and kills. With scissors, eh? She kills her husband with scissors! It shows you. Scissors, pokers – if somebody wants to murder a person, hm! Daggers they can find in . . . in . . . in chocolate cakes, if they put their minds to it. Even a razor they can kill somebody with. Present company excepted. With a murderer, everything is a revolver. But what for? Why should she do it to her own husband?"

"For love, I think, Mister Flickenflocker."

"Eeeeh! Love. People should settle down, with a home, and plenty children, with plenty work; happy they ought to be, people. If there's an argument, so sometimes one gives way, sometimes another gives way. For peace in the house, you got to give way. It looks bad to fight in front of the kids. So in the end you have grandchildren. What do they mean, *love*? To *kill* a person for love? In a book they read such rubbish, Mister Wainewright. For hate, for money, for hunger kill a person. For your wife and children kill a person. But love? Never heard of such a thing."

"We'd better leave that to the judge and jury," said Wainewright, coldly.

"We got no option," said Flickenflocker. "We got to leave it to the judgen-jury. Anyway, it didn't have nothing to do with you, thank goodness."

"No?" said Wainewright.

"No," said Flickenflocker, easily.

"It happened in my own house. I was in the next room. It does affect me a *little* bit," said Wainewright, frowning.

"It's all for the best I dessay," Flickenflocker picked up a pair of fine clippers. "Lots o' people'll want to live there now."

"More likely they'll want to stay away from my house, Mister Flickenflocker."

"Don't you believe it! If there was a body (God forbid) in every cupboard, people'd pay double to stay there. For every one that don't like a murder, there's ten that'd rather have a murder than a . . . a . . . a hot-water-bottle. Don't you worry. I know people, so they'd give fifty pounds to have a murder in their place."

"Dry shampoo, please," said Wainewright.

Flickenflocker unscrewed the top of a bottle. "Curiosity," he said.

"Hm?"

"Curiosity. Were they open or shut?"

"Were what?"

"The scissors. The scissors the lady killed the gent with."

"Shut."

"It only shows you, eh? What can cut, can cut out lives from people. *Pssss!* . . . *Hwheee!* Even a road – fall on it from a high roof, and where are you? . . . Scissors, eh? Temper, that's what it is: temper. A stab and a cut, and there you are: you've hanged yourself."

Wainewright did not want to talk any more. He was looking into the mirror. Two men, awaiting their turn, were exchanging whispers and looking in his direction. He knew what they were saying. *That's Wainewright,* they were saying; *that quite ordinary-looking man having the lavender shampoo is Wainewright, the Wainewright who has the house where Tooth was murdered by his wife.*

He smiled. But then old Pewter flipped the linen cover from the man in the chair on Wainewright's right – a big, swaggering man with a humorous, rosy face. One of the whispering men got up and said, in a voice that shook with awe: "Excuse me, but aren't you Al Allum?"

The big man nodded gravely. *"That* is my name," he said.

"May I shake hands with you? Would you mind?"

"Not at all." The big man held out a heavy, manicured fist, caught the stranger's hand in a grip that made him jump, gave Pewter a shilling, and went out with a cordial and resonant "Good-bye".

The man who had shaken hands with him said to Pewter: "I'll give you two shillings for that shilling Al Allum gave you just now."

The old man handed him the shilling with a faint smile. The other man, putting it in his breast-pocket, explained: "It's for my boy. He's crazy about Al Allum: you know what kids are."

Somebody else said: "The greatest comedian alive to-day, Al Allum. Ever see his fake conjuring sketch? Brilliant!"

"Brilliantine?" asked Flickenflocker.

"Cream," said Wainewright.

"Mmmmmyah! . . . There."

As Wainewright was paying his bill he said to the cashier: "Is your clock right?"

The girl replied: "It wouldn't be working in a barber-shop if it was." Everybody laughed. A man said: *"Dead clever, that!"*

Mr. Wainewright went out.

The city muttered under dry dust and blue smoke; the day was warm. Girls passed looking like bursting flowers in their new summer dresses. Wainewright looked at them. Here – passing him, jostling him and touching him with swinging hands in the crowded street – here walked thousands of desirable young women with nothing more than one-sixtieth of an inch of rayon, linen, or *crêpe de Chine* between their bare flesh and his eyesight. Why – ah, why – did his destiny send him out to walk alone? *What's wrong with me?* Wainewright asked himself. *Tramps, cripples, hunchbacks, criminals, horrible men deformed and discoloured and old – they all know the love of women. What's wrong with me? What have they got that I haven't got? I am a man of property . . . still a young man.* He stared piercingly at a pretty girl who was slowly walking towards him. Wainewright felt that his eyes were blazing like floodlights. But the girl, looking at him incuriously, saw only a small ordinary man with mild, expressionless eyes; if she thought of him at all, drawing conclusions from what she saw, she thought of him as a dim and boring little family-man – a nobody – the same as everybody.

Mentally addressing the passing girl, *That's what you think*, said Wainewright. *If I told you who and what I am you'd change your ideas quickly enough, Blondie!* He stopped to look at hats in a shop window. A furry green velour caught his eye, and he decided to buy a hat like that – a two-guinea hat, a real Austrian hat and not a ten-shilling imitation such as Tooth used to wear. That, and a younger-looking suit, a tweed suit; a coloured shirt, even. . . . *Why have I waited so long?*

Wainewright was not a drinking man. Alcohol gave him a headache. But now he felt that everything was changing inside him: he was getting into step with life. Now he wanted a drink. He walked jauntily to the "Duchess of Douro". Tooth had taken him there once before, one Saturday afternoon several months ago. Wainewright remembered the occasion vividly: he had not yet come into his inheritance; he worked for his living then. His aunt was still alive. He was waiting: she could not live for ever. His little Personal Expenses Cash Book said that Wainewright had had seven hair-cuts since then. This made five months since his last drink of beer with Tooth.

Tooth was a tall dark man, strongly built, bright with the sickly radiance and false good-fellowship of the travelling salesman. He resembled one of those wax models that make cheap clothes attractive in the windows of mass-production tailors: he had the same unnatural freshness of complexion, the same blueness of chin, agelessness of expression, and shoddy precision of dress. Tooth wore Tyrolean hats and conspicuous tweeds. He liked to be seen smoking cigars. Yes, with his fivepenny cigars he was a man of personality with a manner at once detestable and irresistible – a way of seeming to give himself body and soul to the achievement of the most trivial objects. He could not accept the finality of anybody's "No". Argument, with Tooth, soon became acrimonious, full of recrimination. Women described him as "masterful": Tooth would shout for twenty minutes over a bad penny, a bus ticket, or an accidental nudge of the elbow.

"Have a drink," Tooth had said.

"I couldn't, really, Tooth."

"You can and will, cocko. There's a girl in the 'Douro' I want to introduce you to. A blonde. Genuine blonde: I found out. Eh? Ha-ha! Eh? Come on."

On the way to the public-house Tooth talked:

"Having the car painted. Just as well: I always seem to get

myself into bother when I'm out in the car. Be lost without it, though. Tell you about the other night? Listen: I'm on my way to Derby. Listen. Listening? Well . . . listen:

"On the way I meet two girls, sisters. Both ginger; one slim and the other plumpish. So I say: 'Want a ride?' And so they say: 'Yes.' And well . . . after a few miles we pull up . . ." Tooth became briefly but luridly obscene. "But listen: the joke of it was this; I ran 'em about fifteen miles further on and we pulled up at a sort of tea-shop place and went in for a cup of tea. Listening? Well, I order tea and cakes and things, and I say: 'Excuse me, my dears, I've got to see a man from the Balkans about a boarhound,' I say. 'Pour my tea out and I'll be right back,' I tell 'em. So I nip out, start up the old jam-jar, and scram before you can say knife. Eh? Ha-ha! Eh? Eh?"

"But what happened to the girls, all that way from home?"

"That's their look-out. I told you I had to get to Derby, didn't I? What was I going to do with 'em in Derby? Have a heart! Ah-ah, now you're coming in here to meet the nicest barmaid in London. No nonsense. Shut up. Come on in now."

He crashed through the grouped drinkers, pulling Wainewright after him. A tall young woman with honey-coloured hair, whose face was strangely expressive of lust and boredom, dragged languidly at the handle of a beer-engine. But when she saw Tooth she smiled with unmistakable sudden joy. Only a woman in love smiles like that.

"Baby," said Tooth, "meet Mr. Wainewright, one of the best."

"Why, Sid! Why haven't you been to see me for such a long time?"

"Been busy. But I've been thinking of you. Ask George Wainewright. We met in the City. He wanted me to go with him to a posh week-end party in Kingston. (He's a very well-to-do man.) But I insisted on coming here. Did I or did I not, Wally?" said this pathological liar.

The compulsion of Tooth's glance was too strong. Wainewright nodded.

"See, Baby? Now, what'll we have?"

"I, ah, a small shandy."

"Oh no, George. Not if you drink with me, you don't. None

of your shandies. Drink that stuff and you don't drink with me. You're going to have a Bass, a Draught Bass. That's a man's drink. Baby, two Draught Bass."

"He always has his own way," said the girl called Baby.

"Skin like cream," whispered Tooth, with a snigger. When the girl returned with the beer he leaned across the bar and stroked her arm. "This evening?"

"No, I can't."

Tooth grasped her wrist. "Yes."

"Leave go. People are looking."

"I don't care. I'll wait for you after eleven."

"I shan't be there. Let go my arm, I tell you. The manager's coming over."

"This evening?"

"Stop it, you'll get me the sack."

"I don't care. This evening?"

"All right, but let go."

"Promise?"

"Promise."

Wainewright saw four red marks on the white skin of her arm as Tooth released her. She rubbed her wrist, and said, in a voice which quivered with admiration: "You're too strong."

"Eh, George?" said Tooth, nudging Wainewright and grinning.

"You must have one more drink with me," said Wainewright, emptying his glass with a wry face, "and then I must be off. . . . Excuse me, miss. One more of these, please."

"Eh? Eh? What's that? Oh no, damn it, no, I don't stand that. You make it two more, Baby. Do you hear what I say?" Fixing Wainewright with an injured stare, Tooth added: "On principle, I don't stand for that kind of thing."

"Very well."

"So I should think! No! Fair's fair! Well, and where are you staying now?"

"In my aunt's place still."

"Hear that, Baby? Looking after his old auntie, eh? His nice rich old auntie. Ha-ha! He knows which side his bread's buttered, George here. No offence, George. I'm going to look you up in a week or two. I want a nice room, reasonable."

"We're full right up just now, Tooth."

"Ah, you old kidder! Isn't he a kidder, Baby? You'll find me a room all right. I know."

And surely enough, a fortnight later Tooth came, and by then Wainewright's aunt was dead, and there was a room vacant in the solid and respectable old house in Bishop's Square. So Tooth had come to live with Wainewright. Yes, indeed, he had blustered and browbeaten his way into the grave, as luck ordered the matter; for there Mrs. Tooth had found him.

And therefore all Britain was waiting for a Notable Trial and, under rich black headlines, the name of George Wainewright was printed in all the papers, called by the prosecution as witness in the Victoria Scissors Murder.

Mr. Wainewright smiled as he entered the "Duchess of Douro": this pub had brought him luck. In this saloon bar he had found power.

* * * * *

The barmaid called Baby was still there. Wainewright stood at the bar and waited. "What can I get you?" she asked.

With a gulp of trepidation Wainewright said: "Whisky."

"Small or large?"

"Ah . . . large, please."

"Soda?"

"Yes, please."

"Ice?"

"Please."

He looked at her. She did not recognise him. He said: "You don't remember me."

"I've seen you somewhere," she said.

"I was in here some time ago with a friend of yours."

"Friend of *mine*?"

"Tooth."

"Who?"

"Tooth. Sid Tooth."

"Sid! I didn't know he was called Tooth. I thought his name was Edwards. He told me his—— Well, anyway . . ."

"If you didn't know his name was Tooth, you don't know about him, then," said Wainewright, gulping his drink in his excitement.

"Know what?"

"Victoria Scissors Murder," said Wainewright.

"What's that? Oh-oh! Tooth! Was that Sid? Really?"

"Yes, that was Sid. It happened in my house. I'm Mr. Wainewright. I'm the witness for the prosecution."

She served another customer: Wainewright admired the play of supple muscles in her arm as she worked the beer engine.

"Want another one?" she asked, and Wainewright nodded.

"Will you have one?"

"Mustn't drink on duty," she said. "So *that* was Sid! Well."

"I'm sorry to be the bearer of sad tidings," said Wainewright.

"Sad tidings? Oh. I didn't know him very well. We were just sort of acquaintances. Scissors, wasn't it? Well, I dare say he deserved it."

Wainewright stared at her. "I was in the next room at the time," he said.

"Did you see it?"

"Not exactly: I heard it."

"Oh," said the barmaid. "Well . . ."

She seemed to bite off and swallow bitter words. "WELL what?" said Wainewright, with a little giggle.

She looked at him, pausing with a glass in one hand and a duster in the other, and said:

"That makes one swine less in the world."

"I thought you liked him," Wainewright said.

"I don't like any man."

"Oh," said Wainewright. "Um . . . ah . . . oh, Miss!"

"Yes?"

"Tooth. Did he . . . ah . . ."

"Did he what?"

"Oh, nothing."

"Yes he did," said the barmaid.

"Did what?"

"Nothing." She turned away. "Excuse me."

Wainewright wanted to talk to her. "May I have another?" he asked. "Do you mind?"

He emptied his third glass. "You don't like me," he said.

"I don't know you."

"Do you want to know me?"

The barmaid called Baby said: "Not particularly."

"Don't go," said Wainewright.

She sighed. There was something about Wainewright that made her uneasy: she did not like this strange, dead-looking, empty-eyed man. "Do you want something?"

He nodded.

"Another double Scotch?"

Wainewright nodded absently. Baby replenished his glass: he looked at it in astonishment, and put down a ten-shilling note.

"You've got some silver," she said.

"I haven't got anything at all," said Wainewright, "I'm lonely."

The barmaid said, in a tone of hostility mixed with pity: "Find yourself somebody."

"Nobody wants me. I'm lonely."

"Well?"

"I've got eight thousand pounds and a house. A big house. Big, big . . ." He spread his arms in a large gesture. "Twenty years I waited. I waited. God, I waited and waited!"

"What for?"

A buzzer sounded. A voice cried: "Order your last drinks please, gentlemen! Order your last drinks!"

"She was eighty-seven when she died. She was an old woman when I was a boy."

"Who was?"

"Auntie. I waited twenty years."

"What *for*?"

"Eight thousand pounds. She left it to me. I've got eight thousand pounds and a house. Furnished from top to bottom. Old lease. It brings in seven pounds a week clear."

He groped in a fog, found himself, and dragged himself up.

"Pardon me, Miss," he said. "I ought not to drink." He felt ill.

"That's all right," said the barmaid.

"Will you excuse me, Miss?" asked Wainewright.

The girl called Baby was turning away. Something like rage got into his throat and made him shout: "You think I'm nobody! You wait!"

A doorman in a grey uniform, a colossus with a persuasive voice, picked him up as a whirlwind picks up a scrap of paper, and led him to the door, murmuring: "Now come on, sir, come on. You've had it, sir, you've had enough, sir. Let's all be friendly. Come on, now."

"You think I'm nobody," said Mr. Wainewright, half crying.

"I wish there was a million more like you," said the doorman, "because you're sensible, that's what you are. You know when you've had enough. If there was more like you, why . . ."

The swing-door went *whup*, and Mr. Wainewright was in the street.

He thought he heard people laughing behind him in the bar.

"You'll see, to-morrow!" he cried.

The doorman's voice said: "That's right. Spoken like a man. Here you are, then, sir. Where to?"

A taxi was standing, wide-open and quivering.

"77, Bishop's Square, Belgravia," said Mr. Wainewright.

"Bishop's Square, Victoria," said the taxi-driver.

"Belgravia," said Mr. Wainewright.

The doorman was waiting. He fumbled and found coins. "Here," he said. The doorman saluted and the taxi-door slammed. Everything jolted away. At Whitehall, Mr. Wainewright realised that he had given the doorman four half-crowns instead of four pennies. He rapped at the window.

"Well?" said the driver.

"Oh, never mind," said Mr. Wainewright.

Let them all wait until to-morrow. They would know then to whom they had been talking. . . .

But on that Sunday, for the first time in ten years, the editor of the *Sunday Special* cut out John Jacket's article. Twenty minutes before midnight, formidable news came through from Middle Europe. Jacket's page was needed for a statistical feature and a special map.

Mr. Wainewright went over the columns, inch by inch, and found nothing. He telephoned the *Sunday Special*. A sad voice said: "Mr. Jacket won't be in until Tuesday – about eleven o'clock. Tell him what name, did you say? Daylight? Maybright? Wainewright. With an E, did you say? E. Wainewright? Oh, George. George E. Wainewright? Just George? George. Make your mind up. George Wainewright. I'll give Mr. Jacket the message. 'Bye."

On Tuesday, Mr. Wainewright arrived at the offices of the *Sunday Special* before half-past ten in the morning. Jacket arrived at a quarter to twelve. He saw that the little man looked ill.

"How are you, George?" he asked.

"Mr. Jacket," said Mr. Wainewright, "what's happened?"

"Happened? About what?"

"I hate to disturb you——"

"Not at all, George."

"We met, you remember?"

"Certainly I remember. Hm?"

"The piece you were going to put in the paper about . . . about . . . my views on the Tooth case. Did you . . . ?"

"I wrote it, George. But my page was cut last Sunday. On account of Germany. Sorry, but there it is. Feel like a drink?"

"No, nothing to drink, thank you."

"Coffee?"

"Perhaps a cup of coffee," said Mr. Wainewright.

They went to a café not far away. Jacket was aware of Mr. Wainewright's wretchedness: it was twitching at the corners of the nondescript mouth and dragging down the lids of the colourless eyes. "What's up?" he asked, as if he did not know.

"Nothing. I simply wondered. . . . I wondered . . ."

"About that story? Take it easy, George. What is there that I can do? Bigger things have happened. As for this Tooth murder case – if you can call it a case. Martha Tooth is certain to get off lightly. Especially with Concord defending. I must get back to the office."

In Fleet Street Mr. Wainewright asked him: "Is the trial likely to be reported?"

"Sure," said Jacket.

"I suppose I'll be called, as witness?"

"Of course."

"But I'm detaining you, J-Jack."

"Not at all, George. Good-bye."

"Good-bye, sir."

Jacket hurried eastwards. Mr. Wainewright walked deliberately in the direction of the Strand.

* * * * *

Sumner Concord was perhaps the greatest defender of criminals the world had ever known. He could combine the crafty ratiocination of a Birkett with the dialectical oratory of a Marshall Hall, and act like John Barrymore – whom he closely resembled. The louder he sobbed the closer he observed you. In cross-examination he was suave and murderous. Birkenhead himself was afraid of Sumner Concord. Yet Concord was an honest man. He would defend no one whom he believed to be guilty.

"Tell me about it," he said, to Martha Tooth.

"What do you want me to tell you?" she asked.

"You must tell me exactly what happened that evening at Number 77, Bishop's Square. The truth, Mrs. Tooth. I want to help you. How can I help you if you do not tell me the truth?"

She said: "There isn't anything to tell."

"Now you are charged——" began Sumner Concord.

"Oh, what do I care? What do I care?" cried Martha Tooth. "Charge me, hang me – leave me alone!"

Sumner Concord had strong tea brought in before he continued. "Tell me, Mrs. Tooth. Why did you visit your husband that night?"

Martha Tooth said: "I wasn't well. I couldn't work. There were the children. I wanted Sid to do something about the children. I *was* his wife. He *was* my husband, after all. . . . I only wanted him to give me some money, just a little, till I could work again."

"Work again at what, Mrs. Tooth?"

"I'd been doing housework."

"And it had been some time since your husband had given you any money?"

"Three years."

"You had been supporting yourself and your two children all that time?"

"Yes."

"He had sent you nothing?"

"Not a penny. I left Sid over three years ago."

"Why did you leave him, Mrs. Tooth?"

"He used to beat me. I couldn't stand him beating me in front of the children. Then – it was when we had two rooms in Abelard Street near the British Museum – he brought a woman in."

"Are there, Mrs. Tooth, by any chance, any witnesses who could testify to that?"

"Mrs. Ligo had the house. Then there was Miss Brundidge; she lived downstairs. I ran away with the children and went to my aunt's place. She still lives there: Mrs. Lupton, 143, Novello Road, Turners Green. Her friend, Mrs. Yule, she lives there too. They both know. We stayed with them once. Sid used to knock me about. The police had to be called in twice. He wanted to kill me when he'd been drinking."

"... *In twice*," wrote Sumner Concord. "Novello Road. Novello Street Police Station, um? Take your time. Have some more tea. A cigarette. You don't smoke? Wise of you, wise. He was a violent and dangerous man, this husband of yours, then?"

"Yes."

"He threatened, for instance, to kill you, no doubt?"

"No," said Martha Tooth, "he never threatened. He just hit."

"And on this last occasion. You called to see him. Hm?"

"Yes, that's right."

"You hadn't seen him for some time?"

"About three years."

"How did you find out his address?"

"From his firm, Poise Weighing Machines."

"You hadn't tried to find out his address before, eh?"

"All I cared about was that Sid shouldn't find out my address."

"But you were at the end of your tether, hm?"

"I was supposed to be having an operation. I've still got to have an operation. And I thought Sid might let me have something ..."

"There-there, now-now! Calm. Tears won't help, Mrs. Tooth. We *must* be calm. You saw Sid. Yes?"

"Yes, sir. But . . . he'd been drinking, I think."

"Tell me again exactly what happened."

"I called. A lady let me in. I went up, and Sid was there. He said: 'What, you?' I said: 'Yes, me.' Then he said – he said——"

"Take your time, Mrs. Tooth."

"He said: 'What a sight you look.'"

"And then?"

"I suppose I started crying."

"And he?"

"He told me to shut up. And so I did. I think I did, sir. I tried to. I asked him to let me have some money. He said that I'd had as much money as I was ever going to get out of him – as if I'd ever had anything out of him!" cried Mrs. Tooth, between deep, shuddering sobs.

"There, there, my dear Mrs. Tooth. You must drink your tea and be calm. Everything depends on your being calm. Now."

"I said I'd go to his firm. I told him I was ill. I told him I'd go to his firm in the City. Then he hit me, sir."

"Where?"

"In the face – a slap. I started to cry again. He hit me again, and he laughed at me."

"He hit you in the face again?"

"Yes, with his hand."

"This is very painful to you, Mrs. Tooth, but we must have everything clear. Your hand was wounded. How did you hurt your hand?"

"All of a sudden . . . I didn't want to keep on living. I was so miserable – I was so miserable – I was——"

Sumner Concord waited. In a little while Martha Tooth could speak again.

"You hurt your hand."

"I wanted to kill myself. There was a knife, or something. I picked it up. I meant to stick it in myself. But Sid was quick as lightning."

There was a ring of pride in her voice, at which Sumner Concord shuddered, although he had heard it before.

"What happened then?" he asked.

"He hit me again and knocked me over."

"You fell?"

"Against the bed, sir. Then Sid hit me some more and told me to get out. He said: 'I hate the sight of you, get out of my sight,' he said."

"Above all, be calm, Mrs. Tooth. What happened after that?"

"I don't know."

"After he hit you the last time – think."

"I don't know, sir."

"You got up?"

"I can't remember."

"You can't remember. Do you remember going out of the room?"

"I sort of remember going out of the room."

"You got back to your home?"

"Yes."

"You remember that?"

"Yes, sir. I know, because I washed my face in cold water, and moved quietly so as not to wake the children up."

"That, of course, was quite reasonable. That would account for the blood in the water in the wash-bowl."

"I dare say."

"Your throat was bruised, Mrs. Tooth. Did your husband try to strangle you?"

"He got hold of me to keep me quiet, I should think, sir."

"Before you picked up this knife, or whatever it was? Or after?"

"I couldn't say. I don't know. I don't care."

"I suggest that you picked up this sharp instrument, knife, scissors, or whatever it may have been, *after* your husband took you by the throat."

"Very likely," said Martha Tooth, drearily, "I don't know. I don't care."

"You must pull yourself together, Mrs. Tooth. How can I help you if you will not help yourself? You picked up this knife, or pair of scissors, *after* your husband began to strangle you with his hands. Is that so?"

"I should think so."

"He was an extremely powerful man, I think?"

"My Sid? Sid was as strong as a bull, sir."

"Yes. Now can you give me a list of the places – rooms, flats, houses, hotels, any places – in which you and your husband lived together from the date of your marriage until the date of your separation?"

"Yes, I think I could, sir."

"You lived together for several years, didn't you?"

"Nearly seven years, off and on."

"He ill-treated you from the start?"

Martha Tooth laughed. "He beat me the first time two days after we were married," she said.

"However, you managed to keep this matter secret?"

"Oh, everybody knew."

"Hush, hush, Mrs. Tooth. Everything depends upon your self-control! He can't hurt you now."

"I'm not crying because of that . . ." Martha Tooth bit her sleeve and pressed the fingers of her free hand into her eyes. Still, tears came out between her fingers.

"Why are you crying, then?"

"You're so good to me!"

"*You must be calm*," said Sumner Concord, in a cold, hard voice.

She stopped crying. "Everybody knew how he treated me," she said.

"You must try and remember everyone who might make a statement concerning the manner in which your husband treated you, Mrs. Tooth. You must try and remember. Is that quite clear?"

"Yes, sir, but I'm afraid. I'm afraid of being in the court. They'll make me swear black is white. I don't know what to do. I don't know what to say. I don't——"

Sumner Concord stopped her with a gentle, but imperious gesture, and said: "Mrs. Tooth, you mustn't persuade yourself that there is anything to be afraid of. You will be given a perfectly fair trial. The clerk of the court will say to you: 'Martha Tooth, you are charged with the murder of Sidney Tooth on the 7th May of this year. Are you guilty or not guilty?' And you will say: 'Not guilty.' This I believe to be the truth. I believe that you are not guilty of the murder of your husband. I believe that, desperate with grief and pain and terror, you picked up the scissors intending to kill yourself, and not to kill your husband."

Martha Tooth stared at him in blank astonishment and said: "Me, pick up a pair of scissors to kill Sid? I shouldn't have dared to raise a hand to Sid."

"Just so. He had you by the throat, Mrs. Tooth. He was shaking you. Your head was spinning. You struck out wildly, blindly, Mrs. Tooth, and it happened that the point of that sharp pair of scissors struck him in the soft part of his neck and penetrated the subclavian artery. You had not the slightest intention of hurting him in any way," said Sumner Concord, holding her with his keen, calm, hypnotic eyes. "What happened after that, Mrs. Tooth?"

"I don't know what happened," she cried. "As he let go of my neck, I ran away from him, that's all I know."

"Exactly. You ran away blindly, neither knowing or caring where you were going. Is that not so? And later they found you wringing your ice-cold hands and crying, while the children lay asleep in your poor furnished room. Is that not so?"

"My hands were ice-cold," said Martha Tooth in a wondering undertone. "How did you know my hands were ice-cold?"

Sumner Concord smiled sadly and with pity. "Be calm, my dear lady, be calm."

"But how did you know my hands were ice-cold?"

"They frequently are in such cases," said Sumner Concord. "And now you must eat your meals and rest and get your poor nerves in order again, Mrs. Tooth. You are to banish this matter from your mind until it is necessary for us to talk about it again. You are to leave everything in my hands. I believe that you have been telling me the truth, and in that case I give you my word of honour that I believe that no great harm can come to you. Now you must rest."

"I don't care what happens to me, sir, but the children – what about the children?" asked Martha Tooth, twisting her wet handkerchief in her skinny, little chapped hands.

"Put your mind at rest, they are being well looked after, I promise you."

A shocking thought seemed suddenly to strike her and she

gasped: "They can send me to prison for years. And then what would happen to them?"

Rising, and laying large, gentle hands on her shoulders, Sumner Concord replied: "Even if you had known that you were striking your husband, you would have been striking him without premeditation, and in self-defence, because in the hands of this crazy drunken brute you were in peril of your life, and if there is any justice in the world, you need not necessarily go to prison at all."

Then he went away and obtained the statements of Mrs. Ligo, Miss Brundidge, Mrs. Lupton, Mrs. Yule, and half a dozen others. He obtained certain evidence from the police at the Novello Street Police Station. A few days later, everybody began to take it for granted that Martha Tooth would get away scot-free.

* * * * *

Because it was Sumner Concord who was defending Martha Tooth, the Central Criminal Court was crowded. Mr. Wainewright, glancing timidly from wig to horsehair wig, felt his heart contract and his stomach shrink, and when his fascinated gaze fell upon the hard, white, turtle-face of Mr. Justice Claverhouse, who sat in his great robes under the sword, he was seized by an insane impulse to run away and hide. Yet, at the same time, he was aware of a certain spiritual exaltation as witness for the prosecution in Rex v. Tooth.

Mr. Sherwood's speech for the prosecution was longer than one might have expected. He had put a lot of work into it. If he could hang Martha Tooth, snatching her from the protective arms of Sumner Concord, he was a made man. His manner was cold and precise. His voice was – as one journalist described it – winter sunlight made articulate. As he spoke, members of the public who had hitherto believed that Martha Tooth could not possibly be convicted changed their minds. One or two sportsmen who had laid five to four on her acquittal began furtively to try to hedge their bets. Mr. Sherwood's sentences struck home like so many jabs of an ice-pick. Here was an angry woman, may it please His Lordship and the members of the jury. Here was an embittered woman, a jealous woman. Here was a woman scorned. She had brooded over her real or imaginary wrongs until at last she had decided on a bloody revenge. Under the cover of the gathering darkness, she had gone stealthily out of her house, to the house of her husband. And there she had stabbed him to death with this pair of scissors, paper-cutting scissors with a shagreen handle. (The pair of scissors was unwrapped from some tissue paper in a little cardboard box, into which they had been packed with loving care.) She left the scissors in the wound, knowing that no fingerprints would be visible on the rough shagreen. Then she slunk out of the house. But her cunning had not been quite deep enough. She had forgotten to wipe her fingerprints from the door-knob on the inside of Mr. Tooth's bed-sitting-room door. There were witnesses who could swear to having seen her come and seen her go. Medical evidence would prove that this murderous stab in the throat, which had gone down through the subclavian artery, had been inflicted at such-and-such a time. She was arrested almost literally red-handed, for she had not yet had time to empty certain blood-stained water from a basin in her room. While her husband's innocent children lay asleep in her bed, the murderess had crept back to wash away the evidence of her guilt, and so on and so forth. And now with the assistance of his learned friend, Mr. Bottle, he would call the evidence before the court.

At this point, Mrs. Madge was called. She remembered everything. She had let Mrs. Tooth in on the evening of the murder. She knew at exactly what time she had let that party in. How did she know the time? She had every reason to know the time because it was time for Mrs. Madge to go home and she had paid a certain amount of attention to the clock. She was not a clock-watcher but she did her duty, and was not paid to stay more than a certain number of hours. On this particular evening she had an appointment with a friend, Mrs. Glass, with whom she had arranged to go to the pictures in time for a certain performance. Therefore she had particularly desired to get away in time to change her clothes and make herself decent. Therefore – give or take half minute – she could say fairly exactly at what time the lady came to the door and asked for Mr. Sidney Tooth and she could swear to the lady: she was in the habit of keeping her eyes open; it was her hobby, sizing people up. Mrs. Tooth was wearing a very old loose black coat, the sort that the Jewish shops sell for a guinea, and one of those black hats you could get for three-and-sixpence at Marks and Spencers. She was carrying an old black handbag, and her shoes must have been given to her by a lady, a bigger lady than Mrs. Tooth who had worn them out and was about to throw them away. She could take her oath on it that Mrs. Tooth was the person she had let in on that fatal evening.

Then came Mr. Wainewright. He had bought a new suit for the occasion – a smart, well-cut suit, with the first double-breasted coat he had ever worn. He had gone to the West End for a shirt that cost eighteen shillings. His tie must have cost as much again, and there was a pearl pin stuck into the middle of it. An equilateral triangle of white handkerchief protruded from his breast pocket. He looked respectable and intensely uncomfortable as he gave his evidence, which was as he had outlined it to John Jacket that evening in the "Firedrake".

Cross-examined, he gave the defence nothing to work on. It was apparent that Wainewright was telling the truth. Then came the turn of the defence.

To the astonishment of the public, Mr. Sumner Concord did not attempt to break down the evidence for the prosecution. There was no doubt at all, he said, that the unfortunate Mrs. Tooth had called on her husband at that time. But he happened to know that she had called in order to plead with him. Tooth had callously deserted her and his two children. He was earning a good salary and substantial sums in commission, which he devoted entirely to dissipation. Mrs. Tooth, the deserted woman, had been compelled to support the children and herself by menial labour. Medical evidence would indicate that it was necessary for this lady to undergo a serious internal operation in the near future. She had visited her husband merely in order to beg – to beg on her bended knees if necessary – for the wherewithal to feed their children, his children and hers, until such time as she could find strength to go out again and scrub other women's floors to earn the few shillings that she needed to maintain them.

Sumner Concord drew the attention of His Lordship and the jury to the fact that Mrs. Tooth had a separation order but had never received a penny: her forbearance was inspired by mercy and also by fear, because Sidney Tooth, as he was about to prove, had been one of the most murderous bullies and unmitigated scoundrels that ever polluted God's earth. This poor woman, Mrs. Tooth, did not care whether she lived or died – her husband, by his persistent brutality and ill-treatment had beaten the normal fear of death out of her. Evidence was forthcoming which would prove that this wretched, persecuted woman had for many years gone in terror of her life and had frequently interposed her broken and bruised body between the drunkenly raging Sidney Tooth and the undernourished, trembling bodies of his children. Mother-love was stronger than the terror of bodily harm. Knowing that in a little while her exhausted frame could no longer support the strain imposed upon it – knowing that the time was fast approaching when she must go into hospital – Martha Tooth went to plead with her husband, and he mocked her. He laughed in her face. He struck her. She, driven to desperation, God forgive her, driven to self-destruction, picked up that pair of scissors to stab herself. In doing so she wounded her hand. Then Tooth, who was drunk and who – a brute at the best of times – was murderous when drunk, as evidence would prove, took her by the throat and began to strangle her. She struck out blindly and he let her go. She went weeping, she ran out blindly into the night. Mr. Sumner Concord did not deny the validity of the evidence of Mr. Wainewright and Mrs. Madge. Mrs. Tooth believed that she must have killed her husband, and she was horrified at the very thought of it. As for killing him by intention – she could never have thought of that, she loved him too much and she feared him too much. She wanted to kill herself. There was medical evidence to prove that the blood in the hand-basin was her own blood from her own hand which she cut in so blindly snatching the scissors with which Tooth had been killed. That her life was in danger might be indicated by the evidence of eleven witnesses, three of them doctors. . . .

Mr. Wainewright, wondering at the complexity of it all, looked away. He looked away from the face of Sumner Concord, scanned the faces of the jurymen (one of them was surreptitiously slipping a white tablet into his mouth) and blinked up at the ceiling. A piece of fluffy stuff, such as comes away from a dandelion that has run to seed, was floating, conspicuous against the panelling. It began to descend. Mr. Wainewright's eyes followed it. It came to rest on the judge's wig, where it disappeared. Mr. Wainewright was conscious of a certain discontent.

After that nothing of the trial stuck in his mind except Sumner Concord's peroration, and Mr. Justice Claverhouse's verdict.

The peroration was something like:

"Here was a beast. He tortured this woman. She trusted him and gave him her life. He accepted it brutally and threw it away. She had been beautiful. He had battered her with his great bony fists into the woman you see before you. That face was offered to Tooth in the first flush of its beauty. He beat it into the wreck and ruin of a woman's face – the wreck, the ruin that you see before you now. She did not complain. He mocked and humiliated her. She was silent. She wept alone. He made her an object of pity, this mad and murderous bully, and she said nothing. He deserted her, leaving her with two young sons whom she loved very dearly: she was sick and weak, and still she never spoke! The prosecution has raised its voice: Martha Tooth suffered in silence. She worked for her children, happy to bring home a little bread in her poor cracked hands.

"You have heard the evidence of those who have known her. She was a woman without stain, a woman undefiled. But when, at last, she went ill – dear God, what was she to do? She wanted nothing for herself. But there were her children. Her husband was prosperous. She asked him only for bread for his children – he laughed in her face. He struck her and ordered her to go. She pleaded – and he beat her. She cried for mercy and he abused her, reproaching her for the loss of her beauty, the beauty he himself had savagely beaten away.

"At last, driven mad by despair, she picks up the first thing that comes to hand, a pair of scissors, and tries – poor desperate woman – to kill herself. Laughing, he takes her by the throat. These hands, strong enough to break a horseshoe, are locked about her frail throat. Imagine them upon your own, and think!

"She struggles, she cannot speak, she can only struggle while he laughs in her face, because these murderous thumbs are buried in her windpipe. She strikes out blindly, and this great furious hulk of bestial manhood collapses before her. Sixteen stone of bone and muscle falls down, while seven stone of wretchedness and sickness stands aghast.

"And looking down she sees the scissors embedded in that bull neck. By some freak of chance – by some act of God – she has struck the subclavian artery and the great beast has fallen. She runs blindly away, weeping bitterly, half demented with anguish, and when the police find her (which was easy, since she had not attempted to conceal herself) she is crying, and the blood in the basin is her own blood. The children lie asleep and she begs the police to take her away, to take her away anywhere out of this world. She asks for nothing but death, and there, there is the pity of it! . . ."

After an absence of twenty-five minutes the jury returned a verdict of Not Guilty.

* * * * *

Then, although everyone said he had known from the beginning that Martha Tooth would be acquitted, London went wild with delight. The *Sunday Extra* sent Munday Marsh to offer the bewildered woman five hundred pounds for her life-story. Pain of the *Sunday Briton* offered a thousand. She shook her head wearily and dispiritedly. "Twelve hundred and fifty," said the *Sunday Briton*. The *Extra* said: "Fifteen hundred."

"I can't write stories," said Martha Tooth. "Anyway———"

"I can," said Pain.

"Calm, gentlemen, calm," said the sardonic voice of John Jacket. They turned, and saw him dangling an oblong of scribbled paper between a thumb and a forefinger. "I've got it."

The *Sunday Special* had given Jacket authority to pay as much as two thousand pounds for Martha Tooth's story. Ten minutes before Munday Marsh had arrived, Jacket had bought the story for six hundred pounds.

"Oh well," they said, without malice, and went away. Pain

said: "To-day to thee, to-morrow to me, Jack," and they shook hands. Ainsworth of *The People* said nothing: he knew that in a year's time the whole business would be forgotten, and then, if he happened to need a human-interest murder-feature, he could re-tell the story from the recorded facts.

So John Jacket wrote fifteen thousand words – four instalments, illustrated with photographs and snapshots – under the title of DIARY OF AN ILL-USED WOMAN. What Jacket did not know he invented: Martha Tooth signed everything – she still could not understand what it was all about. Soon after the first instalment was published she began to receive fan-mail: half a dozen religious leaflets, letters urging her to repent, prophecies concerning the Second Coming, and proposals of marriage, together with frantically abusive notes signed *Ill-Used Man*. She also received parcels of food and clothes, and anonymous letters enclosing postal orders. An old lady in the west country, saying that she had wanted to kill her husband every day for forty years, enclosed sixty twopenny stamps.

Martha Tooth was taken in hand by a lady reporter, who carried her off to a beauty parlour, compelled her to have her hair waved, and showed her how to choose a hat. In three weeks she changed; paid attention to her finger-nails and expressed discontent with the Press. The Press, she complained, wouldn't leave her alone, and everyone wanted to marry her. Before the fourth instalment appeared she had received eleven offers of marriage. Martha Tooth had become whimsical, smiled one-sidedly, and took to lifting her shoulders in a sort of shrug. "Men," she said, "men! These men!"

After the fourth week, however, she got no more letters. She was out of sight and out of mind.

She went to the offices of the *Sunday Special* to see Jacket. Someone had told her that she ought to have got thousands of pounds for her story, and that there was a film in it. When she told Jacket this, he drew a deep breath and said:

"Mrs. Tooth. Your story is written, read, wrapped around fried fish, and forgotten. You forget it too. Be sensible and forget it. You've lived your story and told your story. Go away and live another story." He added: "With a happy ending, eh?"

She went away. Soon, a paragraph on the gossip page of an evening newspaper announced that she had married a man called Booth. Her name had been Tooth – there was the story. Mrs. Tooth married Mr. Booth. He was a market-gardener, and, strangely enough, a widower. Mr. Booth had proposed to her by letter.

John Jacket had forgotten the Tooth case when Mr. Wainewright came to see him for the second time, twelve weeks later.

* * * * *

It struck Jacket as odd that Mr. Wainewright was wearing a jaunty little green Tyrolean hat and a noticeable tweed suit.

"Is it fair?" asked Wainewright. "Where do I come in?"

"Come in? How? How d'you mean, where do you come in?"

"Well," said Mr. Wainewright, shuffling his feet, "I mean to say . . . I hear that Tooth's good lady got thousands and thousands of pounds."

"A few hundreds, George," said Jacket.

"It isn't that, Mr. Jacket. It's——"

"The credit?" asked Jacket, twitching an ironic lip.

"Who is *she* to be made a heroine out of?" asked Wainewright, looking at his finger-tips.

"What exactly are you trying to get at, George?" asked Jacket.

"Get at? Who, me? Nothing, Mr. Jacket."

"Then what do you want? What do you want me to do?"

Mr. Wainewright looked at the ball of his right thumb and shook his head. "There was nothing about me at all in the papers," he said. "I've got a story, too."

"Be a pal," said Jacket, "and go away. I've got work to do, George, old man, work. So be a pal."

"Right." Mr. Wainewright got up.

"Don't be angry with *me*. Things come and things go," said Jacket, "and a story is a nine-days' wonder. Wash this murder out of your head."

Mr. Wainewright said: "Well, you know best. But I've also got a story——"

A telephone bell rang. "See you some other time," said John Jacket, lifting the receiver. "So long for now, George."

Wainewright went out without saying good day. Shortly after he had gone, John Jacket, hanging up the telephone, found himself wondering about something. There had been something wrong with Wainewright. What?

Jacket gnawed a fat black pencil.

He had eaten his way to the last letter of the pencil-maker's name before he knew what he was trying to remember. He laughed, and said to himself: *That silly little man has gone and got himself up in a furry green hat and a tweed suit. What on earth for?*

Jacket felt that he was on the verge of a discovery – not a *Sunday Special* story, but something interesting all the same.

Then his telephone rang. By the time he had stopped listening new things were in his head, and Mr. Wainewright, being gone, was forgotten.

* * * * *

Three weeks later, as Jacket was leaving the office at lunch-time, he heard Mr. Wainewright's voice again. The little man came breathlessly out of the cover of a doorway and said: "Mr. Jacket, sir. Please. One moment. Just *one* moment."

"Well, what is it?" said Jacket, looking down at him with an expression of something like loathing. "What is it now, Wainewright?"

"It's something important, sir. Something very important. I give you my word, my word of honour, you'll never forgive yourself if you don't listen to me."

"I'm in a hurry."

"I've been waiting for you here in the street for an hour and a half," said Mr. Wainewright.

"You should have telephoned."

"If I had, you wouldn't have spoken to me."

"True," said Jacket. Then he blinked, and said: "What the devil have you been doing to yourself?"

Mr. Wainewright was dressed in a tight-fitting, half-belted jacket of white stuff like tweed, an orange-coloured shirt and a black satin tie with a diamond horseshoe pin, blue flannel trousers, a panama hat, and brown-and-white buckskin shoes. He had trimmed his moustache to a fine straight line, above and below which Jacket could see a considerable area of tremulous white lip, beaded with perspiration. And he could smell lavender-water and whisky.

"Doing to myself? Nothing, sir," said Mr. Wainewright.

"I like your hat."

"It's real panama."

"Um-um!" Jacket considered him for a second or two, and then said: "Come on, then. Tell me all about it. Come and have a drink."

"It's very private," said Mr. Wainewright. "It's not something I could talk about if there was anybody around. Look, Mr. Jacket, it'll be worth your while. Come home with me, just for a few minutes."

"*Home* with you?"

"To Bishop's Square – ten minutes in a taxi, no more. I've got plenty of drinks at home. Have a drink there. Ten minutes. I'll show you something. . . . I'll tell you something. Please do! Please do, Mr. Jacket."

"All right, then. But I haven't long," said Jacket.

They got into a taxi. Neither of them spoke until Mr. Wainewright said: "After you," as he unlocked the street door of Number 77, Bishop's Square. "Lead the way," said Jacket. The little man bobbed in a shopwalker's obeisance. They passed through a clean, dim passage hung with framed caricatures out of *Vanity Fair*, and climbed sixteen darkly-carpeted stairs to the first floor. Mr. Wainewright opened another door. "This used to be my auntie's room," he said, rather breathlessly.

"Charming," said Jacket, without enthusiasm.

"It was Tooth's room, too."

"Oh I see. The room in which Tooth was murdered, eh?"

"Yes, sir. It's my bedroom now."

"And is this what you brought me here to see?" asked Jacket.

"No, no," cried Mr. Wainewright, splashing a quarter of a pint of whisky into a large tumbler, and pressing the nozzle instead of the lever of a soda-water syphon. "Please sit down."

"That's a massive drink you've given me," said Jacket. He observed that his host's drink was not much smaller.

"No, not at all."

"Cheers." Jacket emptied his glass in two gulps. Mr. Wainewright tried to do the same, but choked; recovered with a brave effort, and forced the rest of his drink into his mouth and down his throat. Jacket could hear his heavy breathing. "Now, tell us all about it," he said.

"There was," said Mr. Wainewright, swaying a little in his chair, "there was a . . . an astounding miscarriage of justice."

"In what way, Wainewright?"

"In every way, Mr. Jacket, sir. In every way. What I have to say will shock you."

"Go ahead."

"Sid Tooth died just about on the spot where you are sitting, sir."

"Well?"

"The rug, of course, is a new one. They couldn't clean the old one. . . . But your glass is empty."

"I'll pour drinks. You go on," said Jacket, rising.

"Listen," said Mr. Wainewright. . . .

* * * * *

Mr. Wainewright said, dreamily:

"What I want to know is this: where's your justice? Where's your law? If justice is made a mockery of, and law is tricked – what do I pay rates and taxes for? The world's going mad, sir. A woman is accused, sir, of killing her hubby with a pair of scissors. It's proved that she did it, proved beyond doubt, Mr. Jacket! And what happens? This woman, a nobody mind you; this woman does not pay the penalty of her crime, sir. No. She is made a heroine of. She is cheered to the echo. She has her picture in all the papers. She has her life-story published. She marries again, lives happy ever after. Is that fair? Is that right?"

"What's on your mind, Wainewright? It was pretty well established as a clean-cut case of self-defence."

Mr. Wainewright, with extraordinary passion, said: "She was

lying! Tooth was still alive when she left this house! He was hale and hearty as you or me, after the street door closed behind Martha Tooth. Alive and laughing, I tell you. She's a perjurer . . . a perjuress. She's a liar. She got what she got under false pretences: all that money, all that sympathy. 'Ill-Used Woman', as you called her! She never killed Tooth. The world must be going mad."

"What about your evidence?" asked Jacket, skilfully pouring half his drink into his host's glass.

Mr. Wainewright snapped: "Evidence! Don't talk to me about evidence!"

"You drink up your nice drink," said Jacket, "and go over it all again."

"I hated that man," said Mr. Wainewright. "Who did he think *he* was, that Sid Tooth? He was no good. And all the women were in love with him. He was a bully, a dirty bully. A drunkard, a bad 'un – bad to the backbone. He practically *forced* his way into this house. A laugh, a joke, a drink, a bang on the back – and before I knew where I was, there was Tooth, in auntie's old room. I'm not used to that sort of thing, Mr. Jacket, sir. I'm not used to it. He borrowed money in cash, and ran up bills. He told me he'd done a deal with a new department store, for weighing machines – over a thousand pounds in commission he had to collect. So he said. All lies, sir, all lies, but I swallowed 'em. I swallowed everything Tooth said. Bad, sir, bad! He was bad to the backbone."

Jacket asked: "Why didn't you tell him to get out?"

"I meant to," said Mr. Wainewright, "but he always saw it coming. Then it was a laugh, and a joke, and a drink, and a bang on the back. . . . To-morrow: he'd pay me to-morrow. And to-morrow, he said, to-morrow. And then he had to go to Leeds, or Bristol. It was drinks and women with him, sir, all the time. He used to bring women into this very room, Mr. Jacket, sir, into this very room. And I was next door. No woman ever looked twice at me, sir. What's the matter with *me*? Have I got a hump on my back, or something? Eh? Have I?"

Jacket said: "Far from it, old friend."

"And I sat in my room, next door, with nothing to do but get my scrap-book up to date."

"What scrap-book?" asked Jacket, refilling the little man's glass.

Mr. Wainewright giggled, pointing to a neatly-arranged pile of red-backed volumes on a shelf by the bed. Jacket opened one, and riffled the pages. Mr. Wainewright had meticulously cut out of cinematic and physical-culture magazines the likenesses of young women in swimming suits. He had gummed them in and smoothed them down. Here, between the eight covers of four scrap-books, lay his seraglio. His favourite wife, it appeared, was Ann Sheridan.

"You think I'm pretty terrible," he said, rising uncertainly and taking the book out of Jacket's hands.

"Go on," said Jacket.

"No, but I don't want you to think . . ."

"I'm not thinking anything. Go on, pal, go on."

"I think there's something *artistic* in the human form, sir. So for a hobby, you see, I collect it in my scrap-books."

"I understand, I understand," said Jacket. "You were sitting in your room next door to this, with nothing to do but get your scrap-books up to date, when – go on, go on, George."

"I asked you here to tell you this," said Mr. Wainewright. "You don't need to . . . to draw me out. I'm telling you something. A story – worth a fortune. No need to screw your face up. No need to pretend to treat me with respect. I know what you think. You think I'm nothing. You think I'm nobody. Let me tell you."

"You were sitting in your room——"

"I was cutting out the picture of the young lady called Pumpkins Whitaker, sir – an artistic figure – when Mrs. Tooth came to visit *him*."

He pointed to the floor under Jacket's chair.

"Go on."

"Yes, Mr. Jacket. I listened. What happened was as I said in court. They quarrelled. She cried. He laughed. There was a scuffle. In the end Mrs. Tooth ran out. Just like I said, sir."

"Well?"

Mr. Wainewright leaned forward, and Jacket had to support him with an unobtrusive hand.

"Then, sir, I went into Tooth's room, this very room, sir. I knocked first, of course."

"And there was no answer?"

"There was an answer. Tooth said 'Come in'. And I came in, Mr. Jacket."

"You mean to say Tooth was alive when you came in here, after his wife had left?"

"Exactly, sir. I was curious to know what had been going on. I made up an excuse for coming to see him just then. I'd borrowed his scissors, you see, the ones she is supposed to have killed him with. I'd been using them – they were very sharp – for cutting things out. They were part of a set – scissors and paper-knife in a shagreen case. I came to give them back – it was an excuse. Actually, I wanted to know what had been going on."

"Go on, George," said Jacket, quietly.

Mr. Wainewright said: "He was sitting on the bed, just about where you are now, in his shirt-sleeves, laughing and playing with the paper-knife. He started telling me all about his wife, Mr. Jacket, sir – how much she loved him, how much the barmaid at the 'Duchess of Douro' loved him, how much every woman he met loved him. His collar was undone." Mr. Wainewright paused and moistened his lips. "His collar was undone. He had one of those great big thick white necks. I had that pair of scissors in my hand. He threw his head back while he was laughing. I said: 'Here's your scissors.' He went on laughing, and coughing – he was a cigarette-smoker – at the same time. 'Here's your scissors,' I said. I think he'd been drinking. He roared with laughter. And then, all of a sudden, something got hold of me. I hit him with my right hand. I couldn't pull my hand away. It was holding on to the scissors, and they were stuck in his neck, where his collar was open. He made a sort of noise like *Gug* – as if you'd pushed an empty glass into a basin of water, sir, and simply went down. I hadn't intended to do it. I hadn't even shut the door of this room when I came in. But as soon as I saw what I'd done I wiped the scissors with my handkerchief, in case of fingerprints, and I slipped out, shutting the door from the outside, and went back to my room. Do you see?

"Martha Tooth never killed anybody. It was me. I killed Sid Tooth, Mr. Jacket, in this very room.

"And so you see, sir. There was a miscarriage of justice.

Martha Tooth hasn't got any right to be made a heroine out of. She never killed that beast, sir. I killed Tooth. But she," said Mr. Wainewright, with bitterness, "*she* gets acquitted. *She* is made a fuss of. *Her* life-story is all over your paper. *Her* picture and *her* name is all over the place. And the honest truth of it is, that *I* did it!"

John Jacket said: "Prove it."

* * * * *

Mr. Wainewright drew a deep breath and said: "I beg pardon, sir?"

"Prove it," said Jacket. "Prove you did it."

"Do you think I'm crazy?" asked Mr. Wainewright.

"Of course you're crazy," said Jacket.

"I swear before the Almighty," said Mr. Wainewright, with passionate sincerity, "I swear, so help me God, that I killed Tooth!"

Jacket, who had been watching his face, said: "I believe you, Wainewright. I believe you *did* kill Tooth."

"Then there's your story," Mr. Wainewright said. "Eh?"

"No," said Jacket. "No story. It's proved that Martha Tooth killed her husband and was justified in killing him. It's all weighed and paid. It's all over. You can't prove a thing. I believe you when you say you killed Tooth. But if you weren't a lunatic, why should you go out of your way to tell me so after everything has been resolved and poor Martha Tooth has been comfortably provided for?"

Mr. Wainewright sat still and white. He was silent.

Jacket rose, stretched himself, and said: "You see, George old man, nobody in the world is ever going to believe you now." He reached for his hat.

"Still, I did it," said Mr. Wainewright.

"I begin," said Jacket, "to understand the way you work. Tooth was a swine, a strong and active swine. I see how you envied Tooth's beastly strength, and shamelessness. I think I get it. *You* wanted to ill-treat Tooth's wife and betray his girl friends. You were jealous of his power to be wicked. You wanted what he had. You wanted to be Tooth. No? So you killed Tooth. But all the while, George, in your soul, *you were Tooth!* And so you've gone and killed yourself, you poor little man. You tick unheard, George; you move unseen – you are a clock without hands. You are in hell, George!"

John Jacket put on his hat and left the house.

He did no work that afternoon. At five o'clock he telephoned Chief Inspector Dark, at Scotland Yard, and said: ". . . Just in case. That little man Wainewright has just been telling me *he* killed Tooth in Bishop's Square."

Chief Inspector Dark replied: "I know. He's been telling the same story around here. He was in yesterday. The man's mad. Damned nuisances. Happens every time. Dozens of 'em always confess to what they haven't done every time somebody kills somebody. Have to make a routine investigation, as you know. But this Tooth business is nothing but a lot of Sweet Fanny Adams. Pay no attention to it. Wainewright's stone crackers, plain crazy. Forget it."

"Just thought I'd tell you," said Jacket.

"Right you are," said the chief inspector, and rang off.

* * * * *

So Jacket forgot it. Great things were happening. Everyone knew that England was about to go to war against Germany. The nights were full of menace, for the lights were out in the cities. London after dark was like something tied up in a damp flannel bag. Jacket, who preferred to work a little ahead of time, was preparing certain articles which, he was certain, were going to be topical. He wrote a thousand words about a gas attack, under the title *They Thought This Was Funny*, and had it set up, illustrated with a cartoon from a 1915 issue of *Simplicissimus*. He wrote an impassioned obituary on the first baby that was to be killed in London, for immediate use if and when the war broke out. He compiled and elaborated monstrously scurrilous biographical articles about Hitler, Goebbels, Goering, etcetera.

But one evening, as he sat refreshing himself with a glass of beer and a sandwich in the "Duchess of Douro", he saw Mr.

Wainewright again. Mr. Wainewright could not see him: a twelve-inch-square artificial mahogany pillar stood between them, and the hot, smoky bar was crowded. Mr. Wainewright, dressed in a tight-fitting black suit with red chalk-stripes, was conversing with a thick-set sweaty man in a light tweed sports coat.

The conversation had touched the perils and the dangers of the coming night. The thick-set man was saying:

"Buy torches! Buy bulbs, buy bulbs and batteries! At any price – any price at all, wherever you can lay your hands on them. Buy torches, bulbs, and batteries. Prices are going up by leaps and bounds. A good torch is going to be worth its weight in gold. Everybody is stumbling about in the dark. There's going to be accidents in the black-out. Mark my words. Accidents. And crime. Look out for crime."

"Crime?" said Mr. Wainewright.

"Crime. Forgive me if I can't offer you a drink," said the thick-set man.

"Oh please, have one with me."

"No, no! Well, a small one. You're very kind. . . . Yes, crime. Robberies, murders – the black-out sets the stage for robberies and murders."

The barmaid whom Tooth had called Baby said, as she put down two drinks: "Are you still on about murders?"

Mr. Wainewright, paying her, said: "You look out. This gentleman is right. You can't be too careful. What's to stop anybody following you home in the dark and sticking a knife in you?"

The thick-set man said: "Exactly, sir. Exactly."

"I don't go home. I've got no home," said the barmaid. "I live here. You and your murders!"

"Yes, but you go out sometimes," said the thick-set man.

"Only on Tuesday," said the barmaid, with a tired laugh. "If you want to stick a knife in me, you'd better wait till Tuesday." She pushed Mr. Wainewright's change across the bar and served another customer.

"Tuesday," said Mr. Wainewright.

The thick-set man was pleased with his idea. He said: "I'm a man who is as it were *professionally* interested in crime." He looked sideways and laughed.

"Oh, indeed?" said Mr. Wainewright.

"As a *writer*," said the thick-set man, suddenly grave. "My name is Munday Marsh. You may have come across one or two of my little efforts in the *Roger Bradshaw Detective Library*." He cleared his throat and waited. Mr. Wainewright said:

"Oh yes, yes I have indeed!"

"I hate to have this drink with you because I can't return it. . . . No, no – not again! You're *very* good! As I was saying. Assume there is a sort of Jack the Ripper; a murderer without motive – the most difficult sort of killer to catch. The lights are out in this great city. The streets are dark. Dark, and swarming with all kinds of men from everywhere. Now say a woman – Blondie there, for instance——"

"She is called Baby," said Mr. Wainewright.

"Baby. Baby is found dead, killed with a common kitchen knife. There are thousands of kitchen knives. I've got half a dozen at home myself. Say I kill Baby with such a knife. All I need is nerve. I walk past her, stab suddenly, and walk on, leaving the knife in the wound. If necessary I turn back as the lady falls and ask 'What's the trouble?' Do you get the idea? I simply kill, and walk coolly on. Who could swear to me in this black-out, even if anyone saw me? Eh?"

"What a clever man you must be!" exclaimed Mr. Wainewright.

Jacket, who could see his face, saw that the scanty eyebrows arched upwards, and observed a strange light in the colourless eyes.

"Of course," Mr. Wainewright continued, thoughtfully, "you'd use – in your story, I mean – any sort of knife. Something anyone could get anywhere. A common French cook's knife, say: a strong knife with a point. Um?"

"Any knife," said the writer who called himself Munday Marsh. "Anything. You don't wait to get your victim alone. No. All you need is nerve, sir, nerve! A quick, accurate stab, and walk calmly on your way. I'd write that story, only I can see no means of catching my murderer."

The barmaid heard the last word and said: "My God, why is everybody so morbid? Murder, murder, murder – war, war, war. What's the matter with you? You got a kink or something?"

"Wait and see," said Mr. Wainewright. "I'm not so kinky as you think."

Jacket, still watching, saw Mr. Wainewright's pale and amorphous mouth bend and stretch until it made a dry smile. For the first time he saw Mr. Wainewright's teeth. He did not like that smile.

The barmaid raised her eyes to the painted ceiling with languid scorn. Jacket observed that she looked downward quickly. Then he heard the *whup-whup-whup* of the swinging door, and noticed that Mr. Wainewright was gone.

* * * * *

A week passed. John Jacket was eating and drinking at the bar of the "Duchess of Douro" before one o'clock in the afternoon, the day being Wednesday.

"How's life?" he asked the barmaid.

"So-so," she said.

"Doing anything exciting?"

She hesitated, and said: "I ran into a friend of yours last night."

"A friend? Of mine?"

"That little man. What's his name? A little man. You *remember*! That funny little man. Old Murders – I forget what he calls himself. The one that gets himself up like a gangster. Used to go about in a bowler hat. Talks about murders. What *is* his name?"

"You mean Wainewright?"

"That's it, Wainewright."

"How did you manage to run into him, Baby?"

"It was a funny thing. You know Tuesday's my day off. I generally go to see my sister. She lives near High Road, Tottenham. I left here about eleven in the morning and there was little what's-his-name. Wainewright. I walked along Charing Cross Road to get the tram at the end of Tottenham Court Road – you like to stretch your legs on a nice morning like yesterday, don't you?"

"Well?"

"I walk to Hampstead Road, and there he is again."

"Wainewright?"

"Yes. Well, I pay no attention, I catch my tram, I go to my

sister's and spend the afternoon, and we go to the pictures. We get the tram back and go to the Dominion. And when we get out, there he is again!"

"Wainewright?"

"That's right. There he is. So my sister says: 'A nice night like this – let's walk a bit. I'll walk back with you.' So we walk back here. Well, when we get to the National Gallery, we wait for the lights to change before we cross the road – there he is again."

"There Wainewright is again?"

"Uh-huh. So I say to him: 'Hallo.' And he says 'Hallo', and walks off again along Charing Cross Road. It was almost as if he was following us."

"That's funny," said John Jacket.

"Coincidence, I dare say. But he's a funny little man. Do you like him, Mr. Jacket?"

"No, Baby, I can't say I do."

"Well," said the barmaid, reluctantly, "he seems to be all right. But somehow or other I don't seem to like him very much myself. What's the matter? What're you thinking about, all of a sudden?"

"Nothing, Baby, just nothing." Jacket finished his drink, and said: "He was outside here. He was at the tram-stop in Hampstead Road. He was at the Dominion. And then he was here again. Is that right?"

"Yes. Why?"

"Nothing. When's your next day off?"

"Tuesday."

"Are you going to your sister's again?"

"I generally do," said Baby, turning away to serve a soldier.

"What time d'you get out?" asked Jacket, when she returned.

"About eleven or so. Why?"

"I just wondered. And you get back before the pub closes, I suppose? Before half-past eleven, I mean. Eh?"

"We've got to be in before twelve o'clock, you know," said Baby. "Why do you ask?"

"Curiosity. Your movements fascinate me," said Jacket.

Then the lunch-hour rush began to come into the "Duchess of Douro", and Jacket went out.

He went to see Chief Inspector Dark. "Listen, Dark," he said, "you know me."

"Well?" said the chief inspector.

"You know I'm not crazy."

Chief Inspector Dark pursed his lips and said: "Well?"

"You remember that crazy little man Wainewright, the witness in the Tooth case?"

"Well?"

"I think he's getting to be dangerous."

"How?"

"You remember how he kept confessing to the killing of Tooth?"

"Well?"

"Well, Dark, I believe he really did do it."

"Well?" said Chief Inspector Dark.

"If I were you I'd keep an eye on Wainewright."

"Why?"

"Because I believe that Wainewright's gone really mad, dangerously mad at last, Dark."

"What makes you think so?"

Having explained why he thought so, Jacket concluded: "Wainewright's feelings are hurt. He is determined to make you believe, at any cost."

"Look," said Chief Inspector Dark. "With one thing and another I'm rushed off my feet. I'm short-handed, and I'm busy. Is this all you've got to say?"

"Keep an eye on Wainewright," said Jacket. "He's after the barmaid, Baby, at the 'Duchess of Douro'."

"Following her about? So would I, if I wasn't a married man, and had time to spare," said Dark. "Keep an eye on Wainewright yourself. I don't think there's anything to it. I'm short-handed, and I'm busy, Jacket. Will you take a hint?"

Jacket said: "Oh well, I can't blame you for not seeing my point."

"Much obliged," said Dark. "See you some other time."

Jacket left, grinding his teeth. *I'll keep close to Baby myself*, he said to himself, as he waited for a taxi in Whitehall. *I'll show them. I'll make Dark feel small!*

But on the following Sunday, Mr. Chamberlain announced that England was at war with Germany, and ten days passed before John Jacket had time to think of Baby and of Mr. Wainewright.

By then, something had happened.

* * * * *

It happened on the night of September 5th, 1939. The Germans had destroyed the 7th Polish Division, and the French Army had engaged the Germans between the Rhine and the Moselle. U-boats had sunk British merchant ships. The blonde called Baby had her day off, and Mr. Wainewright followed her. She did not leave until half-past five that day.

He had learned something of the technique of pursuit. Instinct had warned him to put on again his dark suit and his bowler hat. He wore, also, a grey overcoat. The blonde called Baby could be kept in sight without his being seen. Mr. Wainewright knew how to play his cards. He saw her coming out of the side entrance of the "Duchess of Douro", and kept her in sight: she wore a fur that resembled a silver fox, and a diminutive yellow hat. It was not difficult to keep her within your range of vision.

Mr. Wainewright followed her to St. Martin's-in-the-Fields, and right, into Charing Cross Road. Something had happened to the current of life in the town. There was a new, uneasy swirl of dark-clothed civilians, like tea-leaves in a pot, together with a rush of men in khaki uniforms.

Baby walked on: she had to walk. Once she tried to stop a taxi, but the driver waved a vague hand and drove towards Whitehall. So she walked, until she caught her tram. Baby climbed to the upper deck to smoke a cigarette. Mr. Wainewright sat below. When she got out, he got out. She disappeared into a little house beyond Seven Sisters corner. He waited.

As he waited he thought:

"Nobody believes me. I've confessed to a murder. They throw me out. They laugh at me. They take me for a lunatic. To the police, I'm one of those madmen who go about confessing – saying they've committed crimes they haven't committed. I killed Tooth, and I tell them so. But

no! I'm crazy, they say. Good. I'll kill her. I'll kill her with a common knife. When the papers report it, I'll mark it with a pencil and go along and confess again. Nobody will believe."

The light was fading. Keeping his right eye on the ground-floor window of the house into which Baby had disappeared, Mr. Wainewright stepped sideways into the road. He put his right hand under his coat and chuckled. Then he heard something coming. He hesitated, leapt backwards – saw that the truck had swerved into the middle of the street to miss him, and tried to jump back to the pavement.

But the driver, having seen his first leap in that treacherous autumnal light, spun back to the left-hand side of the road, and knocked Mr. Wainewright down.

The light truck squealed to a standstill as its rear wheels came back to the surface of the road with a soft, sickening jolt. Somewhere a woman screamed, and a man shouted. A policeman came running, and as he ran he switched on the beam of an electric torch which waggled in front of him.

A few minutes later an ambulance came, with a high, flat clangor of bells. Mr. Wainewright was carried away.

He was horribly crushed. But he also had a knife-wound. A long, wide, triangular cook's knife – what they call a French knife – was embedded in his stomach.

The surgeon came to the conclusion that Mr. Wainewright must have been carrying the knife in his inside breast pocket.

* * * * *

When, at last, Mr. Wainewright opened his eyes he knew that he was dying. He did not know how he knew, but he knew. A cool hand was upon his left arm, and he could discern – in a big, shadowy place – a white coat and a white face.

"I killed Sid Tooth," he said.

"There, there," said a voice.

"I tell you I killed Sid Tooth!"

"That's all right, there, there . . ."

Something pricked his left arm, hesitated, went in deep, and threw out a sort of cold dullness.

Pain receded, tingled, and went away.

Mr. Wainewright said: "I swear I did it. Believe me, do please believe me – I did it!"

"There, there, there," said a whisper.

Looking down at his blank, white, featureless face, the surgeon was reminded of the dial of a ruined clock, a mass-produced clock picked to bits by a spoiled child, and not worth repairing.

Flight to the World's End

Peter John Gospel, a poet of independent fortune, and his wife Betty Lou were regaling a critic named Belcher with strawberries and cream at tea-time in World's End Cottage, when the doorbell rang.

"Now who the devil's this?" said Belcher, putting down his spoon.

"Some gypsy selling clothes-pegs," said Gospel.

"Oh, but surely not at the front door," said Betty Lou.

"Let me go and see," said Gospel, and left the room.

Betty Lou said to Belcher: "*Nobody* just pops in. *Everybody* knows Peter John's working. Who on earth——?"

Then the front door closed, and Peter John Gospel's heavy, meditative tread sounded in the passage, together with a hesitant, metallic clumping; someone in hobnailed boots was trying to walk quietly.

"Who on earth can this be?" said Betty Lou.

Her husband came in blinking, bewildered and a little harassed, and said: "I say, Betty Lou, look – you deal with all this sort of thing, don't you? There's a young man here with a message of some sort. Would you mind dealing with it? Do come in, won't you?" He stood aside and made way for a small broad-faced, round-eyed boy in a blue jersey and dark knickers and big boots, who stood clutching a little round cap and a bundle of yellow leaflets.

"What on earth do *you* want?" asked Betty Lou.

The boy blushed and said, looking up at Mr. Gospel: "From the vicar, sir. Just to give it to you, sir, please sir."

Mr. Gospel took a yellow leaflet between finger and thumb, glanced at it, smiled faintly and passed it to Betty Lou, who raised her eyebrows and gave it to Mr. Belcher.

Belcher said: "Oh, ho! What have we here? The Arts, upon my soul! A church concert, Gospel, at St. Timothy's Hall, and I'm a living sinner! The choir at St. Timothy's Church will perform, believe me or believe me not; Miss Orchis Tweed will sing; Mr. Hatherley will impersonate Dickens's characters; and God bless my soul, the Sixweston Dramatic Society propose to freeze our blood with a performance of *The Monkey's Paw*, by W. W. Jacobs. Here's richness!"

"Can I go now, sir, please sir?" asked the boy.

"Can he go now, sir, please sir?" said Mr. Belcher, with a sly smile at Mr. Gospel.

Gospel was in a good humour now. He shook his head and said, in a portentous voice: "This must be gone into, Belcher. Don't you think so, Betty Lou?"

She, entering into the spirit of it, said: "Oh – definitely." The boy blushed again.

"Sit down, young man," said Belcher.

"Anywhere, sir?"

"No, not anywhere, sir. Sit down there," said Belcher, pointing to a chair covered with peach-coloured velvet. "Yes, sit on it, sit right on it. Now, young fellow, what do you mean by ringing a poet's door-bell in the middle of the afternoon in order to hand him atrociously printed yellow leaflets – execrably printed, I may say, by . . . yes, Rugg and Son of Sixweston?"

The boy's voice quivered as he answered: "I didn't mean nothing, sir, please sir. Mr. Bond told me to, sir. The six best boys give 'em out from door to door, sir. One takes the New Road, one takes the Old Road, one takes the Main Way, one takes the Heath Road, mum, one takes the World's End Way, and one takes the Martyr's Way, mum, and we give 'em out from door to door. It's about the church concert, mum."

"Stop calling me mum, I am *not* your mum," said Betty Lou.

"Yes, mum . . . I mean, yes mum," said the boy, picking at his cap, "can I go now, sir, please sir?"

Mr. Belcher assumed a judicial manner and an air of doom. "Go? Go, does he say? A snivelling Jack Presbyter? Go? Ay, I promise you, you shall go, you rogue, forty cubits high like Haman! I see thee dancing on nothing; crop-headed, prick-eared knave! I see——"

"Don't be such an idiot, Belcher," said Betty Lou. She picked up Gospel's plate of strawberries and cream and a spoon, gave them to the boy, and said: "There you are; don't be a silly boy, the gentleman was only joking. Have some nice strawberries and cream. Here, look, let me put some more sugar on them. And now, eat it up."

Wet-eyed, wet-nosed, the boy held the plate and sniffed. He wanted to use his handkerchief.

"I was only joking," said Belcher, somewhat shamefaced. "Be a Briton! Don't you like strawberries and cream with sugar?"

"I don't know, sir," said the boy, "I never tasted 'em."

"Well, taste it now," said Belcher exchanging glances with Gospel and Betty Lou.

"We are not supposed to, sir," said the boy.

"Not supposed to *what*? Exactly what do you mean?" asked Betty Lou.

"Take things, mum, sweets and things, mum, from anybody else."

"Anybody else but whom, for goodness' sake?"

"St. Timothy's, mum."

"What does he mean, St. Timothy's?"

"St. Timothy's Home for Waifs and Strays, mum," said the boy.

"Are you a waif? A stray? If you don't mind my asking?" asked Belcher.

"Yes, sir, please sir."

"What's your name?"

"Henry Ford, sir, please sir."

"No relation to *the* Henry Ford, I suppose?"

Betty Lou said: "Belcher, *do* shut up. The child doesn't understand you're only joking. And how old are you, Henry Ford?"

"Please, mum, thirteen years and five months."

"And have you been at this place of yours for long?"

"Since I was seven and a quarter, mum."

"And you like it there?"

After an uneasy pause, Henry Ford said: "Yes, mum, thank you, mum, very much indeed, mum."

"Do you get enough to eat?"

"Oh, yes, mum."

"Are you happy?"

"Yes, thank you, mum."

"Then why don't you eat your strawberries and cream?"

"We're not supposed to take things from people, please mum."

"What would happen if you did?" asked Belcher.

"If Mr. Bond found out, I dare say I'd get the stick, sir."

"What's that?" asked Gospel, "did I hear you say stick?"

"Yes, sir."

"Do they beat you?"

"Not if you behave, sir."

"Would you mind elucidating that?" asked Gospel.

The boy shook his head and Mr. Belcher said: "What do you mean by behave yourself? In other words, what do you have to do to get the stick?"

" – or it might just be a smack on the head, sir, please sir," said the boy.

"Well," said Belcher, "what do you have to do wrong before they cane you or smack your head?"

The boy began tentatively: "You can get the stick for taking sweets and things from boys at school. Or you can get the stick again if you get the cane at school."

He paused to think, and Betty Lou said, in a voice that trembled with pity: "I promise you nobody shall know if you eat your strawberries and cream."

The boy raised a spoonful to his lips, hesitated, looked anxiously from side to side, and began to eat. In a minute or two Betty Lou took the empty plate and the spoon and said: "Now, nobody is going to punish you for that anyhow. But did you really mean it? Why? Why? I don't understand. This is barbarism, barbarism! Why? Why, Peter John?"

"I suppose the idea is, to impress upon the world at large that they want for nothing," said Belcher. "And tell me, Henry Ford, what else do they punish you for?"

The boy paused, still licking his lips, and left the pink tip of his tongue protruding, as an aid to calculation, from the left-hand corner of his mouth, as he continued: "We can get the stick for whispering on duty, or if we splash the floor when we're washing, you might get a smack on the back; or if you use too much soap scrubbing the floor, well, sir, you might only get a smack round the ear just to remind you. The same as if you cry, or make too much noise getting coal or washing up, or if you clump your feet going upstairs or walking along the landings, or if you run about, or if you walk too slow . . . you can get it for that, the same as when you talk upstairs at any time, or if you make a hole in your socks or your jersey, or if you have an untidy locker or clothes basket. Or you could get punished for making your towel too dirty, sir, or your shirt collar, sir, or going about with your trouser buttons undone, mum, or your bootlaces undone, sir, or if you hold your knife and fork wrong, or if you say your prayers with your eyes open, or if you don't sweep the lobbies and dust the ledges properly, mum. You get it for laughing when you ought not to laugh, or for not laughing when you ought to laugh – I mean looking miserable, being sulky. Or if you get your knees dirty, or go about with untidy hair, mum, or if you don't learn Sunday Collect and the General Thanksgiving properly, sir, or if you lie in bed with your knees raised. And you can get the stick for not eating your dinner. I mean for leaving leavings, or if you eat up what somebody else leaves, or if you use too much boot blacking, or if you're caught not wearing your apron for Duties. Or if you don't keep your scrubbing bucket and floor-cloth clean, and specially if you wet the bed, mum."

"Good God!" muttered Gospel, pacing the floor and lighting a fresh cigarette from the end of his last.

The boy slid off the chair. "You won't say anything, sir?" he asked.

"Say anything? Say anything?" cried Gospel, in a rage, dashing his pale right fist into the pinkish palm of his left hand.

Henry Ford was opening the door. He said: "About the strawberries, sir, sometimes they ask people. We are not supposed to, mum. If they say did this boy go and eat strawberries at your house . . ." he was confused.

"No, no," said Betty Lou, hurriedly fumbling in her purse, "no, no, don't worry. Hadn't you better run along now?" She found a half-crown and put it into the boy's hand.

"Yes, mum, thank you, mum. I am much obliged to you," he said.

"Well, run along now, Henry Ford, and if there is anything we can do for you, you *will* let us know, *won't* you? Good-bye."

"Yes, mum, thank you, mum."

Henry Ford, having run himself to a standstill fell into a breathless, hopping walk at Six Ways Circus. He was late, and he would catch it. He was yearning now to avoid punishment, and panting to escape a beating, sweating heavily under his dark jersey and durable heavy knickers that marked him as one of the waifs and strays of St. Timothy's. In his wet hand the yellow leaflets had been crumpled to pulp. He remembered that he ought to have delivered them, and now it was too late. What was he to say? He reasoned: *If I tell the truth, I'll cop it. I'll get the stick for sure if I tell the truth. If I tell a lie, and say I put all these bits of paper in people's letter-boxes because I couldn't get an answer when I rang the bell, I might just about get away with it, with luck. But if I tell the truth, I cop it. Better tell a lie and chance it.*

He rolled the sweaty leaflets into a hard ball and threw it as far as he could into the scrub. It disappeared in a gorse bush. There remained only the half-crown which the beautiful lady had given him at Honeysuckle Lodge. He opened his hand and looked at it. Half-crowns, strawberries and cream, and sugar; velvet chairs; there was a way to live! He would never forget how nice the lady was. Even the gentleman who shouted – he was only joking. But the lady – there was somebody for you. Her hands might have been modelled out of scented soap. The big yellow jewels on her fingers must be worth millions of pounds; and what a nice voice she spoke with! A lady, a proper lady if ever there was one. And the way she said: *"Run along now, Henry Ford, and if there is anything we can do for you, you will let us know, won't you? Good-bye!"*

Henry Ford wanted to cry now. He had the half-crown, which was a lot of money; but the strawberries and the cream and the sugar and the velvet and the scent – these were gone, and St. Timothy's stood red and square around the next corner. Mr. Bond and Mrs. Bond were waiting there. Looking from side to side to be sure that nobody was listening, Henry Ford said aloud: "Rotten old Bond, you bloody big bully! Why don't you hit somebody your own size?" When he came in sight of the

Home he whispered: "Our Father which art in Heaven, let me get away with it this time and I swear on my dying oath not to tell any more lies afterwards as long as I live, Amen."

Then he was at the gate of St. Timothy's Home for Waifs and Strays. He slid the half-crown into a pocket, wiped some of the dirt from his boots and went in.

It seemed that God had heard his prayer.

But it isn't easy to get away with anything in Sixweston.

As you pass through the tiny town, curtains stir, little triangles of face appear, and then, as you look up, quickly disappear. You are being watched. Windows have eyes, walls have ears, and the very stones seem to whisper. Woe to the transgressor in Sixweston! Nothing escapes the eyes of the watchers by day and ears of the listeners by night. For example, a certain lady, who had taken everybody in at first by an appearance of unassailable virtue, a soldier's wife with three children, appeared, after a trip to London, in a smart fur coat. Sixweston knew her wardrobe to a handkerchief, and took a grave view of this coat. Some doer of good by stealth, signing himself or herself "Well Wisher", wrote to the lady's husband saying: "Far be it from me to make mischief, God forbid, but I think it is scandalous for your wife to go gallivanting around in expensive fur coats while you are roughing it at Camp . . ." The husband came roaring home with a bayonet, and there might have been bloodshed if his wife had not made it perfectly clear that the fur coat had been given to her by his own sister. He recognised the coat and was perfectly satisfied; but Sixweston was not, and to this very day the lady with the fur coat is regarded as a loose woman, and men leer knowingly at her when they pass her in the street.

Here you must weigh your word, measure your intonation, and watch your step.

The war had its effect on Sixweston, of course. Some of the population went away into the Services. Strangers came in. The Royal Barracks spread itself and became a training camp for recruits from all over the country. Gnashing and rattling, great tanks tore up sections of the common and the heath. On Sundays bored soldiers loitered about the Circus, occasionally whistling after the girls. Outlandish voices were heard – sentments Yorkshire voices, frozen-mouthed Midland voices, glottal Cockney voices; and later, the *Oink-oink-oink* of New Jersey and the drowsy *Eeeah . . . eeeah . . .* of South Carolina. Some of the inhabitants lost sons. Others made money. Like every other place in England, Sixweston got itself a gallon of private grief and a pint of recorded glory. A number of nobodies proved that they were great; several solid citizens demonstrated that they were shrewd. A farm labourer of Dogworth Hill went into the Commandos and got a posthumous V.C.; a poultry farmer of Dogworth Valley went into the black market and got his wife a mink coat. But – by God's grace! – there is virtue left in the world! The pub called "The World's End", where World's End Cottage is, in World's End Way, still lives by the goodwill of the old beer-drinking men of Dogworth, Nether Bottom, and Sixweston Old Town; and sells most of its wines and spirits to ladies and gentlemen out of the Dogworth Hill Private Sanatorium – the quiet ladies and gentlemen who are allowed out between breakfast and lunchtime if they promise on their honour not to drink.

This sanatorium is a respectable cupboard for all kinds of skeletons – a lumber-room for living junk – a repository for every sort of hereditary – and acquired – stuffed owl, broken clock, chipped bust, rusty sabre, gutted sofa, and mouldy writing-desk with secret drawers. Here, storage is paid for certain useless heirlooms which one cannot in decency chop up and burn – husbands who cannot forget, wives who cannot remember, younger sons and stray daughters destroyed by lust, drugs, drink, love and hate. There are some mighty strange cases up in the Dogworth Hill Private Sanatorium; creatures of the twilight. But the inmates have one of the best views of all England. On one side they can see the pretty little town, plainly visible in the clear air, calm and yet remote, like a toy village inside a glass paperweight. From Dogworth Hill in a summer twilight Sixweston is unbelievably tranquil, delicate and beautiful, as the rosy tail-end of the sunlight touches the roofs and the spires, and passes like a blush over the sturdy, square-blocked Saxon church. You can see the six winding roads running away from the Circus, and Martyr's Hill surmounted by the stone cross which marks the place where the Sixweston Heretics were burned back to back in the days of Bloody Mary, singing to the last. Beyond the Hill, the Martyr's Way runs down into the new grey road which goes, straight as a steel tape, to London.

Beyond the town the matted heath rolls away, full of strong, long-drawn curves; dark yet colourful, unkempt, alluring; familiar yet remote like a gypsy woman, it keeps itself to itself and has secrets. From time to time, in hot weather, a spark from a passing locomotive or a sunbeam focused through a dewdrop starts a heath-fire which soldiers from the Camp run out to quench. When the smoke has drifted away you may see unlikely objects that the gorse and the heather have kept hidden – tin cans, broken kettles, oil-drums, frying-pans, chamber-pots, buckets, and (once) a rusty revolver. Wherever the heath burns away, rubbish is uncovered.

Who knows what we might find if the canal dried up? It twinkles behind an elegant veil of silver birches – a languid ribbon of almost stagnant water, scummed with green in the proper season, and occasionally visited by swans that make their nests near the Old Bridge. In September, the stationer at Bullockbridge confidently mails an order for a gross of mixed autumnal tints in tubes; local water-colourists love this bit of countryside. He also sells a considerable quantity of metallic paints – ladies collect fir-cones, mount them on bits of wire, brush them with silver, gold, and bronze and give them to the Church Jumble Sale. Visitors buy this painted detritus to give, at Christmas, to people who don't matter; who cry "Lovely!" and throw it in the dustbin.

Every year old soldiers out of the Barracks cut down young fir trees, stand them up in tubs of sand, and decorate them with empty boot-polish tins and rosettes cut out of old Army forms, in memory of Christmas. They have no legal right to mess about with the trees, yet nobody but Mrs. Obscot has ever tried to stop them. One December day when she was out looking at Nature she caught an infantryman in the act of hacking down a fir-sapling with a slash-hook.

"Are you aware that only God can make a tree?" she asked.

The soldier said: "Well, yes'm."

"Did that poor little tree ever do anything to harm you?"

"No'm."

"Then why are you torturing it?"

The soldier was embarrassed. How could he tell this woman that he and his friends wanted to stick the sapling in a tub of sand and decorate it with empty tins?

He said: "None of your business."

She reported the case to the colonel, who announced in Part Two Orders that it had come to his attention that men had been cutting down trees: this practice should cease forthwith.

"Cease forthwith" became, thereafter, a standing joke. Raw recruits were awakened in the dead of the night and asked if they had been asleep. If so, this practice should cease forthwith.

The soldiers hated Mrs. Obscot for the sake of their Christmas tree.

Mrs. Obscot was a grinning, gaunt, staring, pouncing widow of fifty, who appeared to have been stretched and dried in the wind. Even her eyes and teeth looked dry. She rustled and crackled, hunting people down, wearing them to a standstill, sucking them to husks and hopping on from craze to craze. Her neighbours feared her for her maniacal charity, her inability to recognise a rebuff, and her frightful, persistent voice.

More or less intensely, she believed in everything inaudible and invisible. She could understand unspoken languages, reconcile the irreconcilable, and hear unheard-of noises – the brief shrieks of cut flowers, the thin yelping of sliced string-beans, and the *Ow-owch!* of flayed potatoes.

What the devil are they after, these people who weep for the tree and comfort themselves over the burning logs; who pity the lamb and fry the cutlet? Do they see themselves itemised in some celestial filing-system, collecting a muttered, perfunctory *Thank you* here and there with a gift scheme in view, as we used to collect vouchers out of cigarette-packets?

God knows. I cannot make head or tail of them.

Mrs. Obscot had a niece named Tina Pocock who lived with her and made herself useful about the house; she sewed, mended, and made clothes; went shopping, cooked, cajoled tradesmen, scrubbed floors, polished furniture, and laundered the best linen. As she worked, she sang. She was a natural, as they used to call them; a saintly woman of simple mind, pure of heart, who liked to please people. She shed tears of delight if she felt that she had made somebody happy. If you were satisfied, Tina was satisfied. She had a clear, warm, joyous contralto voice.

One afternoon, Mrs. Obscot heard Tina singing "Drink to me only".

"Why, Tina," she said, "you sing like an angel!"

"No, do I really, Aunt Phyl?" said Tina, smiling.

"You do! Oh, you do! Sing some more, please."

Tina sang "Caller Herrin". Her aunt said: "Tina, I am going to put you on the map."

"Aunt Phyl; let me make you some tea."

"Oh, yes, do make some tea. Make some tea like a good girl, Tina. But all the same, I am going to make a star of you. You're not good-looking, but with a voice like yours – my goodness, they can fake you up to look like anything on earth. Most of these actresses are all paint and powder. You make some tea, Tina, and leave it to me. Why didn't you tell me you could sing?"

Mrs. Obscot asked the vicar to let Tina sing in the concert.

"I'm going to get her on the stage, or into the films," she said.

"Why not, why not indeed?" said the vicar. "Who knows? Why not? Our little concert is, after all, a start. One can never tell where such things may lead to, don't you think, Mrs. Obscot? Everybody comes to our little concerts. For instance, the author, Peter John Gospel. He has highly influential friends. For example, the critic, Mr. Belcher, is stopping with Mr. Gospel for a week or two. A word from him, for instance, might go a long, long way."

"I'll go and see him at once," said Mrs. Obscot, rising.

The vicar got between her and the door and said: "My dear Mrs. Obscot, I shouldn't if I were you. Mr. Gospel is a shy man, a reticent man. He'll come to the concert, Mrs. Obscot, have no fear."

"Will he?"

"Oh, he will, I promise you, he will, he will! Apart from the posters pasted on the walls, Mrs. Obscot, we have our door-to-door canvassing, if I may employ the phrase. Mr. Bond sends the most reliable of his boys from house to house with leaflets, a fortnight before the concert. Good boys, grateful and reliable boys – they never fail us, Mrs. Obscot, so set your mind at rest."

"I dare say you know best. I'll be guided by you, Mr. Reason."

Mrs. Obscot went out. Near the gate of St. Timothy's Home for Waifs and Strays, she met Mr. Bond. He lifted his black hat. Mrs. Obscot said: "Now mind, Mr. Bond, mind you send out all the invitations for the concert!"

"Without fail, dear lady," said Bond.

"*Do* see that Mr. Gospel is invited, won't you?"

"The literary gentleman, my dear madam? The gentleman over at World's End? Without fail!"

"I shall be very annoyed with you if he isn't there," said Mrs. Obscot.

"Heaven forbid," said Mr. Bond.

She went on her way. Mr. Bond's smile faded. He entered St. Timothy's, hung up his hat, cleared his throat with a great rattling noise, and asked: "Which boy gave out leaflets along World's End Way?"

"Henry Ford, sir, please sir."

"Send him to me."

Henry Ford came, with a fluttering stomach and a pale face. Mr. Bond stared him out of countenance and said: "Ford, I understand you distributed some of the concert leaflets in World's End Way?"

"Yes, sir," said Henry Ford, blushing.

"Right. Do you know a house called World's End Cottage?"

"I think so, sir. Yes, please sir."

"Did you deliver a leaflet there, Ford?"

Henry Ford stammered: "Oh, yes, sir, I did, sir."

"To whom, Ford?"

"I gave it to a gentleman, sir."

"Did you see anybody else, Ford?"

"Yes, sir, another gentleman, sir, and a lady, sir."

"So, Ford, you gave your leaflet to a gentleman, did you? What kind of a gentleman?"

"Please, sir, he looked worried. He walked up and down, sir. He smoked cigarettes, sir."

"And you gave him the leaflet, did you? You're quite sure now?"

"Oh yes, sir, quite sure."

"Go."

Henry Ford went back to his duties, giggling with relief. He had thought for a moment that somebody had been talking about the strawberries and cream. He was convinced now that there was virtue in prayer. That night, for the love of God and for good measure, he said as much as he could remember of the Twenty-Third Psalm.

But that evening Mr. Bond talked with his wife, who was matron of the House; a square-cut, resolute woman whom he addressed as "Mama", although she had never borne a child. She usually had a great deal to say, and uttered every word with decision, inflexibly, and with a suggestion of irony. If she said: "It's a nice day," you felt that she could say a lot more to the day's discredit, if she chose. When she talked she clasped her hands, dovetailed the fingers and pressed the palms together, making one fist out of two.

Mr. Bond was a large, loose, quiet-walking man with a soft thick voice which could roar like a blast furnace when he was angry, but generally sounded as if his throat was full of fluff and dust and crumbs such as you find in the pocket of an old overcoat. When his voice rose his eyes opened; they swelled like bubbles as his wrath boiled up until they strained out of their sockets and glared through networks of bright red veins. His clothes were neither grey nor black. He dressed himself like an impending thunderstorm in an indefinable darkness, relieved only by the whiteness of his collar and a V of shirt front.

His wife, when she was angry, narrowed her eyes, swallowed her voice in a great gulp, and said nothing for the time being. She was a thrifty woman and a good manager – she could make one blast of temper last for three weeks; hashing it, rehashing it, warming it up, slicing it cold, mincing it into bitter little rissoles, boiling the bones of it for soup, and reluctantly throwing the indigestible residue to the dog. But Mr. Bond thought nothing of squandering a rage in five minutes. Still, he was rich in anger: he might grow calm in a little while, but there was plenty more where the last one came from.

They were highly regarded in their circle. There was nothing to be said against them. They were non-smokers, non-drinkers, active in all sorts of good work; and above all, they suffered little children.

* * * * *

Mr. Bond was saying: "Just as I was coming in this evening I saw that Obscot woman."

"Oh, her. And what's *her* trouble now?"

"I didn't ask her, Mama. But she stopped to have a little chat with me. She wanted to be sure that that writing man, Mr. Gospel, was coming to the concert. Now I wonder why. I didn't think that Mrs. Obscot had anything much to do with the Gospels, did you?"

"Oh, *them*. Nobody has much to do with them. But now I come to think of it, that niece of hers, what's her name?"

"Miss Pocock?"

"Poor girl, she's singing at the concert."

"Why, now that you mention it, so she is, Mama. But why the Gospels? What have they got to do with it?"

Mrs. Bond turned down the corners of her mouth and said: "Oh, them. They're very important people. And they have a gentleman staying with them. A very great gentleman, a critic, a very great critic."

"Anyway, Mrs. Obscot made a point of asking me whether we'd sent a concert leaflet to the Gospels."

"Quite right, too. The papers will be full of it. There won't be room for anything else once your Miss Pocock starts singing. It isn't as if she was only a nightingale, is it? She has the looks that go with the voice, hasn't she? I don't doubt for a moment——"

"My dear, what on earth is the use of talking to me like that. You know Mrs. Obscot."

"Oh, her. I know her."

"You know what a dangerous woman she is, Mama. I only mentioned it because of that."

"Oh yes. Very dangerous. I shiver in my shoes at the sight of her. Well, to cut a long story short, have the Gospels got their precious concert leaflet?"

"Henry Ford delivered it."

"Oh, him! *He* did, did he?"

"I particularly asked him about it. But what I meant to say was this: since Mrs. Obscot is making such a fuss about it, I wonder if you could – you know, in the course of passing by – drop in and make certain that they've got their leaflet at World's End Cottage?"

Mrs. Bond's eyes became narrow, and she gulped, and said nothing.

"Oh dear," said Mr. Bond, "don't take it like that."

"So you want me to go canvassing, do you?"

"Mama, you know what Mrs. Obscot is."

"Well, then, since you're such a diplomat, you'd better go yourself," said Mrs. Bond.

"But damn it all——"

"I've yet to see the situation that is improved by the use of foul language," said Mrs. Bond pouring the last cup of tea.

Her husband went out closing the door quietly and deliberately.

He wished to goodness that Mrs. Obscot might choke on her next mouthful of bread. He had a certain dread of strangers; he wasn't the sort of man who enjoyed paying visits. He feared a rebuff as some men fear death, and never knew just what to say, or how, or when to say it. On the other hand, he had a hunger for the society of desirable people. In little, misty day-dreams he saw himself as a friend of the great, invited to fine houses and received as an equal in his own right. He wanted very much to visit the Gospels, but not in this way, it made him feel indescribably silly.

* * * * *

The boy, Henry Ford, feeling that he had been delivered by a special dispensation of Providence from ineluctable torments and punishments, decided to become a Christian martyr, instead of an African explorer. He would get a job as a missionary, with a view to being burnt alive by heathens. He made up his mind that as he burned, he would sing.

To begin, he wanted to sell all he had and give to the poor. But what had he to sell or give? He took stock of his treasures and found that he possessed a broken penknife, with half a blade, a toy magnetic compass, half an indelible pencil which he used for tattooing anchors on his left arm when he wanted to pretend that he was a pirate, a Chinese coin with a square hole in the middle, a cog-wheel out of a clock, which could be spun like a top, a broken cigarette-holder and a little metal case which had contained a cyclamen lipstick, two-thirds of a pocket comb, and the cup-shaped cap of a thermos flask which he carried in case of shipwreck. There was also the half-crown he had got from Mrs. Gospel.

Now he had only to find the poor.

Henry Ford knew several poor boys. There was Baldwin, who had a weak bladder and a nervous tendency to burst into tears whenever anyone spoke to him; a very wretched boy, whom Mr. Bond found particularly irritating.

There was Austin, a snivelling boy with a pasty face who, like Huxley's Ape, was hated for his dirty nose, and whom nobody could possibly love. He, too, was a poor boy, a revoltingly poor boy, to whom tears came very easily, especially at school, where the weakest and most despicable boys with homes of their own kicked him on the shins and punched him in the stomach to enjoy the spectacle of his slobbering grief.

Again, there was a boy named Fred Jones, who was always in trouble because of his touchy temper. At school, Fred Jones got beaten for fighting; at the Home Mr. Bond beat him for having been beaten at school. And still he fought. Recently he had been doubly punished for saying that it didn't hurt; and still he stayed dry-eyed; tense, dark, sullen, always ready for another battle. It was whispered that he had a special sort of skin, like a crocodile, which made him impervious to punishment. But once, in the lavatory – Jones had not been beaten that time – Henry Ford caught him in the act of crying into his sleeve and had asked what was the matter. Jones started up, struck at him, missed, and ran away. Later, Henry Ford gave him the lens out of a broken bicycle-lamp – a burning glass, incalculably valuable on desert islands. After that, they became friends, although they never exchanged fifty words. He wanted to give Fred Jones something, too, and make him happy.

He would get change and give Jones half of his half-crown; or, say, a shilling. Perhaps sixpence.

Next day he sought out Baldwin, the bed-wetter, in the school playground and said: "Come over here, I want to talk to you."

Goggling with trepidation, Baldwin shuffled backwards to the nearest wall. Henry Ford came close, fumbling in a pocket, pulled out the broken penknife clutched hard in a tightly-closed fist, and said: "I've got this for you."

The other boy glancing at the clenched fist, burst into tears, and ran away, crying over his shoulder: "Why don't you leave me alone? I never done anything to you, did I? I'll tell teacher if you don't let me alone!"

Then Henry Ford was sad. His feelings were hurt. He looked at the broken penknife. It was a very good broken penknife. But in an inexplicable rage he threw it away without taking the trouble to see where it fell.

He sat next to Austin in the classroom. During the afternoon arithmetic lesson, while the teacher's back was turned, he fished out his broken cigarette-holder and dropped it in Austin's exercise book. The teacher turned from the blackboard and said:

"I've got my eye on you!"

He had not: it was a stratagem by means of which he kept law and order in the chalky badlands of the classroom, but Austin, bursting into tears, cried: "Oo, I never, sir! Please sir, it was Ford, please sir!"

The teacher was a tired man, a bored man, but not an ill-natured man. "Don't let me have any more of this nonsense from *you*, Ford," he said. "Stop that idiotic blubbering, Austin, and pay attention."

Almost punch-drunk with injustice, Henry Ford whispered: "You wait, Austin – I'll murder *you*!"

The teacher said: "Stop that whispering!"

"Please sir, he said 'I'll murder you'," sobbed Austin.

"Ford! Come out. Stand there. Now stand still and be quiet!"

So he stood in front of the class for the remainder of the period, trying to look as if this kind of thing amused him; winking whenever he caught someone's furtive eye, and occasionally making a grimace which he intended to be expressive of whimsical nonchalance – like the face of Rex Darrell, the Battling Duke, whose fantastic adventures covered four or five pages every week in *The Knockout*. Darrell the Battling Duke was unconquerable; he went to Mars in a space-ship on the seventh of the month, was back on Earth in a continent under the sea on the fourteenth, and up on dry land winning the heavyweight championship of the world by the twenty-first; always wearing a monocle.

Henry Ford unpocketed his half-crown, looked at Fred Jones, and screwed the coin into his orbit. He was sure that the teacher was not looking. Yet the teacher saw, and said: "Ford!"

The half-crown fell; Henry Ford caught it, recovered his balance, and stood, looking foolishly at his feet.

"Ford," said the teacher, "I don't know what can have come over you to-day. Is anything wrong?" He was a good man who in his youth had read Cutcliffe Hyne and wanted to be a wiry little sea-captain with flying fists and a torpedo beard: and here he was, forty-five years old and nailed to a dusty blackboard.

"No, sir," said Henry Ford.

"I'm trying to teach you how to put two and two together. When you grow up and go out into the world, what are you going to do? Give *me* a job at ten pounds a week or so, to tell you how much you earn every month? Eh?" said the teacher, with sad and weary irony.

"Yes, sir," said Henry Ford, before he knew that the words had slipped out of his mouth.

"I don't want to have to punish you, Ford. I'm trying to treat you like a human being; but you won't let me. No," said the teacher, growing angry, "no! You want to make fun of me. You want to – you want to show off at my expense, is that it? Eh?" And he struck Henry Ford a ringing slap on the head. The boy saw his hand descending, and tried to duck; shifted backwards, and received the slap on his left cheek.

A slap in the face is a challenge and an insult. But what can a small boy do about it? Henry Ford felt tears coming, tried to hold them, but had to let them go. He wept. The teacher wanted to take him in his arms. But he said: "It serves you right, Ford. Go and sit down now, and – and – and be a good boy."

"Sir," said Ford, and sat in his place next to Austin, who grinned at him with a certain malevolence and made a wet, bubbling noise with his nose.

"Now, pay attention!" cried the teacher. He gave the class an exercise in compound interest. He was sad, flat and depressed. There was no vice in the man! But once in a while petty irritation gathered and swelled up, throbbing like a whitlow, yearning for a pin-prick. In good time it burst, leaving a pale, flabby emptiness. The trouble was that the thing never burst at the right moment. He never lost his temper with the headmaster, the inspector, the vicar, or any of the governors, although for fifteen years he had wanted to tell them exactly what he thought of them. But no; he became terrible only to small boys, and told them what he did not think of them. And he was ashamed. He walked around the classroom looking over the boys' shoulders, and paused by Henry Ford's desk. For one mad moment he wanted to say: "I beg your pardon, Ford; I didn't mean to hit you, but what with one thing and another I lost my temper" – offering his hand in proper humility.

But then the bell rang and the lesson was over, and a great weight fell upon the heart of Henry Ford, so that even if he could have found words to say he would not have taken the trouble to pronounce them. He turned away. Jones, glaring at Austin, said: "You dirty, rotten sneak!"

He went to join Henry Ford, who was looking at the ground.

"Lost something?" asked Jones.

Henry Ford said: "Penknife. Threw it away."

"Help you find it?"

"Oh, never mind," said Henry Ford. "It's only a broken one. If you find it, you can keep it."

Henry Ford's forefinger was exploring the milled edge of the half-crown in his pocket. He still wanted to share it with Jones, but he felt that he had had enough self-sacrifice for one day. They walked to St. Timothy's without speaking. Austin and Baldwin walked behind them laughing and whispering. Henry Ford was full of hate for these two mean little boys; he despised them for their lack of understanding and loathed them for their treachery. He wanted to hurt them; but at the same time he felt a great love for the taciturn, savage, loyal, tongue-tied friend who walked beside him. He had an inspiration. He stopped, laying his hand on Jones's shoulder, and said: "Wait a minute." Then as Austin and Baldwin came close, he took the half-crown out of his pocket, showed it to Baldwin, who gasped; held it under the nose of Austin who sniffled; and then thrust it into Jones's hand, saying: "Here you are, Jonesey, here's half-a-crown."

Jones said: "You mean you want to give me this for nothing?"

"That's right."

Baldwin gasped and said: "Where did you get it?"

Ford replied: "That, my good fool, is my affair."

"Give us one?" suggested Austin. "Come on – one each?"

Rex Darrell laughed a sinister laugh: "Ha-ha! – You amuse me, my fine feathered friend!"

Then he walked on with Jones, his left-hand in his pocket, which was always full of large-calibre pistol-ammunition and ten-pound notes; his right hand swinging. With his right hand he could fell an ox. Upon its third finger blazed a diamond bigger than a hazel-nut, the gift of the Princess Florabell, who had accompanied him in the rocket-ship when he visited the planet Neptune to kill King Krag, who wanted to destroy the earth with atomic rays.

"Do you want to give me this?" asked Jones.

Henry Ford fell three light-years and found himself on the gravel that led to St. Timothy's Home for Waifs and Strays.

"Eh? Why?"

Jones, with hellish intuition, said: "I thought you just wanted to pretend to give it to me because of those two. I can give you it back when nobody's looking."

Henry Ford blushed and said: "I gave you it for keeps, Jonesy. What are you going to do with it?"

"I don't know," said Jones.

Stepping out of the sunlight and the open air into the shadows that smelt of floor polish and disinfectant, Henry Ford whispered: "Jonesy, where do you hate most – school, or here?"

"I hate them both," said Jones.

"To-morrow's Saturday," said Henry Ford. "No school till Monday."

"I don't care one way or another," said Jones.

"I wish I was twenty."

"What are you going to do when you are twenty?"

"Want to go abroad."

"Where to?"

"Anywhere."

"We could get to Dover and go to Calais," said Henry Ford. He was thinking of the map; the Channel was no wider than his thumb. He had heard that on a clear day the French coast was visible from Dover. Once in Calais, he reasoned, everything would be simple. He would go from Calais to the Bering Strait, arriving in the dead of winter when the sea is frozen. Leaping over the floating ice, he could reach the coast of Alaska, work his way south, picking up whatever gold he happened to discover en route and so get to Dakota. He had a great yearning for Dakota. In a little while he would come back with his pockets full of money and show Sixweston what was what.

"What do we use for a boat?" asked Jones.

Henry Ford was irritated by this question. He said: "It's only twenty miles. People can swim twenty miles. Thousands of people swim the Channel."

Jones said: "Why talk silly: it can't be done."

"You know everything, I suppose. But I bet you a million pounds it can be done."

"You haven't got a million pounds."

Rummaging in his mind for something worth saying, Henry Ford found nothing, and said: "How do you know I haven't?"

"You wouldn't be here if you had."

"Well, I did give you half a dollar just now," he said.

Jones replied: "You can take your half-dollar back if you like."

"I don't want it back."

Later, Jones said to Henry Ford: "You can have my rag if you like."

The boys of St. Timothy's scrubbed the floors of the Home. Sometimes they fought over floor cloths. Jones owned a very beautiful scrubbing rag; the remains of a woollen under-vest which he had found on the heath. None of the boys had dared to try and steal it. A good scrubbing rag was something worth fighting for, and Jones, when he fought, did not care how hard he hit, or where.

Henry Ford was touched. He said: "My scrubber's okay, Jonesey, thanks all the same."

"Well, to-morrow's Saturday," said Jones.

"Then comes Sunday."

"What's the difference?" said Jones, drearily.

Yet the day after next was destined to be an important day in the life of Henry Ford. For on Sunday afternoon, Mr. Bond, driven by dread of Mrs. Obscot's anger, called upon the Gospels at World's End Cottage.

* * * * *

Bond dressed for this visit with particular care, in the black coat and striped trousers which he wore only for the most momentous occasions, and – not without hesitation – stuck a couple of pinks in his buttonhole. Contemplating his reflection in the mirror on the wardrobe door, he decided that, when all was said and done, he was by no means a bad figure of a man – in a way, an impressive sort of person; taller than most Cabinet Ministers, and much better dressed than, say, Mr. Bevin. His new bow-tie really looked very well indeed; it was black with a discreet pattern of white dots; and set off his face, he thought, and gave a touch of squareness to his whole head. His wife watched him, with her sour, ironical smile, and said: "Where's the wedding?"

"I have to go and call on the Gospels, as you very well know."

"Oh dear, oh dear me. However could I have forgotten that? Oh yes, of course, you must make yourself beautiful for the Gospels. Can I cut you a few more pinks for your buttonhole? Or shall I go and ask Lord Sixweston's gardener for an orchid? What a pity you haven't got yellow gloves to wear. Or perhaps I ought to be thankful that you haven't. You look so dashing, I dare say I ought to be afraid that your Mrs. Gospel might lose her head over you."

"I don't see anything to laugh at," said Mr. Bond, dark with anger.

"Of course you don't. Well, enjoy yourself; have a nice time."

At World's End Cottage, Bond paused to dab his face with a handkerchief, and then rang the bell. Suppose they were not at home? A nice thing that would be. Footsteps sounded. The door opened and a beautiful, tall, dark lady appeared. Mr. Bond's heart jumped and fluttered like a frightened bird. He felt himself blushing from head to foot; breaking out in a hot bright redness like a neon tube when the electric current goes thrilling through it. The woman was naked, by heaven, stark naked. At least she would have been, if she had not been wearing a bathing suit, a most sensational bathing suit that consisted of a strip of yellow stuff at the bosom, and a scanty, skin-tight pair of knickers. He looked down and saw her feet. Painted toe-nails protruded through the opening of a pair of strange wooden-soled sandals. She was not at all disconcerted. "Oh, so sorry, coming to the door like this. I thought you might be a friend we were expecting," she said.

Bond did not know where to look. The whole world seemed to be bristling with breasts, bursting with buttocks, and straining under sweaty white skin. He forgot the little introductory speech he had prepared and said: "I – I – I – beg your pardon, Madam. I – I – I hope I haven't disturbed you."

"Not at all."

"Oh, er, Mrs. Gospel, I have a – a – a message. Not exactly a message, no. Well, yes, in a way, yes, a message."

"Well, look, come in, won't you? We are all having a drink in the garden, if you don't mind stepping out there. It seems such a pity to waste all this sunshine, don't you think?"

"Oh yes, you're quite right. If I am not intruding."

"Not a bit, come in – or should I say, come in and come on out?"

Mr. Bond's nostrils, unpolluted by nicotine, detected an odour of strong drink. The door closed. He remembered that the interior of World's End Cottage was unconventionally luxurious, and that it must have cost a pretty penny; but he was too confused to observe much. It was like a dream ... a respectable man walks along a respectable street, knocks at a respectable door; and a naked houri appears, conducts him through half-darkness full of strange shapes which elude recollection, into a beautiful garden full of sprawling pagans drinking the wine of madness out of green glass cups. There were three more people in the garden. Two of them were men, and they were reclining upon ungodly couches of coloured canvas. One of the men was short and burly, nude except for a pair of flannel trousers and a singlet. The other man was wrapped in a long roomy red bath-robe, and was smoking cigarettes with a kind of nervous deliberation, as if he had wagered more than he could afford that he could smoke a certain number of cigarettes in an impossibly short space of time. Between them, in the convenient shade of a little tree stood a low table with a box of cigarettes, a bottle of brandy, and a syphon of soda water. In the full glare of the sun, a great tawny blonde woman lay upon a red blanket. She glistened with oil, her bathing suit was a menace to civilisation; it did not fit closely enough, big as she was, and Mr. Bond knew that if he approached very close, lay flat on his stomach, watched closely, and waited until she moved, he would be able to see things which should never be seen or even thought of.

The man in the robe looked at him with the air of a diabolical high priest as Mrs. Gospel – she had undoubtedly been drinking – said: "This is Mr. Thingummy. What did you say your name was?"

"Bond, of St. Timothy's," said Bond.

"Awfully sorry but you know how it is: I didn't remember for the moment. This is Mr. Timothy. Mr. Timothy, my husband."

"How do you do?" said Peter John Gospel, but his tone indicated that he did not care how Bond did.

"Great honour and privilege——"

" – Mr. Timothy, Mr. Belcher."

"How do you do, sir?" said Bond.

"I do, I do. Do you? Will you?" said Belcher, pointing to the bottle.

"Thanks all the same, but I never touch it. I have never touched it in my life. I neither smoke nor drink, but don't let that stop you," said Bond.

"Thank you, Timothy, I won't let it stop me since you are so kind," said Belcher, throwing Bond into confusion.

Mrs. Gospel said: "The lady you see cooking gently in her own juice is Melissa. She's asleep. Sit down," said Mrs. Gospel, "and if you're sure you won't have a drink———?"

"Perhaps a little soda water."

"Mr. Timothy has a message, Peter John."

"I have come really on behalf of Mrs. Obscot," said Bond, deriving a certain courage out of the sound of the name: "Mrs. Obscot," he repeated.

"Obscot?" said Peter John Gospel, "I don't know any Obscots. I know somebody named 'Scot'. But he's dead. Obscot, odd name. There is a place called Penobscot, I believe. If I remember right, Iroquois squaws tortured to death several European settlers whom they captured near Penobscot." He went on abstractedly: "We don't seem to be able to amass full details of Indian torture; but they must have brought torture almost to a fine art, as the Chinese did, since – I beg your pardon, do go on, Mr. Timothy."

"Excuse me, Mr. Gospel, *Bond*."

"Forgive me, but I'm afraid I don't understand. Obscot, Timothy, Bond – I don't understand! Elucidate, will you have the goodness?"

Betty Lou ran to his side, holding his hand, and said: "You mustn't upset yourself. Mr. Timothy, I'm sorry, but I can't let you upset Peter John. He's in the middle of some very important work." She had become grave, anxious, her expression had changed.

"Better spit your message out and scram," said Belcher, in his off-hand, brutal voice.

Bond stammered: "It, it – it . . . Mrs. Obscot simply wanted you to know that she particularly hoped you would come to the concert. Mr. Belcher particularly. I promised to give you Mrs. Obscot's message. Please pardon my unpardonable intrusion. . . . unpardonable liberty. I did not mean to disturb the gentleman, Mr. Gospel, I'm sure . . ."

Bond rose, dripping with sweat, and clutching his hat. Betty Lou was sorry for him. She said to Belcher: "I do wish you'd be quiet, Belcher – you forget yourself." Then, turning to Bond, she said: "Pay no attention to him, Mr. Timothy. He's just a bully; his bark's worse than his bite. He's got false teeth. But tell me, what concert do you mean?"

"The church concert, Mrs. Gospel."

"Church concert? What church concert?"

"I was under the impression that you had received a notice," said Bond, in an agony of embarrassment.

"Oh, the church concert——" began Belcher.

But Betty Lou silenced him with a glance and said:

"Oh yes, Mr. Timothy, the church concert, of course. When is it to be?"

"I'm ever so sorry. I thought you knew about it, Mrs. Gospel, indeed. Next Thursday at seven o'clock at the Hall. I am told Mrs. Obscot's niece is a – a – a – discovery, and there is *The Monkey's Paw* and, and, Mrs. Obscot was very anxious for you all to come. But I thought you would have had one of the leaflets."

Betty Lou looked at her husband, and then, at Belcher. Turning again to Bond, she said: "What a shame! If only you'd let us know sooner! We'd all have been delighted to come. We were looking forward to it. I'll never forget that last concert, when the girl in green sang: 'Down in the Forest Something Stirred'. If only we'd known. Oh dear, oh dear, what a pity! We all have to go to town on Thursday morning. If only it could have been any day but Thursday," cried Betty Lou with anguish. "Why were we *not* told? We could have readjusted things. But I'm afraid, now it's quite impossible. Out of the question. We just can't do it. You do understand, I hope?"

Bond said: "I hope you'll excuse me, Mrs. Gospel, I hope you'll excuse me, Mr. Gospel. And Mr. Belcher, I hope you'll pardon me——"

Belcher raised two fingers and uttered a benediction: "You're pardoned."

"I don't know what to say, I'm sure. But I *was* informed positively that you, that you, had been informed."

"Unfortunately, no," said Betty Lou. "If only we'd known . . ."

"I thought you would have had one of our leaflets, a programme . . ."

"You know how it is, Mr. Timothy, we get so many leaflets. They get put through the letter-box and one scarcely looks at them. Appeals for this, appeals for that. Peter John is very deep in his new book, and our little world stands still meanwhile. Had we known——"

"Ah, had we but known," said Belcher dramatically.

Peter John Gospel said: "We'll gladly pay for a few tickets. I mean if a pound or two – it is a charitable affair, I believe – if a pound or two, or something like that——"

"No, no," said Bond, backing away, "please, not at all, I assure you. This – this – this——" The word had escaped him.

"Well, well, Mr. Timothy——" said Betty Lou getting to her feet.

"Pardon my intrusion," said Bond, "there was . . . there was . . . a misunderstanding. Someone has blundered as Lord Tennyson says; I beg your pardon. Thank you. Goodbye. Great pleasure. Hospitality, and everything – thank you again. Forgive me . . . better be going."

"Must you?" said Peter John Gospel, looking at his right foot.

"Well . . ." began Bond; but Betty Lou took him by the arm and led him to the garden gate.

"I'm so sorry about all this," said Betty Lou, "if we'd known we would have come. We are awfully disappointed. But there it is. Good-bye, Mr. Timothy. It *has* been *so* nice seeing you, and if there is anything we can do, do let us know, won't you?"

And Bond found himself out of the garden. Betty Lou had got rid of him through the doorway nearest to hand. A previous tenant of World's End Cottage, a colonel's widow, had tacked to this door a plate which said *Tradesmen*.

Bond saw this.

Betty Lou, back in the beautiful garden poured herself a drink, threw herself into a deck-chair and said: "I love them. I'm sorry but I love them. Call me anything you like, but I love these funny men in striped trousers."

The woman who was lying on the red blanket sat up and said: "Oh, couldn't you just tell him you didn't want to go to the bloody old concert and have it done with?"

Betty Lou replied: "We have to *live* here, Melissa."

"I thought you were asleep," said Belcher.

"I was only pretending to be asleep. I didn't want to get involved," said Melissa. "Somebody give me a drink."

"Go and get it yourself, you lazy bitch," said Belcher.

Peter John Gospel began to get out of his deck-chair, but Betty Lou said: "No, Peter John, you relax," and she mixed a drink and gave it to Melissa, with a venomous look. Melissa took both without acknowledgment. The look spent itself in her head like a bullet in a sandbag; the drink lost itself in her stomach, and she lay down smiling and went on sunbathing.

With hate in his heart Mr. Bond was walking back to St. Timothy's Home for Waifs and Strays. His collar was wet and wilted. *Mister Timothy!* His new bow-tie had drooped, his clothes were covered with dust; nothing mattered. He wanted only to get back, to get back quickly so that justice might be done. *Tradesmen!* Thinking of Mr. and Mrs. Gospel he kicked a stone and hurt his foot. *Good!* Mr. Bond looked at his best boots. One of them was scratched. *All the better!* His toes throbbed. Excellent! *Tradesmen*, eh?

Old George, the hedger-and-ditcher, out for a walk with his lurcher bitch saw Bond pass, brick-red and dripping with heat and rage. "There's a hot man for you, Nell old gal," he said, "running about in that Sunday suit." The lurcher blinked her sly yellow eyes. "I wonder what he's after."

Bond was after Henry Ford.

He tried to keep his anger under control, for fear that he might swear or strike too hard. His anger thus compressed, grew hotter. The hotter it grew the tighter he compressed it; and the tighter he compressed it the hotter it grew. At last, in St. Timothy's Home for Waifs and Strays, he called for Henry Ford and said:

"You told me, Henry Ford, that you had delivered the concert announcement to Mr. Gospel. Well? What have you got to say for yourself?"

"I did, sir."

"You did, did you? And what did Mr. Gospel say?"

Henry Ford, feeling guilty on account of the strawberries and cream and the half-crown, hesitated, and Mr. Bond went on, louder and louder: "You are a liar, Ford. You have lied to me, Ford. You lying young dog, you have been making things up.

You never gave that leaflet to Mr. Gospel. You are a deliberate liar, a dirty, deliberate little liar. You depraved young scamp! You lying hound! Can you look me in the face and tell me that you delivered the leaflet, as you said you did, to Mr. Gospel? Look me in the face and answer me, you little rotter!"

Henry Ford looked Mr. Gospel in the face and said: "I did, sir."

His voice was unsteady, and husky with emotion, so that Mr. Bond shouted: "Speak up, you dirty little blackguard and wipe your filthy nose, you disgusting little scoundrel. Look at yourself, you slovenly hangdog liar! Look at your beastly self, with guilt written all over your slobbering face – you criminal, you ungrateful little beast! You did *not* give that leaflet to Mr. Gospel, because I have been there to see. I have been there this very morning to see, do you understand, Ford? You have been lying!"

"No, sir, I haven't been lying," said Henry Ford, "I haven't been lying, sir. I *did* give the gentleman the thing about the concert."

"Oh, you did," said Mr. Bond. "And what did Mr. Gospel say?"

Desperately Henry Ford said: "Please, sir, he said: 'Here's richness!' and sat me down in a velvet chair and . . . and made me eat strawberries and cream."

This was more than Bond could bear. He struck Ford on the cheek with the flat of his fat right hand and shouted: "Now I know you're lying, you cad, you unmitigated rascal, you swinish little cheat, you!" Then, when Ford – overwhelmed by injustice – began to cry, Bond gripped him by the shoulders and shook him, saying: "Own up! . . . Admit that you were lying! . . . Confess! Confess! Confess! . . . Confess, or I'll shake the horrible life out of you, you . . . little beast!"

"I *did* give the gentleman the programme," said Henry Ford.

"You did not!"

"Sir, I did," said Ford, and Bond slapped his face again.

The boy began to sob hysterically, and Bond, remembering that there was to be an inspection on the following day, stepped back, locked his hands behind him and said: "Upstairs, you snivelling creature – upstairs! I'll deal with you later on."

But before he went, Henry Ford said: "I *did* give the gentleman the programme."

"Ford, you are a little liar, and I know it; and you know it. I'll deal with you later."

Later the tough boy Jones saw Ford crying. "What's up?" he asked.

"Nothing."

"What you crying for?"

"I'm not."

"What you done?"

"Nothing," said Ford. "Jonesey, I'm going to get out of here. D'you want to come with me?"

"Where to?"

"Anywhere."

"Where's *anywhere*?"

"I don't care. I'm going to get out of here."

"Walking?"

"Any way."

"Remember what happened to Carr, when he pinched the bicycle. They sent him to the Reformatory."

"I won't pinch anybody's bicycle. I'm going to get out of here. Want to come?"

"No, I'm going to wait. And you wait!" said Jones, through his teeth, "you wait, when I get out! Oh, you wait – just you wait!"

"You wouldn't say anything?" asked Ford.

Jones took a half-crown out of his sock and said: "Better have this back."

"No," said Ford, "you keep that. Oh well. . . . Inspection tomorrow."

"Inspection! The inspector!" said Jones, with a sneer. "'*Are you happy here, little man?*' . . . What are you going to do – say no? You say yes. What are you going to do? The inspector goes away, but here *you* are all the time."

"I'm running away," said Henry Ford. "After the inspection, I'm running away."

"But you don't know where to?"

"I don't know, I don't care. I never did anything. I'm going."

* * * * *

The inspector was always accompanied by the vicar. The boys of St. Timothy's made a group, four deep, and were photographed, smiling. They were ordered to smile at the camera, but some of them could not achieve a smile. Therefore, Mr. Bond organised rehearsals. The tallest boys stood at the back, the smallest boys sat on benches in the front row, and at a certain moment they all said *"Cheese"*, showing their teeth and stretching their mouths. Thus, the boys of St. Timothy's were always smiling, dressed in their best clothes.

"Cheese, now, don't forget your *cheese*," whispered Mr. Bond, as they fell into line for the photographer. But Ford rebelled. He said cheese through his teeth, with a down-turned mouth. When Mr. Bond looked at him he closed his mouth and said *cheese* in a whisper through his nose. His glum, big-boned face made a blot in the group. The inspector said to Mr. Bond: "There is a refractory-looking boy, Mr. Bond."

"The most difficult of them all," said Bond. "And a born liar, I'm afraid. We've had occasion to punish him for lying, I'm sorry to say. There must be some good in him somewhere, and we're trying hard to bring it out. But what is bred in the bone will come out in the flesh, Mr. Rose. Dour, he is, and sulky; unsociable. I hate to have to say it, but there it is. Goodness knows, we're patient."

"He does appear quite deliberately to scowl, Mr. Bond."

"I'm afraid he does. I shudder to think what will happen to him when we have no more influence over him."

"I'd like to have a word with him, Mr. Bond."

"With pleasure, Mr. Rose."

Henry Ford was led into the presence of Mr. Rose, who said: "Come along now, Henry Ford. Up with the little mouth, Henry. Why, my goodness, you almost look as if you weren't happy. Aren't you happy, Henry Ford?"

Ford was silent.

"Has the cat got your tongue?" asked Mr. Rose.

"No, sir."

"You can talk to me, you know, as to a friend, Henry Ford. Do you know, I have a motor-car made by a man named Henry Ford? And he was once a little boy, just like you. Eh?"

"Yes, sir."

"Then what are you looking so miserable about, Henry Ford? You're not hungry?"

"No, sir."

"You have a good home here, haven't you, Henry?"

"Yes, sir."

"You're well treated, aren't you?"

"Yes, sir."

"Well then, why aren't you smiling?"

"I can't, sir."

"Something wrong with your face, Henry Ford?"

"No, sir."

"Then what's the matter with you?" asked the inspector.

"I don't want to say *cheese*, and I don't *want* to smile," said Henry Ford, and then he burst into tears.

Mr. Bond, with an apologetic shrug, said: "You see, Mr. Rose? But we do our best."

Mr. Rose said: "Henry Ford, you had better try and pull yourself together."

The boy could not stop crying. It was as if he realised that the inspector was his last legitimate line of communication with the world, and Mr. Bond had blocked that line. So he wept.

"Poor little fellow," said Mr. Bond.

"Cheese?" said Mr. Rose. "What does he mean by cheese? Do you want cheese, young man?"

"No, thank you, sir," said Henry Ford.

"Go along – run along," said Mr. Bond, with a sweet smile and a bitter glance. "Off you go, Henry Ford. Off you go." When the boy was gone he said to Mr. Rose: "It is by no means easy."

"I quite appreciate that, Mr. Bond; as a matter of curiosity, what does the boy want with cheese?"

"We get them to say *cheese* from time to time. It's an exercise, you see."

"Phonetically?"

"Yes, and gymnastically . . . for the face, the muscles about the mouth."

"I wish one could do more for these boys."

"Ford is not a willing boy, I'm afraid. He's not a truthful boy.

I had hopes for Ford. I let him carry certain responsibilities, Mr. Rose. He seemed at one time to be serious, you know; honourable, conscientious. Then when I gave him certain messages to deliver, I'm afraid I found him out to be a liar, a deliberate liar. I hate to say it: I'm disappointed in that boy. I feel that he has let me down. In a way I feel discredited."

"You have no occasion to feel anything of the kind, Mr. Bond. No occasion at all; there are boys," said the inspector, "and boys."

"How true, Mr. Rose. How well you put it. All the same, this is a great responsibility and, considering how hard we try . . . it's a little discouraging."

"I understand and sympathise. But there are backward and difficult children everywhere – Problem Children. I've come across many of them. Some grow out of it, and others go to the bad. That, I'm afraid, is a Problem Child – intractable, I'm afraid . . ."

The inspector shook his head sadly, and so did Mr. Bond. But then the vicar came up with Mrs. Bond. He was like a partly-melted wax mask of Julius Caesar dripping into and over a collar. Mrs. Bond was dressed for the occasion in pale grey. She was gracious; the vicar was effusive. He said: "Mr. Bond, I am happy, very very happy, at this spectacle of youth in bloom."

Mr. Bond smiled in depreciation, and said: "The little that one can do, one does, sir."

Henry Ford was saying to Jones: "Will you swear on your God's honour that you won't split?"

"I won't split."

"Well, look; after roll call, I'm going to hop it."

"To-day?"

Henry Ford might have said: *"If we go forward we die, if we go backward we die; better go forward."* He said: "Today. Cover up for me if you can, will you, Jonesey?"

"All right. I will if I can. But you know what I'd do if I was you? I'd get out before roll call."

"What for?"

"Why, that'd give me time to nip out to the heath. Then I'd find a place to hide, and lie low till night. And then I'd go on. Old Bond's busy with the vicar and the inspector. If I wanted to nip off, I'd do it now. But where are you going to go to?"

"I'm going to Southampton, and then I'm going off to sea. Jonesey, why not come with me?"

Jones said: "Don't be silly. As soon as old Bond finds out you're gone he'll tell the copper, and they'll have you back in five minutes. I'll wait. It won't be long. And then you wait and see what I'll do! Just you wait and see what I'll do!"

"What'll you do, Jonesey?"

"Never mind. You'll see. You wait. But you'd know what I'd do if I was you? Nip down to the kitchen and get hold of some grub. There won't be anybody down there now. You go and grab some grub."

"Um . . . Well, good-bye for ever, Jonesey."

"Good-bye," said Jones.

The boys had been told to play, and were playing. Mr. and Mrs. Bond, the vicar, the inspector and two or three interested visitors were making conversation in a tight little group. Henry Ford went into the house, crept to the kitchen and foraged for food. He found nothing but a basket of apples; everything else was hidden or locked away. He filled his pockets with apples and, on an afterthought, took a tin sprinkler full of salt.

So, with a toy compass, a Chinese coin, a wheel out of a watch, a part of a lipstick, a broken comb, and the cup-shaped top of a thermos flask, he ran away to sea.

He slunk in the bushes, hiding when a pedestrian or a cyclist passed, loping like a wolf from tree to tree along the canal bank until he reached the gorse and the young birch trees on the common. Having found a hollow, he lay still and ate an apple. Twilight gathered, night fell, and Henry Ford, terrified but happy, believed that he was alone in the world.

He was thinking of Red Indians and listening to the hooting of a distant owl, when a hand that felt like hot iron pincers took him by the neck.

* * * * *

His stomach leapt up to his throat and his heart fell into his belly, while all the blood in his body rushed tingling to his skin.

His head was full of lithe copper-coloured men with tomahawks, who moved, unseen and unheard, under the cover of the dark. But when he turned his head he saw only a little, light-coloured, elderly man. Shocked as he was, after the first glance Henry Ford was not afraid of this man, who might have been fifty or sixty, and had a pitted weatherbeaten, battered face. One of his ears resembled a vegetable. Some appalling blow had beaten in the bridge of his nose. There was grey bristle like a pinch of iron filling on his upper lip, and more of the same on his chin. He was dressed in nothing but a flannel nightshirt, curiously striped, and he had only three toes on his left foot. Yet his eyes were the blank, blue eyes of a baby.

"Leave go of me!" said Henry Ford.

The man in the nightshirt released him immediately, and then it could be seen that he had only three fingers on his right hand. Henry Ford knew – although he did not know how he knew – that this man was mad; that he belonged up the hill in the sanatorium; that he too had run away.

The man said, in a hoarse, unearthly whisper: "Are they after you too, mate?"

"Sir?"

"Do they want to lock you up too, comrade?"

Before he had time to think of what he meant to say, Ford heard himself saying: "Yes, sir."

"Co-mate and brother in exile. Shake hands," said the man in the nightshirt, offering what was left of his right hand. The two fingers and the thumb closed on the boy's wrist, so that he cried: *"Ow!"*

"I'm sorry, brother. Co-mate and brother in exile, I wouldn't hurt you. Where are you off to?"

"I'm going away to sea, sir."

"Ah . . . the sea, the sea, the salt sea unharvested! Lies it behind us, the sea! Bend your oars and your sails to the winds of the morning! Oh Poseidon, show us the shore! . . . Can you navigate?"

"No, sir."

The voice of the man in the nightshirt, although he was still whispering, had developed a rasping note of command.

He said: "I'll teach you. I am a captain. I could take you by the dead reckoning from here around the Horn. Then I felt like some watcher of the skies when a new planet swims into his ken.... Ah me, ah me! When I was your age I was apprentice on the *Olaf Trygvesson* – I too, I too! Even I, mate, even I. What's your name?"

Ford had intended to re-christen himself Rex Beverley, but he said: "Ford, sir."

"Shake. How do you do, Ford? I am Captain Shirley. You are my new first officer. Navigation? I'll show you. We've got a boat, don't you see, a boat . . . a schooner . . . over there . . ." Captain Shirley pointed to the rising moon. "Oh, it little profits that an idle king by his cold hearth beside these barren crags, chained to an aged wife, I mete and dole unequal laws unto a savage tribe that eat and hoard and sleep and know not me. . . . Brother, Mr. Ford, there lies the port! The vessel puffs her sail! There glooms the dark broad sea!"

"Yes, sir."

"Not 'Yes, sir' – 'Aye aye, sir'."

"Aye aye, sir."

"That's better. Ah . . . my mariners, souls that have toiled and wrought and thought with me. . . . You and I are old, eh? But some work of noble note may yet be done, Mr. Ford. I assure you . . . it is not too late to seek a newer world. So push off; and sitting well in order. . . . No, no, don't go. . . . Smite the sounding furrows, Mr. Ford, for my purpose holds to sail beyond the sunset and the paths of all the western stars until I die. . . . D'you know what, they insisted on giving me baths up there? To *me*, mark you, Mr. Ford! To me! Soon we will push off, mate. Soon, Mr. Ford! It may be we shall touch the Happy Isles and see the great Achilles whom we knew . . . though much is taken, much abides; and though we are not now that strength which in old days moved earth and heaven; that which we are, we are. Correct me if I'm wrong. We are! We *are*! Made weak by time and fate, but strong in soul to strive, to find, to seek, and *not* to yield! . . . Very good, Mr. Ford. Carry on, Mr. Ford."

He had Henry's wrist in a terrible grip again, and his mutilated hand was hot and rough like a dog's paw. Somewhere behind the burning dry heat of that hand, Henry Ford felt a quick urgent pulsation and looking at the captain, in a fading light, he saw that he was very ill. So he said:

"Can I get you anything, sir?"

"Thank you, Mr. Mate, you can get me a drink if you will be so good. I'm thirsty. All night long . . . all night long . . . night after night, night after night. . . . And there's a pampero blowing, a wild pampero. . . . Get me something to drink, Mr. Ford, if you will be so good . . ."

"You wait here," said Henry Ford," and I'll be back."

"Rest? Rest? Shall I not have all eternity to rest in? . . . Ah-ha! A star! So near and yet so far! The stars in their courses fought against Sisera. Rest? Oh, now I shall rest, Henry Ford! Get me something to drink, Mr. Ford."

Now Henry Ford performed a noble deed. He knew that the people who ran the sanatorium must be looking for Captain Shirley, and believed that the gentleman of St. Timothy's, together with the Sixweston policeman, were searching for him. Yet he crawled through the gorse to the canal and filled his cap and the cup-shaped top of the vacuum flask with water, scummed with green algae. The woollen cap leaked. He abandoned discretion and ran. There was not much more than a gill of dirty water left when he arrived, and the little old man in the nightshirt was delirious. But he drank the water and said: "That was good. What was that?"

"Water, sir."

"Nor any drop to drink. . . . Water is a very good servant, but it is a cruel master. More. More, Mr. Mate. More."

But Henry Ford had heard footsteps crunching in the gravel by the canal, and he said: "In a minute," and wrung the wetness out of his cap into his little cup. The old captain sucked it down like dry sand, and said again: "Water!"

It was then that Henry Ford became sublime. Not forgetting the homecoming to St. Timothy's, the little matter of the stick, and the melancholy vista of the years ahead, he said: "Look. Let me put my jersey over you, and you lie still just for a minute, and I'll go and get you a doctor."

The old man in the nightshirt got his head up between two

waves of delirium, and said, quite sanely: "No, please don't. I don't want any more doctors. Just leave me alone. I've had doctors for years. Who are you?"

"Henry Ford, sir."

"And what are you doing here?"

"I'm going away to sea, sir."

"Where do you come from?"

"St. Timothy's Home, sir."

"You mean the Home?"

"Yes, sir. St. Timothy's, sir."

Captain Shirley made a lowing noise and said: "Dee-dee-dee-dum. . . . Dee-dee-dee-dum. . . . Dee-dee-dee-dee-dee dee-dee-dee-*dum*. . . . Beethoven. Number Five. D'you know that, Mr. Mate?"

"No, sir."

"*There* is the only important thing in the world, Mr. Ford. *There* is the most important thing in the world, Mr. Ford. Be like *that* man! Ah, the greatness of it! . . . Oh, lovely night! . . . Mine enemy's dog, though he had bit me, should have stood that night against my fire, Mr. Mate!"

"You stay there, sir, and let me get you a doctor," said Henry Ford.

The old man in the nightshirt was making a strange disturbing noise, somewhere between the back of his throat and the centre of his stomach; a noise that reminded Henry Ford of the noise that might be made by dragging a dry stick across a grating.

"Pray do not mock me. . . . To tell plainly, I feel I am not in my perfect mind," said the old man, fumbling at the collar of his nightshirt. ". . . All the skill I have remembers not these garments; nor I know not where I did lodge last night. Do not laugh at me . . . do not laugh at me . . . an old man . . . a few goats, señor, a few goats. An old man with a few goats. Do not laugh at me. I am dying, Egypt, dying. . . . Finish, good lady, the bright day is done and we are for the dark. And so, Mr. Mate, let us roll our sleeves and show our scars and for God's sake . . . For God's sake, Mr. Ford, sit down. . . For God's sake let us sit upon the ground and tell sad stories of the deaths of kings. Ah me! Let's stop to sleep now . . . I am the enemy you killed my friend! So let's sleep now. Oh, greatness! Oh, the wonder of it! The pity of it, Mr. Mate! Iago, Iago, the pity of it—— Oh, Iago, Iago, the pity of it, Iago, oh, Iago, Iago, the pity of it, the pity of it, the pity of it . . ."

Henry Ford tried to cover the captain with his jersey, but the old man pushed it aside. A nightingale sang in the distance.

"Let me tuck you up in this, sir."

"Ah-ha! A bird! While little birds enjoy their song without a thought of right or wrong, I turned my head and saw the wind was not far from where I stood, dragging the corn by her golden hair into a dark and lonely wood. . . . The Crime! The *Crime*! . . . Oh, pardon me, thou bleeding piece of earth, that I am meek and gentle with these butchers. Fare thee well. I know not, gentlemen, what you intend . . . who else must be let blood. . . . Away, away with your robes, Mr. Mate! . . . This was a city built of wondrous earth, Mr. Ford, and life was lived nobly here to give such beauty birth. Believe me or believe me not, beauty was in this eye and in the eager hand, Mr. Ford. Death is so dumb and so blind, Death does not understand. Death drifts the brain with dust and soils the young limbs, glory . . . Death sends the lovely soul to wander under the sky. Death opens unknown doors, Mr. Ford, it is most grand to die."

Henry Ford, having wrung out his damp cap, put it on the captain's head. "Just wait. I'll be back in a minute," he said, and ran away. He remembered that the lady at World's End Cottage had said: *"If there is anything we can do for you, you will let us know, won't you?"*

World's End Way and the New Road make an almost geometrically accurate Sign of the Cross. Having arrived at the point of intersection, where the Roll of Honour stands, carved out of marble, in commemoration of the men who fell between 1914 and 1918, Henry Ford stopped. The night was dark and the world was wide. Before dawn he could put twenty miles between himself and Mr. Bond. The devil tempted him: he went to the left. But a hundred yards away from the main road, he stopped again. He did not know how to leave the old man in the nightshirt sick and alone in the bushes. This was something he could not do. Still, he wanted to escape; he needed to be free; and he knew that if he raised a voice for Captain Shirley heavy hands would fall upon him and drag him back to St. Timothy's.

He paused; then inflated his chest and ran to World's End Cottage. The Gospels had not yet gone to bed; Peter John Gospel opened the door and said: "What d'you want? Who are you?"

"Please sir, I'm Henry Ford, sir. Please, sir, there's an old gentleman, sir . . ."

"What's that?" asked Betty Lou.

"I'm afraid I don't quite understand, my dear. The young man says something about an old gentleman. Can you . . . perhaps . . . ?"

"Now look here. I've had enough of your concerts," said Betty Lou. "We really have had quite enough of your concerts, so will you *please* go away!"

"Oh but, mum, it isn't a concert. It isn't a concert," said Henry Ford.

"What do you want this time?"

"Oh please, mum, there's an old gentleman, and he's ill. He's not well, mum, not a bit well. You said . . ."

"Peter John, what does the boy mean? Old gentleman? Not well? What does he mean, Peter John Gospel?"

"There's an old gentleman who isn't well, sir, please sir."

"But why come to me?"

"The lady said – " Henry Ford began, and then he stopped.

Betty Lou said: "But what is it to do with us? And what is it to do with you?"

Then Henry Ford, like Danko in the legend, tore out his heart and threw it away so that it burst in a shower of sparks, as he said: "Please, mum – please, sir – I couldn't tell nobody because I run away. I run away. And you said . . ." He was crying, but managed to continue: "Please, sir, please, mum, don't tell anybody I'm here. But the old gentleman on the heath . . . the old gentleman's ill. He's not well. I've run away. I'm going to sea. Only please, sir, look after the old gentleman. Please look after the old gentleman."

"But how is it possible to understand this boy?" said Peter John Gospel. "What old gentleman?"

"Peter John, you are positively not going to set foot out of this house to-night!" said Betty Lou.

Henry Ford said: "Oh please, sir. He's not well."

Gospel said: "Wait." Then he put into his pocket the first bottle that came to his hand – a bottle half-full of Orange Curaçao – and covered his elephantine head with a big grey hat. "Lead on," he said.

Henry Ford said: "I don't know who the old gentleman is. I think the old gentleman comes out of the sanatorium up the hill."

"But what made you come to me, boy?"

"The lady said, sir . . . I don't know, sir."

"You said you ran away, didn't you?"

"Yes, sir."

"From what?"

"St. Timothy's, sir."

"*To* what?"

"To sea, sir."

"*For* what?"

"To go to sea, sir. Please hurry," said Henry Ford, "the poor old gentleman is burning hot."

They had got beyond the crossroads and were on the heath. Peter John Gospel, with a start, said: "But, my God, why didn't you call a doctor?"

"I don't know, sir."

"You put me, you know, in a very false position."

"I didn't mean it, sir. I'm running away."

"Ah yes, I remember. St. Timothy's. Poor boy, poor boy."

"Here he is," said Henry Ford.

Peter John Gospel said, to the old man in the nightshirt: "Is there anything I can do for you?"

Captain Shirley said: "Let me be gathered to the quiet west, if you don't mind. The sunset splendid and serene. What said Sophocles? Death is not the greatest of ills; it is worse to want to die and not to be able to. Oh, greatness! Oh beauty! How happy I am! Oh Death! How thou followest the happy and fliest the wretched . . ."

"My dear sir!" said Peter John Gospel.

"Ah! What said St. John Chrysostom? What is death at most? It is a journey for a season; a sleep longer than usual. If thou fearest death, thou shouldest also fear sleep. Yes, yes, a man can die but once, and I owe God a death. Oh amiable, lovely death! Death hath a thousand sand doors to let out life. Oh, divine democracy of death! Sir, I am an old sea captain. And between ourselves . . . I think I am a little crazy. Finish, good lady, the bright day is done and we are for the dark. Excuse me," said the old man in the nightshirt; and then, with the smile of a contented child, he pillowed his head on his arm, sighed deeply and died.

"Is he dead, sir?" asked Henry Ford in a hushed whisper.

"Yes," said Gospel, also whispering.

Henry Ford started to walk away. His throat seemed to have closed so that he could not say good-night. But Gospel said: "Don't go." He was afraid of the dark, now, and did not want to be alone. "Walk back with me."

"I've got to hurry, sir."

"But where, at this time of night?"

"To Southampton, sir. I've got to get a move on."

Now a tremendous pity came into the soul of Peter John Gospel, so that suddenly, in that moment, he conceived something like love for this sad and lonely boy. He said: "You poor little fellow. Oh dear, you poor little fellow. I can't let you go on alone at this time of the night; not all alone in the dark. You must come back with me and sleep in my house, and to-morrow we'll see what is to be done about you. Don't be afraid. I won't tell anyone that you're here. I'll hide you if you like. Come." Then he put out his hand, which the boy took, shyly.

"But, sir . . . can we leave *him* like this?"

"What else can we do? We can't carry him. I must inform the police about the poor old gentleman, and the people at the sanatorium must deal with the matter. Don't fret, little boy, he is happy."

"Yes, sir."

"There now, don't cry."

"No, sir . . ."

"Lost your handkerchief?"

"Yes, sir."

"Here," said Gospel, giving him his own handkerchief, an expensive silk one, carefully embroidered with his monogram.

But as he was about to use it, Henry Ford said: "Please sir, didn't we ought to . . . sort of cover up his face?" In all the stories he had read, one covered the faces of the dead.

"What a strange boy you are. Do you *want* to cover his face?"

"Yes, sir, please, sir."

"Then cover it."

"Could I use this, sir?"

"Use it and welcome, my poor child."

"You could get it back afterwards, sir."

"It's yours to do what you like with."

So Henry Ford covered the dead man's face. But first he took his ridiculous little cap off the cool, still head.

"I'm afraid I haven't another handkerchief with me. How about your nose?"

Henry Ford wiped it on his sleeve, and they walked hand in hand, without speaking, until they reached the crossroads. Gospel found something strangely satisfying in this boy. He liked the feel of his hot, damp hand. He liked the appearance of his broad, homely, melancholy face in the moonlight. Gospel had had little to do with children. When he looked back – and he was looking back – his own boyhood seemed to be veiled by the mists of centuries; and he had never begotten any children of his own. Betty Lou had told him, twenty years ago, that a great poet must live for great poetry; his verses were his children; he must father fine words, not shouting sons and screaming daughters.

At the crossroads he said: "You are a good boy, I like you, my boy."

Henry Ford did not know what to say in reply, but instinctively he squeezed Gospel's hand, and the poet said to himself: *By God, I've half a mind to adopt the boy!*

It would be a very pleasant thing, he thought, to have a sturdy, upstanding, ready-made son in the house – a strong yet sensitive boy like this, obviously capable of receiving into his blond, solid, healthy head all the beauty which Gospel felt he had ready to give away.

But soon they reached World's End Cottage and Betty Lou, in a blue-and-gold housecoat with a Medici collar came out to meet them with a cry of relief for Peter John and a half-suppressed exclamation of distaste for Henry Ford. Gospel said: "My dear, we must get on the telephone to the police. An old man has died up there on the heath."

"But what old man?"

"Somebody from the sanatorium, I'm afraid."

"But why should that concern us?"

"I don't know why it should concern us, Betty Lou. The fact remains, darling; somebody's died over there, and the police must be informed."

"Dearest! You're all white and shaky.... This is all your fault, you inconsiderate little boy! How dared you come here and disturb Mr. Gospel? What did you do it for?"

Henry Ford stammered: "I thought ... that time ... you said ..."

"Please leave him alone, Betty Lou," said Gospel. "Do you think we could find him a little something to eat? Just something?"

Betty Lou's lips had disappeared into a crack, and her eyes had grown narrow. She said: "Darling, how many things am I supposed to do at once? Telephone the police, telephone the sanatorium, and prepare meals for visitors all at the same time at this hour of the night?"

Gospel's anger was rare, brief, and diluted. Nevertheless, he was capable of anger. He became very angry now. "The man from the sanatorium is on the heath not far from the crossroads, Betty Lou. Will you be so kind as to telephone to that effect?" he said coldly, with a frown. "And as for 'preparing meals', I will perform the arduous task of giving this charming boy a bit of bread and a glass of milk."

Betty Lou went indignantly to the telephone, the wide skirt of her housecoat swinging dangerously, like an alarm bell, while Gospel took the boy into the kitchen and hacked irregular slabs off a cottage loaf, sawed lumps out of a cheese, poured milk with a trembling hand, mutilated a ham, and opened a pot of caviare. He found a cold chicken, and served that too, on a bread-and-butter plate; laid out a fruit knife, a meat fork, and a teaspoon, and said: "Fall to, my friend. Fall to!" Then, as Henry Ford hesitated, Gospel nervously tore off the legs of the chicken and put them on to the plate; and got himself a glass of apricot brandy to steady his nerves, and sipped it while the boy ate. He was uneasy. Betty Lou's anger was deep-rooted, and of hardy growth. It could strangle an oak tree. It clung. It was ineradicable. Cut down here, it sprouted again there. Thinking of it, Gospel fortified himself with another glass, and then, feeling stronger, he said: "I think you said that your name was Henry Ford?"

"Yes, sir."

"Have some more chicken. Have some more cheese. Eat it all up. Henry Ford . . . I suppose they call you Harry?"

"No, sir. Ford, sir."

"I'm going to call you Harry. Do you like me?"

"Yes, sir."

"There's no need to call me sir all the time, you know."

"Yes, sir."

"Why are you running away from that horrible place of yours? You've been ill-treated, is that it?"

"I never done anything, sir, and I *did* deliver the programme. And it's not fair."

"Harry," said Peter John Gospel, helping himself again, "how would you like to come and stay with me?"

"Please, sir?" said Henry Ford, stopping in the middle of a bite, while the remains of a chicken-leg hung in his hand like a ragged banner.

"How would you like to live with me?"

"I don't know what you mean, sir."

"To live with me and be my son. How would you like me to be your father? Do you think you'd like that?"

"Oh yes, sir," said Henry Ford, putting down the chicken-bone.

Then Gospel exclaimed: "By God! Excuse me – I forgot something." He went into the room where the telephone was, and just as Betty Lou was ringing off, said: "I forgot to tell you . . . on no account mention that little boy. God knows how I managed to overlook it, but please don't on any account mention that he's here. I promised him, you see. I hope you didn't say anything about him, Betty Lou? It's my fault, of course – I should have mentioned it. You didn't say anything about him, did you?"

Betty Lou said: "I do wish, Peter John, I *do* wish you'd get your friend to use his handkerchief."

"He lost his handkerchief."

"I hope he found his supper satisfactory."

"Yes, yes. But you didn't mention his being here, did you?"

Betty Lou wept as she said: "Oh, Peter John, Peter John! Darling, I really do try hard, so hard! All these years I've tried and tried. I have, I have! I *have* tried to keep you free to work. I've tried and tried to keep you from being disturbed and interrupted. I've denied myself motherhood. I——"

" – Betty Lou! You did not deny yourself motherhood. You insisted——"

" – For whose sake, Peter John? Tell me, for whose sake?"

"For my sake, I suppose."

"You *suppose*!"

"But tell me——"

Betty Lou left the room, slamming the door, and went to bed. She had said to the local police station: ". . . It seems that somebody escaped from the sanatorium and is dead on the heath. Will you ring them or shall I? . . . Oh, there's a poor little boy who's run away from What-do-you-call-it? – St. Timothy's Home for Waifs and Strays, or something, and he's in the house now. I should think you might as well pick him up now. He said he was running away to sea. Well, I mean to say . . ."

"Very much obliged to you, madam. We've had a notification about that. We'll come right along. Thank you very much indeed, and very grateful for the information."

Henry Ford was yawning. Gospel found a blanket, a Kelim rug, two cushions and a leopard skin, and put him to sleep on the divan in the drawing-room. Then he drank three more glasses of apricot brandy and put himself to bed. Gospel was exhausted, and somewhat drunk. He slept heavily. His wife, still wearing her housecoat, lay on her stomach reading a book. At a quarter past one in the morning she heard footsteps and went downstairs. She recognised the heavy, measured tread of big boots on the gravel, and opened the door a second before the policeman's thumb touched the bell-push.

He said: "It's about that boy, mum."

"Do be quiet, won't you? Mr. Gospel's asleep."

"Yes'm," said the policeman, whispering.

"Wait just a moment." Betty Lou went to where Henry Ford was sleeping. She hated to disturb him; he was sleeping so peacefully that his relaxed face was like the face of a dead child. For two crazy seconds she feared that he had died in his sleep; but then he sighed. Betty Lou sighed, too, with relief. Her purse was on the sideboard. She rummaged in it and found two pound notes, a ten shilling note, and sixpence. She took out the ten shilling note, but hesitated; put it back and picked up the sixpence, which she dropped into Henry Ford's left-hand pocket. After that she shook him until he was awake and said: "Time to go! Time to go!"

He arose, drugged with sleep, and she led him to the door. The policeman said: "Come on, son. Home we go."

"Home?"

"Home we go, home we go."

"I was asleep. The gentleman said . . . I suppose I must have been dreaming," said Henry Ford, rubbing his eyes and yawning. "I was asleep."

"Here you are, son, have a lift," said the policeman, who had three children of his own. He picked up Henry Ford, made a cradle of his powerful arms, and carried him. The boy, dazed and bewildered, between sleep and wakefulness, knew that he was going back to St. Timothy's to be punished.

He would be beaten, but he was not afraid of that. He would be pricked off as incorrigible, branded as a lost soul, and ear-marked for hell. This did not worry Henry Ford. Drowsing in the arms of the policeman, wearily rocking between the nightmares of sleep and the bad dreams of wakefulness he thought, with a pain in the heart, of the large, slow kind gentleman in World's End Cottage, who said that which was not. He thought, also, of Captain Shirley, the mad old gentleman in the striped nightshirt – his fellow-fugitive – whose face he had covered. Then he dozed, and dreamed of falling. The policeman was lowering him to the ground.

"Sorry, son. My wind isn't what it used to be," said the policeman, and gave him a penny.

"Thank you, sir."

"Cheer up, son," said the policeman, "it can't last for ever. One little breather, and off we go again. You'll be a man soon. What're you going to do then?"

To the policeman's astonishment, Henry Ford said: "I'm going to be rich, and strong. I'm going to keep my promise to people. When anybody comes to *me*, I bet you *I'll* help him get away. I won't send nobody back. I'll help everybody to get away. I bet you I will."

The policeman lifted him again and said: "Come on, son."

The policeman was very warm, and tired. Henry Ford could hear the wheezing of his chest and the beating of his heart; and he could see, in the moonlight, the gleaming silver buttons on his dark-blue bosom. "I can walk," he said.

"You can walk later on," said the policeman.

The boy relaxed. His eyes rolled away from the silver buttons of the blue policeman to the silver stars of the sky. The warmth of the man, the feverish heat of the exhausted boy, the buttons, the stars, the hot blue cloth and the cool blue night ran together and made a beautiful darkness. "I'll be so good to children," said Henry Ford, and then he fell asleep in the policeman's arms, and was carried back to St. Timothy's Home for Waifs and Strays.

Fairy Gold

PART I

That was the Friday afternoon when a well-known silk merchant died of the heat in St. Paul's Churchyard while laughing at a funny story. Suddenly he folded up joint by joint and died before they had time to loosen his collar; and the weather was so oppressively hot that his friends had not sufficient energy to express surprise or simulate grief. Collars were wet, grey bandages. People were irritable and careless. Water, poured in at the mouth, poured out at the forehead. In the stuffier City offices people were uncomfortably aware of the fact that their neighbours had feet. The minutes dragged, clogged with heat and moisture and gritty with dust. Everybody was thinking: *To-morrow is Saturday, which is a half-day. The day after is Sunday. Then, thank God, comes August Bank Holiday, so there will be nothing to do until Tuesday.* This thought, alone, was enough to unsettle many precise minds, and draw attention away from letters to be perused and books to be balanced. Old, tried clerks, accustomed to detecting at a glance one pennyworth of error in ten thousand poundsworth of figures, were horrified to find their concentration out of focus: they paused toward the feet of red or black columns, bit their lips, banished from their minds insidious fantasies of quiet afternoons in the garden; rushed irritably back to where they had started and, line by line, climbed down again. The stenographers sighed, and there was a great deal of irritable tongue-clicking and some irritating grating of cogs and ratchets as they twirled back the platens of their machines to rub out foolish errors – or ripped away whole sheets before starting again with wet faces and set teeth. Everyone was thinking of cold water or cold beer, green grass or cool shade.

In St. Martin's-le-Grand a solicitor named Pismire, having read a short letter addressed to Forty Richards and Co. Ltd., scribbled an impatient signature and told his managing clerk to have the letter posted. "And now let's get out of this," said Mr. Pismire.

This managing clerk was famous, in the City, for his cunning and his caution. He re-read everything five or six times, even his tram tickets. It was said of him that he had dismissed an office boy for wasting too much pencil in the mechanical sharpener. But the day was so hot that, having looked at the letter, he threw it languidly to a typist and told her to send it off at once.

At any other hour of the day he would have noticed that there was something out of the ordinary in the feel of this letter. The firm of Pismire went in for a characteristically elegant notepaper, very thin but beautifully white and opaque, expensively die-stamped with the letter-heading. The managing clerk knew that such sheets tend to stick together, but did not notice, this afternoon, that the typist had used two top sheets of headed notepaper instead of one. She, thinking of something that could never be, pushed the folded letter into an envelope, which she threw into the letter-box.

Mr. Pismire's letter was not important. It informed Forty Richards that an instruction of such and such an *ultimo* had been received, and that Pismire was proceeding in the case of a man named Greatheart who had accused Forty Richards of stealing his formula for a patent medicine which was becoming vastly popular under the name of *Formula* 40-R. The litigant was obviously mad. *Formula* 40-R was nothing but precipitated chalk, which Forty Richards packed in a pocket-size tin with a tricky cap. When you twisted the cap a square hole appeared, out of which you could shake a balanced dose. He sold it with the assistance of ingenious slogans: *The Wind In Your Stomach Will Fill A Balloon*, and *Every Square Inch Of You Supports A Pressure of Fifteen Pounds. One Hiccup Lifts Tons*, and *Don't Let Your Stomach Break Your Back*.

Pismire's letter was delivered at Forty Richards's office by the first post on Saturday morning. Forty Richards's secretary looked at it and, dabbing her upper lip with a handkerchief, said: "It's only Pismire – proceeding according to instructions."

"Good. File it."

"Yes, Mr. Forty Richards," said the secretary. She was a fat woman, almost overwhelmed by the heat of the day. As she closed her employer's door she saw one of the clerks, walking sedately with a manilla folder under his arm.

"Oh, Mr. Trew!" she said. "I wonder if you'd mind putting this letter in the general file, under *Pismire/Gen/Inst.*?"

"Only too delighted," said Mr. Trew, and he walked jauntily to the file. Having found the right section he opened the filing cabinet and put the lawyer's letter in its proper place. Having done this, and slammed shut the deep green steel drawer, he observed that a sheet of paper had detached itself from the letter he had filed, and was lying on the floor. His first impulse was to kick it out of sight under the filing cabinet, but then the secretary passed on her way back to her little office, and Mr. Trew stooped and picked up the paper with exaggerated care, blowing it free of imaginary dust. The secretary disappeared, puffing and wheezing, and Mr. Trew, looking at what he had picked up, was at first disgusted to see that he had wasted good energy on a perfectly blank sheet of notepaper.

But the obvious costliness of the notepaper made him pause in the act of throwing it away: it felt so like a Bank of England note that he stopped to wish that it were, and to listen wistfully to its crisp, dry crackle as he shook it gently between a thumb and forefinger. Thinking of banknotes and looking at the name of Pismire he said to himself: *Lord, say I woke up to-morrow morning, and found a letter on paper like this, telling me somebody'd died and left me fifty million pounds! Well, of course, it couldn't be to-morrow morning, because there's no post on Sunday. Well, all right. Say I get home this afternoon with my lousy four pounds ten in my pocket to last me over the Bank Holiday and all next week. I open the door of the old digs. I'm a month behind with my rent; I've promised faithfully to let the landlady have a couple of weeks' on account this Saturday. She knows Friday's pay-day, but I've buttered her up with a yarn about a Bank Holiday bonus. I'm racking my brains for some new fairy-tale. I can generally get round her by telling the old girl a funny story, and doing a funny act and getting her on the giggle. Get 'em on the giggle, and you've got 'em, but I'm not in the mood. I couldn't make anybody laugh if I tickled them under the arms, not to-day – it's too hot.... Laugh, clown, laugh!* ... said Mr. Trew to himself, with a brave smile, so pathetically that he drew from himself a tear of pity. . . . *Pagliacci! To act with my heart maddened with sorrow, ha-ha! . . . All right! Go in. Letter in the rack – afraid to open it – most likely a bill. Feel it. Crackle-crackle. It doesn't feel like a bill. Pluck up courage and open it. And lo and behold, somebody's gone and left me fifty million pounds! God! . . .*

Pretending to be busy at the filing cabinet, Mr. Trew played with the idea of writing himself such a letter on Pismire's notepaper and brandishing it in the face of his landlady, for the sake of a few more days' grace. But he reasoned that even the most skilful application of charm and the most carefully devised excuses could not procure him more than a week or ten days more credit in her house; for she was only half stupid, and really did owe rent to her landlord. Furthermore she knew where he worked. Mr. Trew's instinct warned him that, easygoing as she was, his landlady might raise the devil if she felt that he had taken advantage of her credulity. She would come to the office, make a scene, and get him the sack.

No, it would not be honourable to play such a trick. . . . She'd come down on me like a sackful of wild cats. Oh, she was ready enough to let me cheer her up when she was depressed. She didn't mind letting me talk myself hoarse, telling her funny stories when she was crying her eyes out that Sunday when the bath overflowed.

Mr. Trew was thinking of a wretched affair; a little tragedy which his comic genius had transmuted into a good joke. Early in the spring his landlady had ordered a female tenant who claimed to be a milliner to leave the house at short notice. The milliner left, but before leaving she wedged the rubber stopper tightly into the plug-hole of the bath and turned both taps on full. The landlady, who was out shopping at the time, came back to find the plaster of the kitchen ceiling lying in four inches of water on the floor. The water had penetrated to her little sitting-room, and the carpet was ruined. Then all the miseries and humiliations of the past forty-five years came back in a rush. The poor old widow threw herself into a sodden stuffed chair, and wept helplessly. Mr. Trew, coming home just then, felt that it was necessary to do something. The landlady had a pin-cushion – a pathetic souvenir of some steamboat trip to Ramsgate – shaped like an old-fashioned life preserver. She had never stuck a pin into the red plush part of it, because it had a sentimental value: it stood on the mantelpiece close to a photograph of her husband as a young man. Mr. Trew hurled the pin-cushion at her, shouting: "Ahoy! *Lusitania* ahoy! Captain Trew to the rescue! Women and children first!" Then, sitting on the soaked carpet he pushed himself in her direction with his heels, pretending to pull imaginary oars. The pin-cushion fell into the water. The landlady looked at it and had hysterics. She laughed and cried at the same time. Her laughter was so piercing and so prolonged that Mr. Trew congratulated himself for having made the most successful joke of his career.

But when he repeated it, with embellishments, to friends in the City, drawing a ludicrous picture of the silly old fat lady shrieking in her chair with a life preserver no bigger than a saucer in her fat white hand, while he, the comedian, got up out of a puddle, nobody laughed until Ted Middleton said:

"You both had a good laugh, Trew, old man, but you were the only one that . . . made your trousers wet. Perhaps the old lady saw only half the joke."

This was the only funny thing Middleton had ever said. Uttered as it was in his timorous, hesitant voice, it struck like a thunderbolt. There was a half-second of astounded silence, followed by a bellow of laughter that blew Trew's narrative out of time and attention, and killed it for ever. He had lain awake half the night weighing every word and measuring every ludicrous angle of that story, for he was the acknowledged joker of the tea-and-bun shops around Cheapside, the Sidney Smith of the milk bars; an important man in his circle. His acquaintances enjoyed his company in the lunch-hour. He was free entertainment. There was no funny story that he did not know by heart. Consequently he found other men's jokes curiously stale and dry. If, taking advantage of some few seconds of silence, while Trew's mouth was full of pie or hot tea, one of his friends managed to tell a little story of his own, Trew generally looked blank, and said: "And what happened then?" Or: "I'm sorry, old man, I don't think I quite get the point of that one . . . and that reminds me. Did you ever hear the one about the Irishman, the Scotchman, the Welshman, and the Jew? . . ."

He loved to tell stories in dialect, for he was proud of a certain knack of mimicry, and had a mobile, expressive face. As a caricaturist of deformity, he was unequalled; a young man whose mother had died the day before had forgotten his grief in a big laugh at Trew's imitation of a man with a dislocated hip and a hare-lip. He was so popular that the proprietor of a certain Italian restaurant allowed him credit – Trew was always followed by so many younger men.

He had, as you will observe, a formidable reputation to maintain. To be funny all the time is the hardest work in the world, for a man who is not born with wit: the strain of it drives men mad. Days of knuckle-biting and feverish nights of intense thinking go to make the mildewed joke that raises the half-hearted laugh in the half-empty theatre in the provinces. Once in a blue moon a petty comedian happens upon something all his own, which strikes him as excruciatingly funny. Then, more often than not, this masterpiece, this calculated laugh-maker, is destroyed by something unpredictable. In a carefully-timed split second of silence, a miserable fly comes out of the tobacco smoke and tickles someone's nose: there is a sneeze, and people laugh – at the wrong thing. Or perhaps some impatient person, determined to have his laugh in any case, lets out a mad guffaw, in which everyone else automatically joins, drowning the masterpiece in uproar. On such occasions, the bitterness of the jester is terrible, and his hate so murderous that, like Caligula, he wishes that the whole had had one throat, that he might cut it.

In such circumstances it is possible for a professional comedian to be philosophic. . . . The great joke fell flat in Manchester; well, it may hit a jackpot in Leeds, and if it falls in Leeds, there is always Birmingham, or Nottingham, or Bedford. But what is the comedian to do who has the same faithful audience of five or six, every day, day after day? He must bury his joke as dead; and he wishes that he might bury with it the mutilated corpse of the murderer that killed it.

Middleton had murdered Trew's only original joke. Since everyone else was laughing, Trew laughed too, and cried: "Shake hands on that, old man – that was a good one!" When Middleton clasped his outstretched hand, Trew squeezed it, and Middleton uttered an astonished cry and started back, knocking over a glass of water; for Trew had concealed in his palm one of those little contraptions of clockwork that give the effect of an electric shock if they take you by surprise. Then the laugh was on Middleton. He, smiling foolishly, stood up and mopped spilt water from his trousers with his handkerchief.

"Are they wet enough for you now, Middy?" said Trew.

There was another roar of laughter, and for a moment Trew was almost grateful to Middleton for having unconsciously helped him to a new, unexpected climax. Then Middleton, in his artless, silly way, pointed to a little wet patch on his left knee and, letting the company see that his right leg was perfectly dry, said, with a giggle: "Look . . . He-he! . . . That was only half a joke, see?"

Heaven knows what there was to laugh at there, yet everyone laughed again. Trew squeezed the thin whey of sour, curdled laughter through tightly clenched teeth.

"Ten minutes to two," said Middleton. "Back to the office, I suppose."

Trew had heard a humorous character in an American film say: "Don't take any flannel dimes." This struck him as excruciatingly funny, and he had been storing it for use on some appropriate occasion. But now, demoralised as he was, he felt the need to improve on it, to give it local significance, and to bring it home to the hearts of unsophisticated young men who did not know what a dime was. At all costs Trew had to get the last laugh. "Well, old man," he said, heartily, "don't take any paper pound notes."

Nobody laughed. The joke fell flat. The audience reasoned: since pound notes are made of paper, why should one not take them? Trew cursed himself. If he had said *flannel pound notes*, he might have raised that essential, memorable, conclusive laugh. Even Middleton said "Eh?" and looked blank, for he worked in the mail order department of Coulton Utilities: hundreds of pounds-worth of paper money passed through his hands every day.

If only I had said "flannel postal orders"! thought Trew. He tried it:

" – Or flannel postal orders."

But it was too late. Only a junior clerk in an insurance company sniggered tentatively, as he always did when Trew said something. Trew went back to his desk. This had been one of the most miserable mornings of his life. That afternoon he made three foolish mistakes, through sheer inattention. His mind was not on his work; he was thinking of revenge.

Now a great comedian must be a great man – a man of fine instincts, because he must never hurt the weak, mock the noble, deface the beautiful, distort truth, or undermine virtue. Great comedians are honourable, merciful, intelligent, and selective in marksmanship. No missile in the world takes more careful aiming than a custard pie thrown at the right time to the right place. A great comedian, therefore, helps to destroy evil by making you laugh at a tyrant, a coward, a poseur, or a fool; if he wishes to attack the abject, he personifies himself as all that is despicable, and tears himself down. He does what he has to do the hard way, because great men naturally take the hard road. But may God save us all from the little would-be comedian; the one who says "Anything for a laugh"! He will dress in rags to make hunger despicable, or humiliate himself in a silk hat to make prosperity hateful. He will get a laugh out of you at all costs. Unsuccessful comedians are the unhappiest of men. Their unhappiness breeds malice – but their malice becomes madness. Would-be comedians are often mad. Their madness takes the easy way. Where a great comedian almost automatically tries to make you laugh yourself out of the misery of the world, a little comedian tries to make you feel strong by laughing at some degradation deeper than your own. A good comedian loves all laughter. A bad one despises any laughter that he has not personally provoked, and hates the man who dares to raise such laughter.

Trew never forgave Middleton for the humiliations of that terrible morning. They had always been close friends, and continued to meet every lunch-hour. Trew cracked five hundred more successful jokes, and Middleton never cracked another. Still, Trew could not forget that Middleton had murdered his joke – cut the throat of his child.

But he was so discreet in his hate that Middleton continued to think of Trew as his best friend.

* * * * *

An aspiring clown's best friend is the man that laughs longest and most constantly at his jokes. The time had been when Trew could not sneeze – he had a highly humorous sneeze – without choking his friend with laughter. Middleton was a sponge out of which he could squeeze tears of joy on any occasion. Since they had lodgings in the same shabby square, Wheeler Square off the Gray's Inn Road, they made a point of meeting every morning at half-past eight and, on fine days, walked together to the City, where they parted reluctantly and went to their offices, to meet again in the lunch-hour, when they generally arranged to stroll home together at five o'clock. Middleton was an excellent companion for Trew: it was impossible to hurt his feelings. If you pulled away his chair just before he sat down, he would begin to laugh before he hit the floor.

But then Middleton fell in love with a pretty brown-haired waitress who worked in a restaurant where they used to eat an eighteen-penny lunch every Friday, when they had their pay envelopes in their pocket and felt prosperous.

Now Trew became grave and anxious, and gave his friend a great deal of good advice. "Look here, old man, I'm a little older than you . . ."

"Four years, Trewie, old boy. You're only thirty."

"I know a bit about life, you know, old man. Don't be a mug, Middy. Laugh it off, laugh it off, old man. I know women – there's nothing to 'em. They drag a man down. You and your Love's Young Dream! Get out! Where does it get you?"

He was unpleasantly surprised when Middleton replied, with a certain asperity: "I don't know and I don't care, old boy. You and your gay bachelor life, where does that get *you*?"

"Good Lord, you're not going to tell me you want to *marry* the girl!"

"What did you think I wanted to do with the girl, may I ask, old boy?"

"No, but I mean to say, old man," said Trew, shocked. "A waitress!"

"Would you mind telling me what's the matter with being a waitress? It's an honest living, isn't it?"

"Well, old man, so is sweeping the streets . . . and that reminds me. Did you hear the one about the two sparrows——?"

" – No, I didn't, Trewie, and with all due respect I don't want to!" cried Middleton, astonishing his friend with an unprecedented flash of anger. "What were you saying about street sweepers? Do you mind repeating?"

"I only said it was an honest living. Keep your hair on, old man."

"Never mind about my hair, old boy. Look after your own hair" – this was a hit, because Trew's light, colourless hair was already thinning on top – "Louisa and I are going to get married, Trewie, and I won't hear a word said against her!"

"But, old man, I was only speaking for your own good. How can you go and get married on four pounds a week? Answer me that."

"Louisa says . . . Well, anyway, we'll manage."

"Got any money saved up?"

"I've got about sixteen pounds left in the bank out of what Mother left. We could start off with just two rooms . . . get the furniture on the never-never system. I won't always be earning four pounds a week."

Trew asked: "What about your rich uncle?"

Middleton had sometimes talked rather wistfully of his Uncle Joseph, his father's brother, who had gone to Australia at an early age and made a fortune out of wool. His mother had made a point of sending an expensive greeting card with a carefully chosen message in verse every Christmas – a practice which he had continued, by habit rather than hope. Trew, of course, had made a joke out of it.

Mr. Joseph Hugh Middleton lived in a place called Wagga-Wagga. For months after he saw the address, Trew greeted Middleton with a joyous bark, shaking his hind quarters, and saying "Wagga-Wagga, old man, Wagga-Wagga!"

"No harm in trying," said Middleton and he wrote a long, affectionate letter to his uncle, who did not reply. So, romantically penniless, he married Louisa at Caxton Hall. Trew was best man, very spruce in a light grey suit with a pink carnation which squirted water into Middleton's face when, after a pressing invitation, he stooped to smell it.

The bride and groom went to live in two rooms (with use of kitchen and bath) on the fourth floor of the same house in which Middleton had lived alone and unattached when he was a bachelor. Middleton carried her over the threshold, and they were happy.

But there came a pay-day two or three months later, when the friends met at lunch-time in a tea-shop and Trew ordered steak and kidney pie, fried potatoes, cabbage, bread-and-butter, boiled golden roll, and a large cup of coffee; while Middleton ordered a crust of bread-and-butter and a cup of tea.

"Lost your appetite? Falling in love again?" asked Trew, as if he did not know.

"I'm not very hungry, thanks, old boy," said Middleton, picking up stray crumbs.

They were alone that afternoon. Trew said: "Look, old man, I'm broke myself, but I could lend you four or five bob till the middle of next week if you like."

"Oh no, thanks all the same, Trewie old boy; I'm very much obliged to you for the offer, but I wouldn't dream of borrowing where I couldn't be sure of repaying."

"Why, poor old man! Bad as all that?"

Middleton said: "Well . . . there was the down payment on the furniture, and a new suit, and a few flowers for Louie. The ring was an item, too . . . and, you know, a little present . . . a little wrist-watch, you know, and so we started housekeeping on a capital of five pounds ten." He smiled wryly. ". . . Well, the rent's a bit high, of course, and then there's gas. A pound a month to pay off for the furniture. All kinds of little items – you know, things like soap, furniture polish – Louie's proud of that furniture – needles, washing, thread, boot polish. And then again you've got to get your shoes mended, and get your hair cut. And shoe-laces, and metal polish. You can't help it if a cup gets broken, or a plate – it mounts up, Trewie old boy, it mounts up like the devil. You have to get your suit cleaned once in a while, however careful you may be: and there goes three-and-sixpence!

I've cut out smoking, it's true . . . but there's hairpins, darning wool. If it rains, as you know, old boy, a man's got to take a bus. Newspapers, of course, a man can do without. But sometimes a girl must go and get herself all sorts of little things. . . . I mean a bit of face powder; that kind of stuff, etcetera etcetera. Things don't last for ever, Trewie old boy. Take stockings; take underclothes. All in all, you need to economise, go easy, because apart from everything else you've got to eat, haven't you? . . . Oh I don't mean stuffing yourself up with meat and stuff in the middle of the day, which only makes you sleepy. I mean you've got to keep body and soul together. You know what I mean? But Louie's a wonderful manager – marvellous! You ought to see her shopping! She can make one shilling do the work of five – honestly, I give you my word, old boy."

"Couldn't she get a job, just to help out for the time being?" asked Trew.

Middleton blushed, and said: "Well, I mean, *job*! . . . Run her legs off being a waitress, or in Woolworth's for a few shillings a week? I don't like the idea of it. Besides, Trewie old boy, Louie and I half believe that we're going to – as man to man, Trewie – have a baby."

"No!" said Trew, staring. "No!"

"Why 'no' in that tone of voice, Trewie?" asked Middleton, irritably.

"I was just thinking of *you*, that's all, old man. Well, you can't say I didn't warn you, old man," said Trew.

Middleton's temper was uncertain this morning. He snapped: "Warn me? What d'you mean? D'you suppose I have any regrets, or what?"

"Don't put words into my mouth, Middy old man!"

" – Well, I haven't!" said Middleton.

"Laugh it off, laugh it off."

"I won't laugh anything off, Trewie, and I have not got one iota of regret," said Middleton, snapping his fingers.

They parted with a handshake before two o'clock. Trew went his way with a malevolent inward chuckle. Middleton strode into his office, taut with screwed-up resolution. He was admitted to the general manager's room.

"Well?" said the general manager.

Middleton's fingers were numb, his nails were breaking; his courage, like a wet sail, was flapping away in a black wind, and an unfathomable gulf foamed below; but he found strength to say: "Mr. Mawson – sir. I hope you are satisfied with my work here——"

"You do your work, and are paid for it, I believe, Middleton?" said Mr. Mawson, who knew what was coming.

"Yes, sir," said Middleton. "But I'm a married man, sir, and I thought——"

"*Married?* What do you mean?" said Mr. Mawson.

"I'm a married man, sir," said Middleton, pale but still resolute. "And I hoped that you might see your way clear——"

" – Excuse me, Middleton. How long have you been married?"

"Three months, sir; and——"

Mr. Mawson said: "But if I remember rightly, your salary is in the region of two hundred pounds a year, isn't it?"

"Yes, sir. That is why——"

"Excuse me, Middleton. How could you think of getting married on two hundred a year? Your wife has a little money of her own, no doubt?"

"No, sir, and so I hoped——"

Middleton did not know how to put things into words. All but one frayed handful of courage had gone fluttering down into the gulf. " – I hoped that you might see your way clear to raising my salary a little, sir," he said.

Mr. Mawson looked at him steadily, shaking his head slowly, and said with terrible deliberation: "Middleton. You have been with us for quite a while, I believe."

"Yes, sir. Nearly ten years, sir – since I was sixteen, sir."

"And your salary has been increased according to our system of annual increments, I think. You are now . . . how old?"

"Nearly twenty-six and a half, sir."

"Now look here, Mr. Middleton; I'm surprised at you. I'm disappointed in you. At your age, with the whole world before you, you get married on two hundred a year! And what if there should be little ones?"

"I'm afraid – I mean I hope – I *think* there are . . . there *is* going to be," said Middleton.

"Just as I said! Middleton, I like my little team of assistants to come and tell me their little troubles. But I think you have been rash, very rash. You must realise, of course, that you have prejudiced your entire career. I have had confidence in you, Middleton. How am I to have confidence in you in the future? Do you realise that some of the greatest banks in the world do not allow their clerks to marry until they have attained certain positions of responsibility? And rightly so! A young man in a position of trust is unsettled by family responsibilities. He is more easily tempted than a young man without responsibilities. You, Middleton, in the mail order department, are in much the same situation as the cashier of a bank. Middleton, I'm glad you told me of this marriage of yours. Pity, pity, pity . . ."

Middleton said: "Mr. Mawson, sir! If you feel that I am not to be trusted, just because I happen to be married——"

Then his throat closed, and he had to swallow to get it open, while he blew his nose hard to ease a certain pressure at the back of his eyes.

"God forbid, Middleton! I am glad that you have been candid enough to make a clean breast of it," said Mr. Mawson.

"Sir, excuse me – I wasn't making a clean breast of anything," said Middleton. "I thought that since I'd been with you so long, you might find it convenient, all things considered, to raise my salary——"

The general manager shook his head, and said: "Quite out of the question. Not within my power to do it, even if I wanted to, Middleton. You should have controlled yourself, Middleton, you should have played the man. I was forty before I thought of marriage."

"Yes, sir," said Middleton, and then a high-pitched buzzer sounded. Mr. Mawson turned to a little oblong box bristling with levers grouped about a hole covered with gauze. He knocked down one of the levers and a voice, strained thin through the gauze, said: "Oh Mr. Mawson, Mrs. Mawson is here to see you."

The general manager changed colour and said: "Ask Mrs. Mawson if she wouldn't mind waiting just a moment," and snapped the lever back. ". . . So, Middleton, you'd better get back to your work. I'm sorry if you're in trouble, but you have no one but yourself to blame. That will be all."

"Yes sir."

" – Oh, one other thing, Middleton. I know that young men who have been foolish enough to place themselves in your position are frequently foolish enough to get even deeper into the mire – buy things they can't pay for, fall into the hands of moneylenders. I don't say you're as foolish as all that, but I give you fair warning; if I hear of your doing any such thing, you leave this office at a second's notice. You know Lord Herring's sentiments. Go along now. On your way out ask Mrs. Mawson if she'll kindly step in, will you?"

"Yes, sir."

But Mrs. Mawson did not wait to be asked; she shouldered Middleton aside and went right in. He caught a glimpse of a massive, elderly woman with the jowls and bulging eyes of an old white bulldog; her head was thrown back so that she might have been straining to balance a preposterous little hat on her powdery forehead. Then the door slammed, and Middleton went back to his desk, his throat tight, his eyes hot; perilously near tears.

The firm of Coulton Utilities manufactured, or caused to be manufactured, almost everything a housewife needs – kitchen cabinets, enamel-top tables, ironing boards, blankets, sheets, canteens of cutlery, brass-plated fire-irons, carving sets, washing machines – all the dreary, necessary paraphernalia of the pinched, half-hungry household. Coulton Utilities also conducted a prosperous mail-order hire-purchase clothing business: you sent sixpence in stamps for a Measure Yourself Chart, a Fashion Book ("State whether Ladies or Gents"), a book of patterns, a free tape-measure, and a hire-purchase form. Coulton Utilities managed to make a profit even on the bait, since the whole envelopeful, postage and overheads included, cost them exactly fourpence farthing. Thus they sold hundreds of thousands of suits of ladies' and gents' outfits, on the easiest of easy terms. A million hard-working, hard-up readers of the advertisements in the Sunday papers were still half-heartedly paying the two shillings a week that had seemed so little in the first flush of enthusiasm, months after their suits, costumes, and overcoats were worn out.

At the same time the president of Coulton Utilities, Lord Herring, a staunch Baptist, sternly warned his employees that they had better not get into debt. Debt led to worry, and worry to loss of concentration; loss of concentration led to day-dreaming; day-dreaming led to the loss of your job, and so, by easy stages to hunger, theft, murder, the gallows, and hell. Every month he sent to every one of his twenty-five hundred employees a little printed sermon full of good advice and biblical references, and pregnant with thinly-veiled menace. A man who let himself be persuaded to buy an article for which he was not absolutely sure he could pay was a weakling and a cheat, said Lord Herring. Also, he was a coward, because in trying to buy what he could not afford to buy, he was cringing away from his duty as a private soldier in the battle of life. He was guilty of cowardice in the face of the enemy; and soldiers in battle are put to death for that. To sum up: weaklings fall by the wayside, and perish; thieves go to prison, and sink lower and lower until they murder and are hanged; cowards are shot. *"The Wages of Debt is Death,"* said Lord Herring, in one of the best-worded of his monthly sermons.

"Liars and hypocrites!" thought Middleton as he cut the string that bound one of the bundles of letters on his desk. The bundle – two hundred tightly-bound sealed envelopes – jerked upwards and over, opening like a concertina. The music, the agonised wailing of that paper concertina, was yet to come. Middleton knew that more than half of the letters contained postal orders. Last Sunday Coulton Utilities had advertised another bargain, not to be missed. *Don't delay, write to-day* – for a twenty-three-piece genuine MacLennan tea service, genuine willow pattern, only ten shillings post free! He knew that the lid of the teapot was included as a "piece".

All over the country housewives would be rushing out to look for the parcel-post. Here were God knows how many pinched pennies of pin-money, saved for little surprises, or bits of finery.

Middleton knew how it went: on Sunday afternoon the tired woman sits down to read the paper for the first time in seven days, easing her poor old feet; she sees the Coulton Utilities advertisement, with the cut depicting a family sitting down to tea at a table covered with fine china. The husband, comfortable and happy, sits at one end of the table. She, young and gay, pours tea from a pretty teapot at the other end. A sturdy son and a pretty daughter and a couple of hale and hearty grandparents sit in their places, smiling in anticipation. Somewhere in the background a cosy fire burns bright. . . . *Free Offer – Real Stamped Willow Pattern Tray.* . . . And that settles it! Out come two-shilling-pieces squeezed down out of twenty-four pennies, worn shillings, smooth sixpences, and silver threepenny bits that appear no bigger than drops of sweat and evaporate faster. One morning the poor woman goes to the post office, changes her silver for a paper postal order, fills in the coupon, scrapes up the price of a stamp to mail it; and waits, dreaming of something pretty for the house.

Middleton knew. And he knew that the other letters in the bundle contained first payments on the Klever Kitchen Kabinet. In this little handful of letters, eighty or ninety harassed women were signing away their peace of mind, agreeing to pay only five shillings a month for two years. "After all, it's only eighteenpence a week," they said to themselves, "and only five shillings with order."

Then Middleton understood exactly what is meant by "Bitterness". He had taken his first taste of it. It was as if his mouth was full of copper coins, green with verdigris. One by one these green copper coins slipped down his throat, until the weight of them dragged his heart and stomach down and down, and there was nothing in the world but an awful heaviness that no sigh could lift; a turbulent emptiness in his head, and in his mouth a bitter taste which he associated with bad pennies.

He washed his face, took a long drink of water, and went back to work – to work like a madman, chasing lost time.

Wherever he turned, Middleton felt a slimy little fish writhing from the back of his collar to his waist-line and escaping with a cold shudder down one or other of his legs. This slippery fish was the general manager's eye. Middleton had made himself conspicuous, now. That coldness was always between his shoulder-blades. If he had been an unmarried man he might have walked out of the office and taken his chance in the world. But Middleton said to himself: "If I was single, with nobody but myself to consider, the situation wouldn't have arisen. As it is, here I am – a married man, a father, most likely, in five or six months. Only four months ago I was my own master. Now I'm a slave under three masters: Louie, the baby, and Mr. Mawson. A slave, that's what I am, a slave. . . . Oh, all right, let it be like that," said Middleton, and went on working.

Middleton had a lucky piece, an old spade-guinea with a hole in it. When he left the office at five o'clock that afternoon, he went to a jeweller's shop, sold it for twenty-three and sixpence, and carried home a flowering shrub in a pot, and a new pound note, both of which he gave to Louisa, saying: "Little bonus for you. A present for a good girl. I want you to buy something nice for yourself. . . . Yes, Louie dear, I *want* you to; it would please me if you did. Go and spend it on something silly."

He was stubborn in his insistence that the pound be squandered in frivolity, so she went to a cut-price hairdresser near Tottenham Court Road, who advertised a permanent wave for only one pound, and had her glossy, straight brown hair curled. The effect was ravishing: Middleton was delighted. She could honestly reassure herself that at least half of the pound had been spent on him. Breathing admiration, and stroking his wife's new curls, he said that he had never seen anything so pretty, while he thought: *Now this is the right way to spend a pound. This is value. What a fool I was to keep that skinny little golden guinea with a hole in it all this time!*

But the poor little potted shrub died in two days. Louisa's hair became straight again in ten days; and things were as they had been before Middleton sold his spade-guinea. All that remained was the dead twig in the little flowerpot. Louisa kept it on the window-ledge where the sunlight could reach it and watered it every morning: refusing to accept death as inevitable, half-hoping for a miraculous resurrection, a new blossoming. Once, she thought she saw green buds. They were nothing but flecks of mildew. Then although she knew that it was foolish to cry over a plant, she shed a tear or two, and threw the flower-pot into the dust-bin.

Louisa disliked Trew and he knew it. Therefore he hated her. He needed admiration: there was a spoiled child wrapped in the thick hide of that irrepressible jester.

Now fingering the fine notepaper of the lawyer Pismire, Trew thought of Middleton, whom he had come to regard as a traitor, and Louisa, whom he saw as a climber, a designing woman, a scheming waitress who had married above herself and taken away his best friend.

Wrinkles appeared at the corners of his eyes. Smiling, he went to his desk, took a pencil, and carefully drafted a letter on a bit of scrap paper. He was not unacquainted with commercial jargon and legal terminology, but he wanted this to be clean-cut, perfect, and unsmudged by erasures. Soon he had it right. His smile became triangular; an office boy, who had observed Trew and understood him, said to another office boy: "I wonder wot old Podgy's got up 'is sleeve."

Out of earshot the office boys called Trew Podgy, because he was prematurely corpulent: they knew that if he overheard them, they would sooner or later feel between their shoulderblades the quick, quiet stiletto of his malevolence. If you forgot to laugh when Trew called a club-footed man "Hoppy", or addressed a one-eyed and one-armed beggar as "Lord Nelson", he might be offended; but if you called him "Podgy", or "Baby Face", he would lie awake at night thinking of revenge.

Trew walked sedately to a typewriter, and carefully wrote a letter to Edward Hugh Middleton, Esquire, of 3, Wheeler Square, W.C.1. He regretted to inform Mr. Middleton of the death of his uncle, Joseph Hugh Middleton, Esquire, of Wagga-Wagga, New South Wales, Australia. He had been advised of Mr. Middleton's present address, and begged to inform him that he, Edward Hugh Middleton, was sole beneficiary in his uncle's will. Joseph Hugh Middleton had left £103,751 6s. 8d.: net personalty £76,100. If Mr. Edward Hugh Middleton would call at his earliest convenience, Mr. Charles Pismire would be happy to clarify the situation. In the meantime, with condolences, he ventured to congratulate Mr. Middleton on his good fortune.

Between the respectful salutation, and the punctiliously typed

CHARLES PISMIRE
Pismire & Pismire

Trew scrawled a black signature.

Then, enclosing the letter in one of Forty Richards's very best white envelopes, he sent it to Middleton, Express. To do so, Trew had to go to the post office. If this had been any other day, his absence, if only for five minutes, might have been noticed; but this was that hot Saturday before August Bank Holiday. The letter was mailed, and Trew was back at his desk before anyone knew that he had left it. He was poring over a great red-and-green ledger when Big Ben struck ten. Counting the chimes, Trew calculated that Middleton ought to receive the letter before three o'clock, and then there would be fun. Pretending to work, he waited. At one o'clock the office closed. *In the good old days*, Trew thought, sadly, *Middy and I used to walk back home on Saturday – we used to walk westward, and have a bite to eat in one of the Italian places around New Oxford Street, or somewhere. Now, of course, he's got his Louie!*

Trew went out to eat alone. A bank clerk to whom he tried to tell a funny story about microbes said that he had to catch a train to Brighton, and ran away. In a few seconds, as it seemed, life departed from the City; dark-coated, shiny-coated swarms disappeared like flies under a Flit spray. Trew, solitary on earth, ate in a restaurant in Charing Cross Road, and killed time with a magazine. He read a newspaper and went for a walk. At three o'clock he went home to take off his dark suit and change into light grey. On the way he was accosted by a flower-seller with a barrow-load of moribund carnations at four for sixpence. Trew bought a shillingsworth. He meant to call on the Middletons, casually, and ask them to come for a walk in the park.

His landlady was waiting for him. Before she could speak, he said: "Here's a nice thing! Had to go and deal with a couple of things in Leadenhall Street – a firm by the name of Koestler and Dunlap, dare say you know them – and when I got back the cashier was gone, all locked up. Never mind, everything will be all right Tuesday."

"Well, Mr. Trew, I sincerely hope so because——"

" – Don't worry. Don't you worry. On Tuesday, mark my words, everything'll be all right. I'm going to have a cold bath. I'm hot."

"I'd hoped you'd be able to let me have something on account, Mr. Trew," said the landlady, vitiated by the heat and thoroughly discouraged. "My rent's overdue, too. I promised——"

" – They can't do anything to you before Tuesday, can they?" said Trew.

"No, but——"

" – Well, Tuesday morning I settle up."

"You've said that so often, you see. I don't like to ask, but . . ." She made a helpless gesture with one hand, and wiped her damp face with the other: she had never dreamed that she would be forced to come down to this. ". . . but what else can I do? I hate asking for money, but . . . When my poor husband was alive, it would have been . . . you promised faithfully, you know. Oh dear me!"

"Would I have walked in this heat if I'd even got the price of a bus-ride?" asked Trew, almost indignantly. "Look at me – wet through. If I say Tuesday, I *mean* Tuesday! Is it my fault if they kept me waiting in Leadenhall Street? D'you think it's pleasant for *me*, having to put you off like this? Eh?"

"No, but——"

" – Tuesday without fail," said Trew, and went upstairs. On the way he stumbled, and the landlady heard a jingling of loose change in his pocket. Then she wanted to run after him, take him by the throat, and kill him, crying: *Liar, liar, liar! You have got money and you did not walk from Leadenhall Street!* But she was overwhelmed by an appalling realisation of her impotence. If she went to Trew's room and said: "Get out!" – what would happen if he replied: "I won't!" What could she do? Throw him out bodily? Scream for policemen? If only poor Dick were alive, this could never have been. She went to her bedroom and sat by the open window, wishing that she had never been born.

In his room, Trew relaxed, keeping an eye on his alarm-clock. Five o'clock, he thought, would be a good time to call on the Middletons.

Trew set the alarm-clock for four-forty-five, in case he fell asleep. The joke was going to be too rich to miss.

* * * * *

As for Middleton, he walked home slowly, with a heavy heart. On the stroke of one the whole City (in a manner of speaking) threw its bonnet over the windmill, and kicked up its heels with a joyous whoop, at the prospect of the Bank Holiday. All the week the clerks had been talking of what they meant to do, and how they hoped to enjoy themselves. Smith, Jones and White, who pretended to be very desperate fellows, were going to Southend-on-Sea for a couple of days; hearing them talk, a naïve stranger might have been tempted to warn Southend that it had better shutter its windows and lock up its daughters. Robinson and Brown were going to Margate on a steamboat – one of those gay boats in which carefree bachelors used to sing sentimental songs until they were hoarse, cool their throats with bottled ale, and, wearing silly little paper hats, brazenly flirt with the girls, who had put on their lightest, brightest dresses and were ready for a little fun, harmless or otherwise. Middleton, in his time, had staggered with a staggering group of jolly good fellows – Trew in the lead, of course – to catch the last train from Southend to Fenchurch Street on Bank Holiday Monday. He, too, had looked forward to August Bank Holiday, putting a little money aside for a little orgy: two Bank Holidays ago he had squandered three pounds in two and a half days. But now he walked homewards heavily, tired and discouraged, thinking with dread of the long week-end. Should he take Louisa to Hyde Park, where they would simply sit on their behinds on the burnt-up grass, cheek by jowl with half a million similar unfortunates, most of them with feverish, sun-scorched children that needed to be smacked or screamed at every five minutes? Or go to the Zoo and make part of a fretful mob, a million strong – half of them children howling their heads off because they couldn't see the lions being fed? Then, suddenly the sky grows black, the rain pours down. There is a stampede for the buses, which are all full. So you stand in the middle of another endless line of fathers and mothers who are beating wet, shivering, terrified children and saying: "Stop grizzling, you little wretch! You're here to enjoy yourself, and enjoy yourself you will, if I have to wring your neck" – or words to that effect. Then comes a peal of thunder; the caged lions, wolves, and apes roar and howl and gibber, and the children kick and scratch at their parents while the parents hiss and strike at their children. If, later, you want to relax in the glamorous darkness of a cinema, you must wait somewhere near the end of a line of a million mothers and fathers, all worrying about their children left at home.

And in a few months, now, I shall be a father, thought Middleton. *I'd rather it was a boy. Perhaps it won't cry very much, though I never came across one that didn't.*

He was near Wheeler Square, walking through a street which, on Saturday, was an open-air market. In the gutters, between two short rows of shops, the street vendors, the barrow-pushers, the costermongers had set up their stalls. They were cutting their prices, now, and shouting like madmen – especially the costers who were selling perishable soft fruits and flowers. By Tuesday, their goods would be rotten. One unfortunate fellow with half a barrow full of peaches still unsold had reduced the price of his fruit from threepence to a penny, and had so exhausted himself with shouting that he could only say, in a husky whisper: "Eech! ... Eech!" Middleton bought sixpennyworth. Then another coster, roaring like a bull, thrust a fourteen-inch cucumber under his nose and said: "Lookatit, lookatit, lookatit, ain't it lovely? Tenpence!" Middleton bought it. Whilst he was counting out the money he remembered what someone had told him – that this was the costermongers' holiday, and that on the Monday they sometimes spent as much as twenty pounds apiece at the fair and in the pubs around Hampstead Heath. The thought must have soured his face, for the coster clapped him on the shoulder, said: "Cheer up, you'll soon be dead – 'ere's a bit 'o creese for the missus" – and slapped a bundle of watercress into Middleton's hand.

When Middleton was on his way the salad-seller turned to his wife and said: "All boot-blacking and no bloody boots. No bread to 'is feet, no boots to eat, eh, gel?"

"Go on, give the stock away! You'd give me away if I let yer."

"'Oo'd 'ave yer?" said the coster, and then, drawing a deep breath, roared at the world again: "Come on, come on, come on! Cucumbers! Cues! Cues 'n creese! Lovely, lovely, lovely! . . ."

Middleton stopped at a barrow loaded with imperishable goods – second-hand books and back-numbers of popular magazines. The proprietor of this stall did not shout: he stood still, stroking his long white moustache. Middleton bought three back-numbers of *Real Love Tales*, for Louisa to read, so that she might keep the dull truth at arm's length over the week-end. For himself, he bought a copy of *Adventure*, so tattered that the old man let it go for twopence. Then he went home. Louisa had prepared a lunch of cold corned beef with a little faded lettuce. The cucumber was just what they needed to make it perfect. With peaches for dessert, what more could a man or woman desire? If all this was not enough, there was something good to read. Middleton sighed deeply, and this sigh loosened something heavy that had been weighing on his back. If Louie was happy, why, then, so was he. They ate heartily of the corned beef, the salad, and the peaches; and drank tea. He complimented her on her housewifery, she thanked him for being such a good provider, they kissed each other, sat down to read their magazines.

Middleton was reading a story about a battle between lumberjacks when his landlady knocked at the sitting-room door, and his head was full of the rumbling of logs and the trampling of cleated boots; the clashing of canthooks and the *By Gars* and *Sacré Dames* of infuriated French-Canadian loggers.

"Yes, Mrs. Gibson?" said Middleton.

"This came for you, Express," she said, giving him a letter. "There was nothing to pay."

"Oh, thanks very much, Mrs. Gibson. . . . Oh I say, Louie, look at this. An Express letter!"

"Oh dear," said Louisa. Urgent communications filled her with nameless terrors: she associated them with death. She watched her husband's face while he opened the envelope, and clutched at her throat when she saw his jaw drop and his cheeks turn grey. "What is it?" she asked, "for God's sake, what is it?"

"Don't upset yourself," said Middleton.

"What *is* it?"

"It's a letter. I mean, it's a letter from Pismire – biggest solicitor in the City. He's Lord Herring's solicitor. Well – you remember my Uncle Joe in Australia?"

"He never answered your letter when you wrote and told him about you and me," said Louisa.

"Well, he's dead, Louie."

"Oh, well——"

" – And he's left me seventy-six thousand pounds, that's all," said Middleton. "Seventy-six thousand pounds, that's all. A mere seventy-six thousand——" he choked.

"Oh no!"

"Well, here's the letter, Louie – read it for yourself."

"*Sole beneficiary*," said Louisa, reading aloud. "What does that mean?"

"Oh, nothing – only that he's left me everything, that's all," said Middleton, half-crying. "A mere seventy-six thousand pounds. . . . Oh Louie, Louie!"

"It seems too good to be true," said Louisa.

"There's the letter," said Middleton. ". . . Let me have another look at it . . ." He fumbled in his pockets, and found twopence. "I'll telephone and confirm," he said. "There might be some mistake."

"Will they be in the office this afternoon?"

"Of course not," said Middleton, "but there can't be many Charles Pismires in the telephone book. I'll ring his private number. Come with me, Louie."

There was no telephone in the house, so they crossed the square and squeezed themselves into the telephone booth on the northern corner. Middleton had some trouble with the thin pages of the directory; some of his fingers were numb; others were wayward, and fluttered in wrong directions. But he found a Charles Pismire who lived in Highgate, and dialled the number. *God, let this be true!* he prayed, while the ringing sound rhythmically buzzed. Then the buzzing stopped, and a loud, expressionless voice said: "Yes?"

Middleton's voice shook as he said: "My name is Middleton. Is that Mr. Pismire?"

"No, sir. Mr. Pismire is not in."

"Oh. It is the right number I'm ringing, isn't it? Mr. Charles Pismire, the solicitor?"

"Yes, sir. Mr. Pismire will not be back before Tuesday. Can I take a message?"

"Well, it's like this," said Middleton. "I received a letter from Mr. Charles Pismire, asking me to get in touch with him. But the office, of course, is closed, you see . . ."

"Was it a matter of business, sir?"

"Yes. I received a letter from Mr. Charles Pismire, informing me of a . . . a legacy – Mr. Joseph Hugh Middleton of Wagga-Wagga, New South Wales, Australia."

"Yes, sir?"

"A matter of seventy-six thousand pounds," said Middleton. "I wanted to have a word with Mr. Pismire and confirm."

The expressionless voice was the voice of Charles Pismire's servant, a man named Sutton. His master had come home, hot and exasperated, before one o'clock, and said: "Sutton, I am going to Paphurst, and I am not coming back before Tuesday morning, whatever happens. I am going to rest. I am spending the week-end with Lord Paphurst, and I absolutely forbid you to disturb me in any circumstances – even if the house burns down. If anyone calls, you will take the message and say I'll be back on Tuesday. Is that clear?" Sutton bowed: he had served Pismire's father, and loved the son.

" – I only wanted to be sure," said Middleton. "I just wanted to make certain that there was no mistake."

"I beg pardon, sir," said Sutton. "I believe I heard you say that Mr. Charles Pismire had already written a letter to you?"

"Yes, but——"

"In that case," said Sutton, "you may rest assured that everything is in order. Mr. Pismire will be back in Town on Tuesday. Is there any message?"

"Only that Mr. Middleton – Edward Middleton – rang, if you don't mind."

"Yes, sir. Good-bye, sir."

Middleton turned to Louisa. "You heard?" he said. She nodded. "You heard him say 'rest assured everything is in order'? Eh?"

"Um!"
"Well, we're rich, Louie!"
"Yes," she said; and fainted.

PART II

Fortunately there was no room in the telephone booth for Louisa to fall. Middleton caught her under the arms as she became limp. A passer-by might have thought that the couple were grappling in a frenzied embrace. It would happen, of course, that a policeman had to pass this point of all points on his beat at that moment. He stopped, and stared.

Crimson with heat and embarrassment, streaming with sweat, Middleton shouted: "She's fainted!" But his voice did not penetrate the heavy glass of the booth: to the policeman Middleton was merely pulling faces, opening his mouth and baring his teeth. For a few exhilarating seconds he thought he had caught a certain sex maniac for whom Scotland Yard was looking at that time. He opened the heavy door, and said: "Now then! What's all this?" As soon as the comparatively cool outside air came in, Louisa recovered. She cried: "Oh Ted!" and burst into tears.

"My wife fainted," said Middleton; and after he had breathlessly outlined the state of affairs, the policeman said: "Well if somebody left me all that money I shouldn't be surprised if I fainted myself. Good luck to you," and went on pounding his beat, day-dreaming. Since he never caught a sex maniac, and no one ever left him seventy-six thousand pounds, he is probably wearing out his big shiny boots on the grey paving-stones of London to this day.

Middleton and his wife walked slowly back to their rooms, hand in hot hand, looking at each other with moist, astounded eyes, not caring whether they walked on the pavement or in the road. They could think of nothing to say just then. Louisa was dumb with dreams. Middleton's head seemed to rattle with the bewildering mixed pieces of fifty jigsaw puzzles trying to shake themselves into place, to make fifty pretty pictures. His mind was muddled, shirred, scrambled, broken up. Every step shook and shuffled his thoughts like numbered bits of paper tossed in a hat in a lottery. It was Louisa who spoke first, when they were passing the newsagent's and tobacconist's shop on the corner. She said, with a great sigh: "Well, I should think it would be all right, now, to get some cigarettes?"

Middleton replied, with a start: "My God, yes, of course, Louie – anything you like," and so they went into the shop and spent six-and-threepence on a box of one hundred of the fat oval Virginia cigarettes that used to cost one-and-three-pence for twenty.

"Would it matter if I smoked one now?" she asked. "I feel I could do with a cigarette now."

They walked along, smoking.

"To tell you the truth, it's the one thing I miss – a cigarette," said Louisa.

"Why didn't you say so, Louie dear?" asked Middleton.

"Well, *you* gave it up, didn't you?"

"Yes, but that's different. You can have anything you like now, Louie dear, you know. Anything you fancy?"

"I'll tell you something funny," said Louisa, laughing, with tears in her eyes, "this morning I fancied some of those Garibaldi biscuits – the ones they call squashed fly biscuits – but I didn't dare."

"Come on, then," said Middleton, "and let's buy a pound – two pounds."

"Not now. Let's go home, Teddy darling. What I want now is a cup of tea, and some aspirin."

So they went back. There were three peaches left from lunch, to be eaten in the evening. One of them was bruised. Middleton picked it up, and threw it out of the window; saw it splash on the hot asphalt of the empty street, and went to the kitchen to put the kettle on. The landlady was there, filling a pepper pot. She was a genteel soul, full of inside information about the peerage; her knowledge of Royal Family affairs was impressive, and society scandal was not a sealed book to her. She said: "Why, Mr. Middleton, how strange you look! I do hope I have not had the pleasure of being the bearer of bad news? When that letter of yours came, it gave me quite a turn, I assure you."

"Read it for yourself, Mrs. Gibson," said Middleton.

Mrs. Gibson wiped her hands carefully, and read the letter. Then she said: "Sev-en-ty-six thou-sand *pounds*! Well, I'm sure no one deserves it more than you do, Mr. Middleton, and I congratulate you, I'm sure."

"I don't mind telling you," said Middleton, "it shook me for the moment."

"I'm sure you deserve every penny of it, Mr. Middleton. If I've said it once, I've said it a thousand times: 'If anyone deserves to have good luck, it's Mr. Middleton.' Seventy-six thousand pounds! The moment you set foot in my house, I said to myself: 'There's something *about* Mr. Middleton. There's *something* about Mr. *Middleton*. You can see *he* isn't one of the mob!' And I was right. Something seemed to tell me. I must be pishic." Then the bell rang, and she went to open the front door. Middleton heard Trew's hearty voice saying: "Mr. Beginnington in? – I mean Mr. Endton. Middleton! *Oi!*" – in imitation of Bud Flanagan. Mrs. Gibson said: "Oh, Mr. Trew, did you hear . . . ?"

Her voice died away. Middleton could not hear what she was whispering. Then Trew roared: "What? *What?* WHAT? Where is he? Where is he? Quick, and I'll borrow a fiver before he blows it all on wine, women and song!"

Trew shook the house as he galloped upstairs. Middleton, leaving the kettle boiling, ran up to the fourth floor and overtook Trew on the landing. "Trewie, old boy, Trewie, guess what!"

"I just heard," said Trew; and added, with malicious deliberation: "Can it be true?"

"I'll show you the letter, old boy. Besides, I rang Pismire's place."

"You did? And what did Pismire say?"

"His clerk, or somebody, confirmed – everything's quite in order."

"Well, I'll be damned," said Trew. "What's the amount, old man?"

"A mere seventy-six thousand," said Middleton, punching Trew in the kidneys, "a mere seventy-six thousand pounds, Trewie, old boy, net personalty – and what do you think of that?"

Louisa, hearing their voices, opened the door. Trew said:

"Congratulations, Louisa; I couldn't be more delighted if it had happened to me." But he assumed a glum, discontented expression; observing which, Louisa became radiant.

She said: "Isn't it wonderful? But you've got to admit, if anybody deserved it, it was Ted."

"Seventy-six thousand pounds – blimey!" said Trew, and fell into an easy chair, so heavily that Louisa winced. She could not forget that the furniture was less than half paid for.

"Net personalty," said Middleton with relish, "net personalty, old boy!"

"Just what do you mean by net personalty, Middy, old man?"

"Well, it says here in the letter that Uncle Joe left £103,751 6s. 8d., net personalty £76,000. I take it to mean that his net personalty was all that was left when all his debts were paid off."

"Would that include death duties, I wonder?" said Trew.

"I don't know about that," said Middleton, "but even say taxes were still to be deducted – say they even knocked off fifty per cent death duties. Looking on the dark side, old boy, that would still leave getting on for forty thousand pounds, wouldn't it?"

"So it would," said Trew, sour with envy. "I suppose you're quite sure it's all right, old man?"

Louisa said: "We rang the solicitor, didn't we, Ted?"

"Yes, I got Charles Pismire's home number," said Middleton. "They said it was all in order. Louie fainted away when she heard it – didn't you, Louie?"

"Well, it did come as a shock," said Louie.

"Naturally, Trew, old boy, a man doesn't get excited about this kind of thing without making sure there's something to be excited about."

"Quite right, too. I was only asking, Middy, old man. I mean to say, accidents will happen in the best regulated families, and——"

" – Not being altogether a fool, old boy," said Middleton impatiently, "I invested a hard-earned twopence on a 'phone call to make sure."

"Keep your hair on, old man, keep your hair on," said Trew. "Well, I'm glad the old feller did the right thing at last. The Lord knows you and Louisa deserve it."

"I hardly remember him," said Middleton. "I couldn't have been more than four or five years old when he left England. Fancy him remembering me at last!"

"Well, old man, you did remind him of your existence now and again," said Trew.

"I sent him the same sort of Christmas cards as everybody sends to their relatives, nothing more."

"Well, and there you are, sole beneficiary, sixty-seven thousand quid to the good!"

"Well," said Middleton, "we were only a little family. Mother was the last on her side, and Uncle Joe was dad's only brother, so on the whole *that* isn't so remarkable. The way I see it, Uncle Joe must have felt the end coming, and I was the only relative he could think of. Blood *is* thicker than water, you know, old boy . . ."

"I can see your point, old man," said Trew, solemnly.

After a pause Middleton said: "I'll tell you something funny, Trewie, old boy. D'you know what? I feel awful. I feel kind of as if I wanted to be sick."

"So do I," said Louisa.

"That's shock," said Trew. "If somebody left me seventy-six thousand quid, God, I'd probably drop dead on the spot. Huh! Fat chance of any of my lousy family leaving me anything. My old man cut me off with a shilling – and he had to borrow the shilling off me to cut me off with, the unnatural old parent." He paused for a laugh, did not get it, and continued: "Cheer up, Middy. Don't let it get you down. You'll soon get used to it – like having one leg, or whiskers. You'll recover, Louisa, and then, of course, you won't know your old pal Trew. And I'll be polishing the seat of my trousers on an office chair, while you're riding up and down the south of France in a white limousine with silver fittings. And as for the seat of my trousers, d'you know what? They're so shiny that if I tore them now I'd have seven years' bad luck."

"Have a cup of tea?" asked Louisa.

"Tea?" cried Trew, "did I hear you say *tea*? What kind of talk is this. Why, actually I came along to take you out for a nice cold beer. I was going to pay for it, too," said Trew, with a hollow laugh. "Tea? Millionaires don't drink tea. As I was saying, I was going to take you two out for a nice cold drink, and so I will, as God is my judge. But being as you've got seventy-six thousand smackers, and I've only got seventeen-and-sixpence-halfpenny, Middy, you are going to pay for the beer I'm going to buy you. Is that clear? Is the beer clear? Come on, come on, it's ten minutes after opening-time."

Middleton looked at the little alarm-clock and saw that it was indeed twenty minutes to six. He turned over the money in his pocket and found that he had only seven shillings. The Middletons lived precariously. They "arrived – like that" – as the French say, putting finger-tip to finger-tip. Middleton was scrupulous in the settlement of tradesmen's accounts. He would not put a penny in his pocket until he had paid the butcher, the baker, the landlady, the furnishing company, the milkman, and the grocer; he hated debt for its own sake, and feared it for Mr. Mawson's sake. Coughing uneasily, he said: "Well, old boy, the fact of the matter is, I haven't got any money."

Trew opened his mouth wide and yelled with laughter. "Seventy-six thousand one hundred pounds, and so now he's got no money!"

"I mean ready cash," said Middleton. "You see, things have been pretty tight just lately, what with one thing and another——"

"Damn it all, man, haven't you got a cheque book?"

"Well, yes, I have, but——"

"Cash a cheque, then, for goodness' sake!"

"I don't like to, Trewie," said Middleton. "Eh? What do you say, Louie? Wouldn't it be better to wait till Tuesday?"

He hoped that she would say Yes, but she said: "Oh well, Ted, I don't know . . . if the solicitor said it was all right I don't actually see the harm."

"Well, in the first place all the banks, naturally, are shut. And in the second place, Trewie, old boy, I haven't got more than about thirty shillings in my account – just about enough to keep the account open. I mean, it would mean taking money under false pretences. You know, drawing on what I didn't have."

Trew roared with laughter and said: "Why, what a holy innocent you are, Middy, old man! The whole thing is as clear as mud, and what could be clearer than mud, ha-ha – eh? All you've got to do on Tuesday morning is, go to – what's the name of that lawyer again? Pismire. You go to Pismire, and naturally he gives you something out of the till for expenses. What they say in a case like this is: 'If we can advance you a little money for this and the other, we'll be very happy, my dear Mr. So-and-So. What about a couple of hundred pounds, let us say?' Right on the spot! And then again, when you show that letter to your bank manager, good Lord, he'll give you the key of the vault. Now don't be silly, Middy, old man, cash a small cheque."

"What do you think, Louie?" asked Middleton.

"All things considered, I don't see why not," she said.

"Well, all right," said Middleton, uncomfortably, "but who's going to cash it?"

"What about the old dragon?" suggested Trew, "I mean, the landlady? What's the matter with her?"

"Well, all right," said Middleton, "let's see."

"Of course," said Trew, with something like a sneer, "if you like, I could advance you ten or fifteen bob until Tuesday . . . but somehow it seems kind of silly, doesn't it?"

"I'll ask Mrs. Gibson," said Middleton, "thanks all the same, old boy." Then he went downstairs to Mrs. Gibson's room in the basement; but she was not there.

On Saturday and Sunday evening, her rents collected and her house in order, Mrs. Gibson took time off to enjoy a glass or two of Guinness' stout in the saloon bar of the "Hero of Waterloo", where she was well known and highly respected by a select circle of respectable householders of that neighbourhood. Generally, they conversed in discreet undertones, of matters too high for the furry ears of the sporting riff-raff that frequented the place; for the landlord of the "Hero" was Jack Duck, a retired heavy-weight fighter, an all-round sportsman and drinker, one of the three ugliest men in London. His face had been smashed to the thirty-two points of the compass, so that mothers frightened naughty children into silence by threatening to give them to Mr. Duck. All the bone and gristle had been surgically excised from his ten-times broken nose; his ears resembled old boxing gloves; his mouth and forehead were made up of strata of scar tissue.

One of his great, blood-shot bull-eyes was fixed sightless in its socket; the other rolled and glared. Having run to fat, Jack Duck weighed two hundred and eighty pounds. Even his flat feet were terrible – they slapped the reverberating floor when he walked. After his last great fight, with Tissot, the Black Killer of Senegal, something went wrong with the left half of Jack Duck's face. There was nothing left of him to spoil but his nervous system, and Tissot's right hand did the trick. When Duck talked you stared at him fascinated. The left-hand side of his face was rigid, like clay; the right-hand side twitched and jumped and winked, leered and snarled. Yet he was famous for his silly good nature: since there was nothing more to be got by fighting, he was a man of peace. When his wife was not watching him, he let people eat and drink on credit. On two or three occasions the late Lord Lonsdale, in passing, stopped to say how-do-you-do and offer one of his huge cigars to Jack Duck. He always said that he would smoke the cigar later, and locked it in a safe: he had Lonsdale Coronas wrapped in tissue paper, and sometimes showed them to his intimate friends.

So, apart from casual droppers-in, bums, spivs, and fly-by-night mystery men who lived one week here and another week there in furnished rooms and carried all their worldly goods in half-empty cardboard suitcases, Jack Duck's customers made two groups – the sporting, and the respectable. Mrs. Gibson was the Emily Post of the householders of Wheeler Square. A man named Joe Gutkes led the sportsmen.

He was a bookmaker, a shrewd, hard man – also shapeless of face – who owned greyhounds, promoted fights, and knew what was going on in the world. He walked with a deep stoop and a heavy limp, in a Napoleonic attitude. His right hand under his waistcoat and his left hand in the small of his back seemed to be holding down some tremendous pressure of inside information. His eyes bulged with inside information; and you felt that if you could take a screwdriver and prize open his lips you might receive such an outburst of inside information that you would never have to do another day's honest work as long as you lived.

This Saturday afternoon, excited by Middleton's good fortune, Mrs. Gibson, dressed in her brightest summer clothes, had left the house earlier than usual. Talking of Middleton's inheritance, she did not lower her voice, for this was something to tell the world.

It was an extraordinary thing, she said, but ladies and gentlemen who stayed with her seemed always to have remarkably good luck. There was Miss Stern, a dressmaker, forty if she was a day and absolutely nothing to look at, who married an immensely wealthy manufacturer of copper cooking pots who lived in the City – an Italian it was true, but a perfect gentleman and enormously wealthy. There was a man – just an ordinary gentleman – who had not had a job for six months: he had not been in her house three weeks before his mother died and left him a house and five hundred pounds insurance. She wished, she said, that she had a pound note for every tenant that had had good luck in her house. And now there was the case of Mr. Middleton: a steady young gentleman, a decent young gentleman, a hardworking, conscientious, quiet, respectably married, straight-as-a-die young gentleman. Not a gentleman to push himself forward in the world, but a gentleman to the backbone. The moment she set eyes on him she knew that he was not one of the common herd. He had been living in her house nearly five years, and when it came to the rent she could say with her hand on her heart that he had never been a minute overdue. He had married, although he could ill afford to do so, a perfect lady, and moved to the two little communicating rooms, unfurnished, on the fourth floor. Reluctant as she had been to let her rooms unfurnished (since it was almost impossible to get an unfurnished tenant out) some little voice had whispered to her: *Mrs. Gibson, this young gentleman is not one of the common herd.* Some people might say that she was gifted with second sight: she did not know. However, to cut a long story short, this very morning Mr. Middleton had inherited a hundred thousand pounds.

Jack Duck said: "A hundred thousand pounds is a lot of money."

"Hell of a lot," said Joe Gutkes, stiff-faced like a ventriloquist, scarcely moving his lips.

One of Mrs. Gibson's respectable friends shook her head and said: "Some people have all the luck, Mrs. Gibson."

"Well, Mrs. Midge, if anyone deserves it it's my Mr. Middleton, and I was the first to tell him so."

Half a dozen men and women nodded and murmured, and big Jack Duck, avoiding the eye of his wife, said: "Have a glass of port in your Guinness, Mrs. Gibson." He was always pleased by good news, especially this kind of good news. He loved a stroke of luck. So did Joe Gutkes, the gambler, who had had a bad day on Friday. He said to himself: *It only goes to show you anything can happen,* and said aloud: "All right, Jack. I'll do this. Make it drinks all round, Jack, will you?"

"Yes, Mr. Gutkes, with pleasure, Mr. Gutkes," said Mrs. Duck, elbowing her husband aside and wagging a finger at the barman. So, although Jack Duck had meant to say: "No, that's all right, this is on the house," the bookmaker paid nineteen shillings for a round of drinks for everyone in the saloon bar. "Here's luck," he said, drinking.

"Here's luck," said all the company. They were pleased. Mr. Middleton's luck had brought them luck – an extra, unexpected drink. Even in the grave – even in Wheeler Square – hope was not lost! No uncle lived for ever. What happened to one might happen to another.

Then Trew pulled open the saloon bar door. He bowed low, shouting: "Make way for the millionaire!" – and Louisa came in, nervously fumbling at her lower lip, followed by Middleton, who looked at his boots and blushed darkly.

"That's him!" said Mrs. Gibson in a penetrating whisper; and there was a chorus of astonished comment:

" – Who would think so to look at him?"

" – You'd never dream, would you?"

" – It only goes to show, doesn't it?"

" – To look at him you'd say he didn't have a hundred thousand farthings, let alone pounds."

" – Ah, but you see, you never can tell. I know a man who goes about (if the ladies will excuse the expression) with his shirt hanging out of his trousers, and he owns rows and rows of houses."

" – Appearances are deceptive, aren't they?"

A quick, bright-eyed little woman, much admired for her

shrewdness, said very quickly, and in one breath: "After all ask yourself a question it stands to reason doesn't it if the young man came into all this money this morning he couldn't be expected to turn up this afternoon in a tailormade suit of clothes driving a Rolls-Royce car – wait a bit and you'll see him parading about like a tailor's dummy and treating you like the dirt under his feet and paying no more attention to you than the flies on the wall."

" – Ah yes, Mrs. Bird, money often spoils people."

" – It can be more of a curse than a blessing, it's true, ma'am."

The humorist of the respectable corner of the saloon bar said: "Without wishing to be blasphemous, I wouldn't mind if somebody went and cursed me with a hundred thousand pounds."

Meanwhile Jack Duck was looking at Middleton with profound interest. He remembered Middleton, now – a quiet young fellow who used to come in on Saturday evening, never alone, always with Mr. Trew. He never drank more than four half-pints of mild ale; never spent more than two or three shillings; would strip at about one hundred and fifty pounds – a nice, ordinary, steady little fellow, whose weekly shilling was worth more, in the long run, than So-and-So's unreliable pound note. Now, Jack Duck looked at Middleton with awe. Here was he, Jack Duck, who had spilt his blood, broken his bones, lost his eyesight and his looks; broken an ear-drum, swallowed his teeth, fractured his wrists, and lived the life of an ascetic; keeping away from liquor, rich food, women, and night life between desperate fights, for thirty-five years. All he had was a pub. And here was a mere boy, with the best part of his life before him, into whose lap the gods had dropped a hundred thousand pounds. Jack Duck thought of himself when he was only sixteen, and remembered bloody, pitiless battles fought for five shillings. He remembered his first fight, which had got him two shillings and a damaged nose. (He had given the two shillings to his mother, who took in washing.) Remembering all this, he was sad – sorry for his dead self. But this sadness passed before he was properly aware of it, and then, he felt an inexplicable tenderness for this fortunate young man who would never know how it feels to look with satisfaction from the reflection of a broken face in a cracked mirror to two silver coins in the palm of a hand that ached so abominably and was so badly swollen that you had to screw it into your trousers pocket when you put the money away. Jack Duck felt that lofty pity which is like love, for this nice little fellow who could not fight his way out of a paper-bag; this meek, mild City clerk who, even if he inherited a hundred million pounds, was not made to know the joy of combat, the glory of battle against heavy odds, and the delight of honourable, unpredicted victory.

Offering his immense broken-and-mended hand, Jack Duck said: "Couldn't be more pleased if it happened to me. You and your good lady, and the gentleman, have anything you fancy on the house. Would you like a bottle of wine? If so, say so – it's on the house."

Middleton could think of nothing to say; he could only smile. But Trew said: "John Chicken – I mean Sir Francis Drake – I mean Jack Duck. *Oi!* If you want to know the fact of the matter, my old pal Middy hasn't got any money. He wasn't in time for the lawyer, because the letter didn't arrive until three o'clock; and the banks, as you know, close at twelve, and he doesn't like to accept what he cannot return."

"That's all right," said Jack Duck, "you don't want to worry about that."

"Oh, but——" said Middleton.

"Have this one on me," said Jack Duck, "and if you're short of a few pounds, well, have anything you like."

"But you don't know me, Mr. Duck," said Middleton. At the word *wine*, catching Duck's eye and understanding his nod and gesture, the barman had brought a bottle of mysteriously labelled champagne. At a nod and a wink he opened it. The cork bounced off the ceiling, and rolled to where Mrs. Gibson's party sat. The bright-eyed woman picked it up, and keeps it for a lucky mascot to this day. A small, furtive man whose name no one knew sidled up to Middleton and said: "Want something for the two-thirty? May I be struck down dead this minute, something on the job, honest-to-God on the job for the two-thirty, Epsom. Put your shirt on Little Sneeze, by Big Draught, out of Wisecrack. Is that worth a tosheroon? It's on the job, I give you my God's honour!"

"Tosheroon?" said Middleton, vaguely.

"Half a crown," said the furtive man, quickly. "Little Sneeze, two-thirty. I'm giving it to you, see? It's a gift, see? Little Sneeze, running in the two-thirty. Isn't that worth a tosheroon?"

Then Jack Duck saw him and said: "You get out of here, I'm warning you – I don't want you in my house."

The little man ran away. Joe Gutkes said, ventriloquially: "A man in your position doesn't want to mix up with that class of person – eh, Jack?"

Duck shook his head solemnly. Mrs. Gibson, who had heard the pop of the champagne-cork, came over to reiterate congratulations, and accepted a glass of wine. Trew said: "Do you know what, ma'am, Middy here has been chasing you up and down the house to try and borrow a few shillings?"

Mrs. Gibson was embarrassed. She said: "Why, as a matter of fact I never keep much money in the house. I bank – I *bank*," she repeated, not without pride, "on Friday. I bank on Friday. Whatever I can do, of course, I will under the circumstances. But I have banked."

Joe Gutkes said: "You're well off now. You know me, don't you? Joe Gutkes? Straight-As-A-Ruler Joe Gutkes. You know my office, Mr. Middleton?"

"Well . . ."

"Ninety-nine Jacobean Place. Turf Commission Agent. Antepost, starting price, anything you like. Everyone knows me. My name's Joe Gutkes. Now that you've come into your money, you'll want a bit of a flutter, Mr. . . . what did you say your name was . . . ?"

"Middleton. I'm afraid I haven't any money yet. Perhaps later. You understand, I can't get any money until everything is confirmed, and——"

"Your credit's good," said Gutkes, "as good as gold. What d'you fancy?"

"Ted, please – don't!" said Louisa, "don't be silly!"

"What's the matter with you, Louie dear?" asked Middleton, sharply.

"I don't know, Ted, darling, but I feel that this is all a dream. . . . Anyway, don't you think it would be just as well to wait till Tuesday? After all, we've got . . . we can . . . after all, it couldn't hurt to wait till Tuesday, Ted, and then . . . You get so excited!"

Middleton said: "I beg your pardon, Louie dear, I do not get excited." Turning to Gutkes he said: "I would like to put some money on Little Sneeze in the two-thirty."

"Little *Sneeze*?" said Joe Gutkes, "did you say *Little Sneeze*?"

"Er . . . yes please."

Trew said: "Little Sneeze please! – Atishoo! – Oi!" A sycophantic barfly giggled, hoping for a drink, but no one else seemed to hear. Everyone was staring at Middleton. He did not feel Louisa's urgent fingers at his sleeve when Joe Gutkes asked: "How much do you want, Mr. Middleton?"

Now, the bad champagne and the good news seemed to rush together in Middleton's head, and explode. He was surprised to hear his voice saying firmly: "Ten pounds!"

"Oh Ted, for goodness' sake! You mean shillings!" said Louisa.

"You're on," said Joe Gutkes, making a note in a leather-covered note-book. "A tenner to win, Little Sneeze for the two-thirty, Monday. Just write your name here, do you mind?" As soon as Middleton had written his precise signature under the note, Gutkes slapped the book shut, slipped it into his pocket, and said: "You're on at fifty to one. It's a long shot, but you can afford it. I'm a fool to myself to take a bet like that from a man starting a run of luck like yours, but my name's Joe Gutkes, and chance it! Have a drink."

"Well, really, really and truly, I think it's my turn," said Middleton, "only I must cash a cheque."

At this point Louisa heard one sporting character whispering to another:

"Blind O'Reilly! Little Sneeze! She started in the two-thirty at Doncaster the other day and finished second in the three-forty-five."

She said, desperately: "Teddy, Teddykins – do listen——"

But Middleton was not listening, because Jack Duck was saying: "That's all right, I'll do it. Tell me what you want." He said it heartily and openly, because his wife, who disapproved of cashing cheques, was in the kitchen, helping the cook to fry sausages and cut sandwiches for the Saturday evening rush.

While Middleton hesitated, Trew said: "He's all right, Billy

Partridge . . . I mean, Tommy Turkey . . . I mean, Jack Duck – *Oi!* Show him the letter Middy, old man!"

"I should have been only too delighted if I had not already banked," said Mrs. Gibson.

As Middleton's hand went automatically to his breast pocket, Jack Duck stopped him and said: "Oh, that's all right. How much do you want?" – and pulled out of his hip pocket a wallet fat with the takings of the past four days.

Still Middleton hesitated, and Louisa's agonised glance went unseen, while Trew, still fighting for a laugh, said: "Listen Sammy Sparrow . . . Robin Redbreast . . . Goosy Gander . . . Jack Duck – *Oi!*" Duck growled a perfunctory *ha-ha-ha*. " – Work it out for yourself. Say *you* came into a hundred thousand quid on August Bank Holiday? Put yourself in my friend's unfortunate position. No banks open till Tuesday. No banks *open till* Tuesday. Why you *open* the *till* – see?" When no one laughed Trew went on: "That one was a bit subtle. Anyway, Middy and his lady wife want to make whoopee. Middy's got a cheque book, and it's good as gold. Empty the till, until Tuesday. Un-till the till, see?"

This witticism, also, glanced off Jack Duck's skull. He simply said: "That's all right. What do you want within reason?"

"Well, I don't know," said Middleton. "I really don't know . . ."

"A tenner?" suggested Duck.

Middleton stared. Trew said: "Don't be silly, what's the use of a tenner? Make it twenty pounds!"

Jack Duck said: "All right, if you like. But make it snappy, will you?" Then he counted out twenty one-pound notes and rolled them into a fat oval, which he thrust into Middleton's outside breast pocket, saying: "There's twenty. Make the cheque out to *Cash*."

So Middleton, in a daze, filled in an open cheque for twenty pounds; which Jack Duck folded, as soon as the ink was dry. He intended to put it in his wallet, but before he had time to do so Mrs. Duck, with a dish of ruddy brown sausages, returned to the bar, followed by the cook, who carried two great trays of assorted sandwiches. Jack Duck knew what would happen if his wife saw him taking out his wallet; there would be a scene; she would show him up in public, discredit him, make him look foolish. Therefore, he slipped Middleton's cheque into a waistcoat pocket. Then Middleton ordered another bottle of sweet champagne, and paid for it with one of Jack Duck's own pound notes.

As he took his change – sixpence – Louisa whispered: "Oh Ted, Ted, why did you do it? Why couldn't we wait till Tuesday? What difference would another day or two make?"

At this Middleton experienced, for a second or two, a strange and awful sinking of the heart. His stomach shrank, his entrails writhed, and his heart contracted as his blood, on the instant, froze and stopped. He had only a few shillings in the bank – scarcely sufficient to keep his account open; and he had cashed a cheque for twenty pounds. If, by some unimaginable quirk of circumstances, Pismire had made a mistake, he was ruined, ruined for ever; lost; utterly cast away.

He went to the room behind the door marked *Gentlemen*, took out the letter, and read it over again twice. The sweet, highly gaseous champagne made him hiccup; and somehow with that little eructation doubt disappeared. He read the letter once again, put it back in his pocket, returned to Louisa, and said firmly but tenderly: "Louie dear, be reasonable. This is a hundred per cent all right. People like that don't go writing letters like this just for the sake of writing them. Why should they? How could Pismire's know about Uncle Joe in Australia – let alone his full name and address? Honestly, Louie, you've got to be reasonable."

"I suppose so," said Louie, "but – twenty pounds!"

Middleton laughed, and said: "You wait till Tuesday morning and you'll see."

"If only we could have waited till Tuesday morning!" said Louisa.

Middleton pressed his lips together and said nothing; and then she saw that he was angry. She said: "Oh, I'm sorry, Ted. Only it did seem sort of too good to be true. I didn't mean . . . I mean, I am sorry if . . . I don't know anything about these lawyers. You know how ignorant I am. I'm sure it's all right. I'm sorry, Ted."

"I may be silly, but I'm not altogether a fool," said Middleton.

"I said I was sorry, Ted," said Louisa, piteously.

Middleton smiled again. "We're going to have the time of our lives," he said. "We're going to celebrate. Dinner in the West End . . . night clubs——"

Trew, who had at last told a funny story, and was well satisfied, came and slapped Middleton on the shoulder and shouted: "Break it up, you two! Look at 'em, like a pair of budgerigars in a gilded cage! I tell you what, Middy, if you lend me a couple of pounds I'll buy you both a drink."

"Trewie, old boy, you're welcome to a couple of pounds," said Middleton, giving him the money, "but to tell you the honest truth I don't think we want any more. This has come as a bit of a . . . a blow, you know, and I want to sort of . . ."

"Sort yourself out, eh?" said Trew. "Well, I'm much obliged to you for the loan, old man."

"Say no more about it, old boy," said Middleton, wet-eyed with friendly feeling.

"You won't recognise me in a week or two from now," said Trew.

"Always the best of friends, Trewie, old boy," said Middleton, in a broken voice. He was about to thank Jack Duck for his kindness, when he observed that the old bruiser, who felt the watchful eye of his wife, was hurrying away to the cellar. So he conducted Louisa out of the "Hero of Waterloo" with the ceremoniously steady walk of a respectable person who realises that he has drunk just a little more than he is used to. Trew followed them out. His face was bright red, and his smile had melted into a loose, wet, ugly grin that fell looser and became wetter and uglier as he talked; he was more than half drunk, and proud of it. Swaying slightly he put his arms around Middleton and Louisa, and hugged them to his damp bosom, saying: "Always the best of friends. Bless you, my children!"

Louisa shook his arm away; but Middleton said: "See you later, Trewie, old boy . . . little later on if you don't mind."

"Oh," said Trew. "Naturally, old man. I understand. You don't need your old friends now. Right you are, Middleton. Au revoir, if not good-bye, Mrs. Middleton. I wish you all the luck in the world."

"Trewie, old boy!" cried Middleton, "it's just that——"

" – I quite understand," said Trew, with pathetic dignity. "The old, old story."

Then the hot evening grew dense with strong perfume, and a harsh nasal voice said: "Pardon me if you don't mind," as a big, overblown woman with dyed red hair pushed between Middleton and Louisa and went through the swinging doors into the saloon bar. In spite of the heat, she was wearing a double silver fox neck-piece, one of the bushy tails of which brushed Louisa's cheek. Louisa shuddered and said: "Ted, I want to go home – please Ted!"

Trew was walking slowly away, looking sad, saying to himself: *There's friendship for you! It's "Trewie, old boy, this . . ." and "Trewie, old boy, that . . ." when they need you. Then along comes a bit of skirt, and it's "Excuse me, if you don't mind, Trewie." And then they can run to you with their troubles, and you can offer to go hungry to help them out of your own pocket – and that's all right. But let them get rich, and it's "Here's a few shillings – run away, Trew." There's life for you! There's gratitude!*

Feeling the two pound notes in his coat pocket Trew decided that to injury Middleton had added insult. He walked back to the "Hero of Waterloo" to drown the memory of the insult and numb the pain of it.

Middleton, aware of the roll of money in his pocket, was almost happy. He and Louisa paused in the street near Mrs. Gibson's house, while they read the letter again. "Why, Louie dear – what is there to look so sad about?" he asked, half petulantly.

She replied, tearfully: "I don't know, Ted. Oh Ted . . . you won't go gambling and getting drunk now we've got all this money, will you?"

"Now just because we celebrate with a bottle of wine, and I put a few shillings on a horse – just to celebrate――"

" – Yes I know, I'm sorry," she said, hastily, "but I dare say it's because of me being like *this*."

"Louie dear," said Middleton, "it's the baby I'm celebrating about; because I don't mind telling you that up to an hour or two ago I used to lay awake at night not knowing which way to turn. Now, let's you and I talk about him."

" – Or her," said Louisa.

"Him or her – you can have anything you like," said Middleton.

"As long as you don't . . ."

"As long as I don't what, Louie dear? Drink champagne and back horses all day long?"

"Oh no, Ted, it's your money, and you're entitled to do anything you like with it. Only . . ."

Louisa was thinking of the big redhead. Her flesh crawled and tingled as she remembered the swaggering shoulders, and the swishing brush of silver fox. Rubbing her cheek where the fur had touched it, and wrinkling her nose in which the stale, expensive, dishonestly-come-by perfume still clung, she added: "As long as you don't let a certain class of people that're only after your money take you away from me."

"Don't be silly, Louie dear," said Middleton, laughing.

"Oh, I know you're different, Ted. But I know what men are . . . and when I see the kind of creatures they go and make fools of themselves with . . . well . . ."

"Don't be silly. Let's talk about you and I and the future," said Middleton. ". . . By the way, what do you mean, you know what men are?"

"Let's talk about you and I," said Louisa.

* * * * *

The big, brazen, scented woman of whom Louisa was thinking had, by this time, jostled her way to the bar with her odorous silver fox neck-piece slung like a blanket roll about her swaggering shoulders. At the sight of her the respectable customers compressed their lips and exchanged frowns; while the sporting gentlemen winked at one another and looked as if they were about to whistle. A certain diminutive, squeezed-up sportsman who seemed to carry with him some of the stale air of a thousand stuffy dressing-rooms, currying favour with a young boxer who had a pound or two in his pocket, whispered:

"Look who's here! Know who she is? That's Wild Rose!"

"Never heard of her," said the young fighter.

"What? You never heard of Wild Rose? Why, years ago, Jack

Duck and Wild Rose—— C'meer, I don't want to shout . . ." He put his mouth to the young fighter's ear.

". . . Is that a fact?" said the young fighter.

"My oath. But keep your trap shut, see?"

"Well, okay, but if I was Jack Duck and you gave *me* to choose that one or the one he got married to, I know which——"

" – Shut up. Look out – here comes Jack. Keep your eyes open."

Jack Duck, coming up from the cellar with an armful of bottles, saw Wild Rose, and dropped a bottle of gin; and when it burst on the cellar floor something seemed to splash up, cold and stinging inside him, while the darkness under the dome of his skull throbbed to the noise of a gong. Instinctively he tucked in his chin and drew a deep breath, shuffling his feet on the top step of the cellar stairs.

But the heart had gone out of him. He felt like a man rooted in a nightmare on a railway track.

Wild Rose was at the bar, unaccompanied, flaunting herself under a sign which said:

LADIES UNACCOMPANIED BY GENTLEMEN
MAY NOT BE SERVED AT THE BAR

Mrs. Duck was behind the bar. The Past and the Present were rushing together. If these two women met there would be a crash and a blinding light; a mushroom of black smoke, a shower of debris, and the end of the world.

"Now for it: Gawd Save the King!" whispered Jack Duck. This was his Lucky Word – his Prayer Before Battle.

Even as he said this a fortunate accident gave him time to think.

PART III

The ruffianly redheaded woman called Wild Rose was feared by navigators in the nightbound currents of the West End as a sort of drifting mine with bristling detonators and likely to go off bang, with fatal consequences, at a touch. Even in repose she was dangerous. Her flaring red hair seemed to be burning its way down over a perilously low forehead, to touch off a fuse between her eyes; and when she raised her eyebrows, and the red point of her "widow's peak" came within an inch of the bridge of her nose, people who knew her took cover. She was all fire and gunpowder. Even in her sentimental moods men winced – when she filled her great lungs with the interminable breath of a tremendous sigh, they thought of a toy balloon, blown tense and certain to burst shockingly at any moment. Wild Rose could not sit still; she had to tap her feet on bar rails and pick the red varnish off her long sharp finger-nails; and at regular intervals she shrugged into position the silver fox neck-piece without which she felt undressed – in the manner of a wrestler who cannot keep his braces in place because of the over-developed muscles of his shoulders.

Now, hitching up one of her silver foxes, she sent the bushy tail flying so that it knocked over a glass of whisky-and-soda, which emptied itself over the light grey trousers of a pink, plump, less-than-half-sober gentleman on her left. Anticipating some protest, Wild Rose turned, clenching a large white hand, upon which she wore a white zircon as big as a bottle-cap. But the man made no protest. He laughed, and said: "Lady, if you want to launch me, break a bottle of champagne over me. Oh well, I'm only a little boat. *Bon voyage!*"

Then Wild Rose laughed heartily, and said: "I like a man to have a sense of humour."

"That's all right then, lady, you like me. A sense of humour is just about all I have got . . . apart from friends. Ha-ha! Friends! Ever have a friend that let you down? . . . Anyway, *you* like a man to have a sense of humour, and *I* like a lady to have a drink. Will you do me the honour?" said Trew, folding a pound note into a paper boat and putting it in a little puddle of spilt liquor on the bar. "A life on the ocean wave – we're launched!"

"Well, I wouldn't say no. To tell you the truth, that's what I came here for. My name's Rose. What's yours?"

"Dick Trew. Hi, Jack!"

Wild Rose stared, slapped her thigh, and cried: "Well, if it isn't Jack Duck!"

"Famous fighter," said Trew.

"Fighter? Don't talk silly," said Rose. "We're old friends – how are you, Jack?"

Jack Duck whispered: "Shush!"

"Who're you shushing, you——"

" – Rosie, be a pal – I'm a married man."

"The beautiful lady and I would like a drink," said Trew.

Wild Rose said, in an astonished voice: "Listen, Jack, tell me – that flyweight in the green dress – is she your trouble-and-strife?"

"Shush, for God's sake!" whispered Jack Duck, winking hideously; and then he shouted: "Certainly, certainly, Mr. Trew! Certainly madam! . . . Oh, Nora, Mr. Trew and his lady friend would like a bottle of champagne!"

Mrs. Duck, her suspicion unaroused, went to get the bottle, and Jack Duck said, as quickly and quietly as he could: "Look, do me a favour, can't you? Come on, Rosie, you always were a sport. Fight fair, Rosie. I played the game with you, didn't I? Do me a favour – don't start no bundles here, will you? I'm a married man, get it?" Before she could reply, he pulled a pound note out of his trousers pocket, pressed it into Trew's hand and continued: "It's all right, the bottle's on me. Pay for it with that. Go and drink it at a table. Do me a favour, Rosie, will you? I'll come and talk to you in a minute."

Then Mrs. Duck came with a bottle of the sweet champagne, which the waiter carried to a vacant table. Trew, pocketing his folded pound note, said nothing. He sat close to Wild Rose, who said: "What's the matter with Jack? Here I am on my way to Euston station – I'm going to Manchester. I've got an engagement, you know. They're putting on lady wrestlers. Why, I haven't seen Jack for years. Me and him used to be the best of friends. What the hell does he mean," said Wild Rose, growing angry, "what the hell does he mean by talking to me in that tone of voice? Married? *Married?* Who cares? He's not entitled to talk to *me* in that tone of voice – him or twenty Jack Ducks! Who's he? Why, I've got a good mind to——"

Then Jack Duck came lumbering over to their table, looking with anguish at Wild Rose, and bellowing: "Everything all right? Everything all right? Everything all right?" Then, tucking his chin into his left shoulder, he whispered: "Listen, Rosie. I'm a pal. You're a sport. I'm a married man. Look, Rosie . . . here's something for a fox fur, or something. I'm a married man, see? I can't go to the till, get it? But this is as good as gold – ask Mr. Trew. Gentleman just came in to a hundred thousand quid. You ask Mr. Trew, here. Didn't he, eh, Mr. Trew?"

"Yes, definitely," said Trew, not very comfortably.

"What *is* all this?" said Wild Rose.

"Catch hold of this, and for God's sake keep it quiet," said Jack Duck, giving her Middleton's cheque. "It's a cash cheque, see? Twenty nicker. Good as gold. Isn't that so, Mr. Trew? . . . Grab hold, quick, Rosie. Mr. Trew, he'll tell you – cheque's as good as gold. Anyway, I'll guarantee it. Man came in to hundred thousand. Ask Mr. Trew. I'd give you the money in cash, but can't. Married man. Cheque endorsed. Be good girl, Rosie – play the game – married man. Let sleeping dogs lie. Be pal."

Then Jack Duck went back to his place behind the bar, and Wild Rose said to Trew: "Now what *is* all this? Cheques? Did Jack think I came to bite his ear?"

Trew said: "Well, a friend of mine's uncle left him a hundred thousand pounds. Jack Duck cashed him a cheque for twenty, that's all." The wine and the whisky had combined to make uneasiness which would not go away, because it was shaken up and thickened by the palpitation of his heart.

Suddenly sober, Trew knew that his joke had gone far enough, and might be ended here. If he said to Wild Rose: "Oh, tear up the cheque and forget it – be big-hearted"; and if she tore up the cheque, Middleton would have had twenty pounds, and no one could be a penny the worse.

But he could not say it, and Wild Rose, drinking the dregs of the champagne, taking him by the shoulder in a terrible grip, cried:

"Come on. I'll catch the later train. You come along with me to Little Lew's. I like a man with a sense of humour, and you bring me luck."

"But——"

"I'm not used to begging people to give me the pleasure of their company," said Wild Rose.

"Whatever you say," said Trew.

When they reached Little Lew's Club in Lisle Street, he learned that Wild Rose had kept the taxi waiting since she had gone into the "Hero of Waterloo" for a quick drink. He gave the taxi-driver the facetiously-folded pound note, and was waiting for seven shillings change, intending to give the man a two-shilling piece, when Wild Rose said: "Keep the change, driver," and dragged Trew into Little Lew's Club.

Now all the humour drained out of Trew, and he was no longer at his ease. Calculating rapidly, secretively fumbling the money in his pockets, he found that he had four pounds ten and a little small change. He had left the office on Friday with four pounds ten. After having paid one or two debts of honour (his landlady could wait) he had gone into the "Hero of Waterloo" with three pounds seventeen-and-sixpence. He could not possibly have spent more than five shillings: Middleton had paid for most of the drinks, and had lent him two pounds. Therefore he should have been able to count nearly six pounds. Where had his money gone? Trew looked up, saw the fierce, implacable face of Wild Rose, and remembered that he was in the company of a woman who could spend thirteen shillings on a taxi-ride and tell the driver to keep the change out of a pound. Then he wanted to go home; but she had him fast by the wrist, and was shouting: "Now here's a man with a sense of humour! I like him, I love him! . . . What did you say your name was?"

"Trew, Dick Trew."

"Hi, there, Nobby – hi there, Muriel! . . . What, is that you, Billy? Come and have a drink with Dick Trew – you too, Sylvia; and bring Wally. Come on over. Meet Dick Trew – a man with a sense of humour. I love him, I want to kiss him!"

Trew put down a pound note. The smoky air in the little club-room seemed to break into ripples which, when Trew coughed, became a curtain of blue-grey watered silk. "Wish you all you wish yourself," somebody said; and Trew, with an empty glass, fumbled for more money, looking left and right for Wild Rose. But she was engrossed in conversation with a very small man in the remotest corner of the room. Trew cried: "Oh, Rose!" – but a woman's voice said: "Leave her alone, dear. Can't you see? She's talking to Tishy. Come on, what I say is, Bank Holiday comes but once a year, so let's all have a drink. Oh, Lew! – Gentleman wants to offer somebody a drink."

"Hm, yes. . . . That's right," said Trew.

The man called Tishy was saying: ". . . I've got a proposition, Rosie. Give you my word of honour. Come on, couldn't you raise me a fiver?"

Wild Rose said: "I haven't got a fiver, Tishy."

It was well known that Wild Rose had a motherly regard for Tishy. Occasionally she treated him to heavy meals – eighteen-ounce steaks, whole chickens, double chump chops, and pints of bottled stout – because Tishy had an air of dumb woe, suggestive of malnutrition, and in his sore pink-lidded eyes there was the wistfulness of a starving waif staring into a pastry-cook's window. He lived like one of those skinny, beaky birds that run forwards and backwards with the ebb and flow of the tide, hurriedly pecking invisible nourishment out of the mud – one of those anxious grey little birds that have to live on the seashore, but apparently hate to get their feet wet. Perpetually advancing and retreating, between waves, Tishy managed to survive in the silt at the edge of the deep. He always knew a man who had a car, a watch, a fur coat, or a greyhound. Whatever you might happen to want (no questions asked) Tishy knew a man who knew a man. He might also be likened to the bird that picks the teeth of the crocodile, or the bird that gets ticks from between the folds of a rhino's hide – any small, quick, omnivorous bird.

"Couldn't we raise a few quid?" he asked, looking up at Wild Rose with his sad starveling's eyes. "I could pay you back double. I know a certain party, a valet, and so this valet worked for a lord. This lord just died, and left a whole lot of clothes. Get it? Suits, overcoats, shoes, silk shirts, hosiery, those red coats and high boots they go and catch foxes in . . . everything – worth a packet. Well, Rosie, for personal reasons this party doesn't want to flog the stuff with any of the gent's wardrobe people, and he's got to have some money by to-morrow, or Monday at the outside. I've got a fiver. If I could let him have, say, a tenner on account I could get the stuff, pay him off on Tuesday, and clear eighty or a hundred nicker. Oh well . . . I'll see what I can fiddle."

Wild Rose said: "I'll tell you what though, I've got a cheque." Tishy groaned, but she went on: "It's as good as gold. Jack Duck gave it to me. I didn't ask him for it, he just gave it to me. It's quite all right; good old Jack Duck doesn't bounce stumer cheques – you can take your dying oath on that. It's for twenty quid."

"Couldn't you get Little Lew to cash it?" asked Tishy, without hope.

"What him? Little Lew?" said Wild Rose. It was said of Little Lew that he had taken the pennies off his dead mother's eyes and replaced them with an IOU.

"No use talking. I'll see what I can fiddle. Still, it seems such a pity," said Tishy. " – But I tell you what. If it's a cash cheque, there *is* just about half a chance I could get this party to take it. You see, he's gone and got himself into a spot of bother with a certain other party, and if he doesn't come up to the mark on Monday, this other party'll raise hell on Tuesday. Do you get what I mean, Rosie?"

Wild Rose understood. In her reckless, contemptuously gesticulating way, she said: "I get it. This valet of yours is a bit of a tea-leaf. His boss snuffs it. This valet half-inches just about as much of the old man's stuff as he thinks he can get away with, before the poor old gentleman is cold. So if somebody turns up and starts shouting the odds, this valet might draw attention to himself. Then there'd be inquiries, and I shouldn't be surprised if they found out that this valet of yours had been half-inching the old gentleman's gold studs, and things, for years and years. So your valet wants to hush it up. Isn't that it?"

"He's not *my* valet, Rosie," said Tishy, humbly. "But that's just about it. I think you've hit it, just about."

"I suppose he got himself mixed up with some woman," said Wild Rose, curling her lip.

"That I couldn't say. I shouldn't be in the least surprised. I'd tell you if I knew, but I don't," said Tishy. "My idea is that this client might take the cheque and use it to stall the other party off with. Well now, say that cheque *is* a stumer. Say it *does* bounce. By the time it bounces my deal will of gone through – I'm dead certain of that – and everybody'll have had time to breathe, and

I can pay off the valet, and everybody's happy. If only I can get him to accept the cheque . . ."

"Wait a minute, wait a minute! Whose cheque *is* this? Where do I come in?" asked Wild Rose.

"Lend me that kite, and I'll cut you in fifty-fifty. Is that fair? If my party doesn't accept, well, you can have your cheque back. . . . But I've got a feeling that he might."

Wild Rose took Middleton's cheque out of her purse, and gave it to Tishy, saying: "Here you are then. Twenty pounds. Now remember, Tishy, this has got a back to it! I'm in with you fifty-fifty. Don't you forget that, now, do you hear? And if you try any funny stuff with me, may I never move from this spot if I don't break every bone in your body – because I've been a good friend to you, Tishy."

"Even if I dared to, I'd never play you a dirty trick, Rosie," said Tishy. "It's a chance, nothing but a chance. Let's try it, and chance it. I'm going to get a cup of coffee. Want a cup of coffee?"

"I'll walk along with you. You ought to have some scrambled eggs, or a sandwich. The trouble with you is, you don't eat half enough," said Wild Rose.

So, at eleven o'clock that night, Trew found himself alone in Soho Square, with sevenpence in his pocket: his legs were rubber and his feet were wool, yet it was necessary to walk a few hundred yards to a bus stop in Oxford Street. He did so, but got on the wrong bus, and, having bought a penny ticket, fell asleep until the conductor shook him at Aldgate and demanded threepence excess fare. From Aldgate Trew had to walk home through the deserted streets of the City. Cats wailed in the dark. Policemen watched him from the shadows. Passing the Old Bailey, Trew looked up at the golden statue of Justice that stands with sword and scales on the dome, and he sneered, cursing the world in general and Middleton in particular. If Middleton had never been born this could never have happened. He cursed Middleton from Hatton Garden to Gray's Inn Road; turned right, inventing new curses; and so, in the remorseful stage of sobriety, reached Wheeler Square at midnight with three pennies in his pocket just as Middleton and his wife were getting out of a taxi at Mrs. Gibson's house.

Bilious with hate, Trew watched Middleton as he paid the taxi-driver, and listened while the flag went up with a sharp ringing noise, and the driver said good-night so politely that Trew could almost hear the tinkle of a substantial tip in a leather-lined pocket. Then he was more than half inclined to tap Middleton on the shoulder and say: "Look here, old man . . . Something I want to tell you. I know you can take a joke, so listen – this is going to make you laugh. About that letter of yours; I wrote it myself. Well, you know me, Middy, old man – anything for a harmless joke, eh?"

But even as he touched Middleton's shoulder, instinct warned Trew that he would be prudent if he kept his mouth shut for the time being. And then gall and acid came up into his throat as he realised that he could never dare, openly, to enjoy his joke; never tell the story. All the world loves a lover, especially a newly-married one, whose silly little waitress of a wife is going to have a baby, and rejoices – strange world! – in his good fortune. The joker who plays the trick with him, therefore, is not funny: on the contrary, he is detestable. Trew shuddered away from a vision of himself as an outcast, shunned and scorned. And he remembered that Gutkes had given credit and Jack Duck had paid money out of pocket, on the strength of his joke. If the story came out Jack Duck would do nothing, but Gutkes might do much. Middleton, again, would be dangerous: apart from the fact that he had a temper, and a pair of hands, he would be compelled to explain and excuse himself when the trick was exposed. Sure as fate, on Tuesday morning Middleton would go to Pismire, who would deny all knowledge of the letter pertaining to the estate of Uncle Joe. After that there would be checking, and double-checking. Without a doubt, Middleton would have the envelope to produce, and this envelope might be traced to Forty Richards. If it were, Trew would have a great deal of explaining to do in the office. Forty Richards might see the joke . . . or then again he might not. He would certainly express, in the strongest terms, his disapproval of a man who filched the firm's envelopes and sneaked other firms' letter-headings out of the correspondence files to play practical jokes.

Then Trew knew that he was in danger, and that his only hope of salvation lay in brazen perjury and consistent lying; in heated denial, emphatic head-shaking, and plausible dissembling.

He could never claim authorship of his masterpiece. The glory was gone, the triumph was void, and there he stood, sick and sorry, with threepence in his pocket and nothing before him but a hopeless August week-end, four interminable hungry days between Tuesday and pay-day – days to be got through by means of hard-found jokes and humiliating loans that would have to be repaid if he starved for a month – and a funny story that could never be told.

So, when Middleton felt his touch and turned, Trew said: "Hullo, Middy," so sadly that even Louisa's heart was softened.

"Why, Trewie, old boy!" cried Middleton. "We've been out celebrating. We went to Romano's in the Strand."

"We made absolute pigs of ourselves," said Louisa.

" – She ate Omelette Arnold Bennett——"

" – A sort of omelette with smoked haddock in it. And a whole roast chicken——"

" – A baby chicken, Trewie, old boy, not much bigger than your fist. And I had——"

" – He had smoked salmon, steak and chips, and a Welsh rarebit——"

" – Louie had peach melba——"

" – We drank a whole bottle of white wine, and Ted had a brandy——"

" – Louie had a Drambuie. Of course we had coffee," said Middleton, "and then we danced. You must come with us sometime, Trewie, old boy. It's not bad at all."

"Expensive," said Trew.

"Expensive! I should say so," said Louisa.

But Middleton said: "Oh I don't know. The whole evening didn't cost us a couple of pounds or so, tips and taxis and everything – did it, Louie dear?"

"Lucky people," said Trew.

"What did *you* do with yourself, Trewie, old boy?"

"Nothing much."

"How about us meeting to-morrow and going out?" said Middleton. "Eh, Louie?"

"If I won't be intruding," said Trew. "I'm not doing anything much that I know of. What time?"

"Well, Louie wants to rest and write a whole lot of letters to her mother and things, so what do you say to about seven or half-past, Trewie, old boy?"

"All right, Middy, old man, see you then," said Trew; and went to his room. He was so tired that he would have gone to bed in his best suit; but reminding himself that next week he would almost certainly have to pawn this suit, he hung it up carefully, and then, throwing himself on to the bed, still wearing his shoes and underclothes, fell giddily into a heavy sleep full of anxious dreams.

But for several hours Middleton lay awake, thinking. His head, frozen by shock, began to thaw, now, in the hot, damp darkness of the little bedroom. Pinprick by pinprick and throb by throb, reason went back where it belonged and Middleton was in agony, wanted to wriggle and shake the brain in his skull, as he had occasionally needed to wriggle and shake a numb foot inside its shoe. Every day for two years, in the mail order department, he had been handling other people's money – good, ready money – postal orders, Bank of England notes, and telegraphed money orders.

If you were an uncivilised person you might see this money as nothing but black-and-white or discreetly-coloured paper, and use it as such. But this paper, to a civilised man, was one of the most important things in the world. Black colliers went into hot dark tunnels a thousand feet underground, to tear the terrific energy of the buried sunlight out of the guts of the world; for bits of paper. Grocers – for paper – sold cakes of soap to wash away the blackness of the pits, and lumps of fat bacon that men ate to give them strength to cut coal to get – paper. You got to work to dig a hole to earn enough to buy the food to get the strength to go to work to dig a hole . . . oh, dreary eternal recurrence! Middleton's head was seething, now. Some great Anarch had taken possession of it, so that his mind flew up in bright spray, whirled down in muddy vortices, rushed up in spouts to kiss the clouds, crashed back in thunder, shrugged sullenly into a languid swell overhung by a fog made up of unsettled particles of itself, and then – unpredictable and uncontrollable – divided like the Red Sea, only to clap back into turbulence again.

. . . Miners mined and weavers wove; farmers farmed, butchers killed pigs and scalded them with boiling water and bled them, and scraped them, and skinned and gutted and smoked them and sold them – for paper – to grocers who sold them for paper again to men who went to work to dig a hole . . . for paper. Paper was life. Paper was death. Middleton thought of his birth certificate; of his father's death certificate. Now, his head was spinning in a rickety way, and he could see his thoughts running inwards to a hole and a pole in the centre of himself – not unlike a phonograph record on an ill-balanced turn-table – shivering white and glittering black, black cut by white, white scored by black. The disc ran down towards the pit, shouting: *You go to work, you go to work to dig a hole to earn enough to buy the food to get the strength to go to work to dig a hole to earn enough to buy the food to get the strength to go to work to dig a hole . . .*

The pit sucked Middleton down, and he found himself falling in spirals in a dark vortex – which exploded, all of a sudden, and blew him up through something mysteriously compounded of froth and light, back into consciousness.

Middleton sat up with a hiccup.

He tried to compose himself, and dozing, remembered an incident over which Trew had made merry a year or two ago. Some fly-by-night trader, advertising some specious bargain, had employed an impoverished man who was too weak to work and too proud to beg, to distribute leaflets on a gusty afternoon in March. The old man's hands were cold. The passers-by kept their hands in their pockets. A bitter east wind was blowing from the direction of the bank. Suddenly, tired of it all, the old man hurled his bundle of leaflets into the wind, pocketed his hands, and walked away. For a second or two the air was white with flimsy bits of paper that seemed to be flying into the setting sun. But they fluttered down into the street and the heavy traffic rolled them into the mud.

And now Middleton felt that inside his head there was a rattling roll of paper, and that the more assiduously he tugged at it the larger it grew. He would have got up and walked about, but he feared that he might disturb Louisa, who was sleeping peacefully in her little bed two feet away. Forcing himself to lie still, Middleton thought of his letter, and of all that might be done with £76,000. £76,000 of capital, invested at five per cent, would bring him an income of £3,800 a year – nearly £75 a week. There were not many safe investments at five per cent. Assume, just to be on the safe side, that a man invested £76,000 at only two and a half per cent. He would have about £35 a week for life, and this was a great deal of money – but not half as much as £75 a week. Still, £35 a week (call it £36) was nine hundred per cent more than the £4 a week for which he was only too anxious to work eight hours a day . . . Middleton tried to laugh at himself.

He tickled his fancy, thinking of what he would say to Mr. Mawson on Tuesday. ". . . Mr. Mawson, as you will see, by this letter, I have come into an inheritance of £100,000, net personalty £76,000, and I have much pleasure in informing you that you may go and——"

. . . Or it might be better to be suave, and say: "Oh, Mawson, I want a word with you." Then Mr. Mawson would glare at him like a maniac; but Middleton would remain calm. Without producing the letter, he would continue: "I have just inherited a very large fortune, and don't intend to work here any longer. Feel like coming to Romano's to-night with my good lady and me for a bit of a farewell dinner, eh, Mawson?"

So, thinking of Mr. Mawson, Middleton remembered all the money he had taken out of envelopes since he had been promoted to the mail order department. The money came in most heavily in the middle of the week; it was posted, generally, on Monday, when the glow of the Sunday advertisements was still warm, and people felt rich. He remembered a certain tremendous Wednesday when he had recorded orders to the value of nearly nine hundred pounds. Then he could see the money in the dark. There were the painfully-scrawled postal orders, the carefully-folded ten-shilling notes, the assiduously-smoothed pound notes. They came into every branch of Coulton Utilities by the million. But he had never regarded this stuff as money – only as something that was not his: paper. . . .

He was almost asleep when he realised that in two years he had dealt with something like a hundred-and-fifty-thousand pounds – all on paper. People bought food to get the strength to go to work to dig a hole to earn enough to buy the paper . . . the Sunday paper . . . paper. . . .

He fell asleep, and then he found himself in a nightmarish Holborn that ran without perspective from a blackness in the east to a fiery redness in the west; and the air was full of falling paper – forty-eight-sheets and postal orders, pamphlets and leaflets, circulars and bank-notes. One pale oblong fell at Middleton's feet, and then, arching itself, crawled away like a caterpillar. "Come back here at once!" cried Middleton. The bit of paper said: "Try and catch me." It stood on end and waited until Middleton was within reach of it, and then slid away like a snake just as he threw himself down upon it. "You had better be careful, Middleton," said Mr. Mawson. But the paper oblong heaved itself up, grew great and flapped its corners derisively before it folded itself into an immense coffin-shaped kite, which caught a dirty wet wind that came rushing out of the darkness in the east, and soared to high heaven. "It escaped," said Middleton; but no one heard him, for he was caught in the tail of the kite. Looking down he could see St. Paul's Cathedral like a pin-head, and the Thames like a twisted wire. And then the kite disintegrated, and Middleton was falling. He could see the world turning, black and glistening – growing larger and larger. The larger the world grew, the less Middleton could see. The world was a wobbling, shiny disc, spinning and spinning, and shouting in a scratched voice that grew louder and louder like the roar of a crowd at a critical moment in a great game . . . and Middleton slid through a silent black hole in the centre of a howling phonograph record, and was profoundly relieved to find himself in bed, and not in the cruel cogs of a dark machine, somewhere in the guts of a howling nightmare.

Dawn was coming, and Louisa was smiling in her sleep. But Middleton could not shake himself free of his dream – the base of his spine still twitched and crawled and his heart was hammering at the walls of his chest. "Now what the dickens is there to be afraid of in a kite?" he wondered.

A psychologist, asked to interpret Middleton's dream, having put him on a couch and cross-examined him for three days, would probably have come out with a terrifying rigmarole, well laced with tasty technical terms and flavoured with some spicy little revelations that would have made his hair curl. He would have told Middleton about the power-symbolism of flying, and the anxiety-symbolism of falling, in a dream. In the end he would, no doubt, have arrived at some kind of conclusion which would have been cheap at half the price. But, after the age-old and unchangeable manner of married men who dream dreams fit to talk about, he told Louisa about it when she awoke an hour later; and she gave him what the carnival fortune-tellers call a "cold reading" on the spot, free of charge. She was a good cockney who, having exchanged back-chat and overheard conversations in a cheap City restaurant, had acquired a fair smattering of slang and unconventional English. She said:

"Dreamt you were flying a kite? Why, Teddykins, you old silly, you! You've just been worrying about that cheque you went and cashed, that's all."

Middleton slapped himself on his tousled head and cried: "Good Lord, what a fool I am not to have thought of that!"

To *fly a kite*, in vulgar parlance, is to put into circulation a questionable cheque. It does not necessarily mean, that a "kite-flyer" is uttering a worthless cheque with intent to defraud ... although it comes perilously close to meaning something like that. For example: an unscrupulous man, knowing that he hasn't a penny in the bank, but knowing that five days must pass before a crossed cheque is cleared, might buy something on cash terms, paying by cheque, and so, in effect, get his goods on credit, since he had bought someone else's property with money that he has yet to find. If he does not find this money, of course, he is likely to find himself in trouble. But somehow he manages things so that his cheque is honoured – even if he has to ask a favour of a "kite-flying" friend and ask for another worthless cheque which he may pay into his account, with a flourish, and so snatch another few days of time. There are few self-made businessmen who have not, at some critical period in their lives, "flown a kite". Still, as a practice, "kite-flying" is generally deplored; it is dishonourable, in principle, because it necessarily involves prevarication, misrepresentation – and if your kite-string happens to break, you are no better than a cheat unmasked.

Now Middleton knew all this. He knew that it was not merely dishonourable but positively dangerous to "fly a kite", and so his cautious and respectable consciousness had kicked the memory of that vulgar expression into the coal-cellar of his memory. He said: "Of course, of course," and was gracious enough to add: "You're a clever girl, and I'm a fool, Louie dear. But my God! Say there's some delay!"

"Well, that's what I was trying to say yesterday, only you wouldn't listen, would you? I don't want to be one of those nagging wives, but I did tell you so, didn't I? But don't worry," said Louisa, smoothing his hair, "all you've got to do is take the letter to the bank first thing Tuesday morning."

"What about the office?" said Middleton.

Louisa said: "Oh never mind your old office! You won't need to worry about your office much longer – you and your old office. You can ring up and tell them you've just come into money. Anyway, you'll have to go to the solicitor's first thing Tuesday, won't you?"

"Yes," said Middleton, sighing with relief. "I'll go to the solicitor first, then to the bank, and if Mawson doesn't like it . . ."

"If he doesn't like it he can lump it. Do you know that, Ted, I'm only just beginning to realise this is true! Wasn't it a lovely evening we had yesterday?"

"To-night," said Middleton, firmly, "we are going to a night club."

"*Ted!*"

"A *night* club, definitely."

"Oh, but Ted, you asked Dick Trew to come along to-night."

"Ah, come on now, Louie dear; don't be so unkind to poor old Trew. Old Trewie does his best, and we've always been the best of friends. Besides, he livens things up."

"I've never forgiven him for what he did the day we were married," said Louisa.

"What, do you mean squirting water in my eye out of that artificial flower? Oh come on, Louie dear, can't you take a joke?

I can. It was well meant. If Trewie had thought for one moment it'd hurt your feelings, he'd never have dreamt."

"All right, Teddykins darling."

Middleton said: "You know what? When I've got everything in order on Tuesday I'm going to take you out shopping – Piccadilly, Bond Street, anywhere you like – and buy you everything you can possibly think of. . . . Louie dear, look: I didn't get a wink of sleep last night, so d'you mind if I take a little nap now so as to be fresh for to-night?"

"There, there, you poor tired Teddykins!"

So Middleton slept, deeply and dreamlessly now, while Louisa, drinking a cup of strong tea, thought of shopping in Bond Street. In her present condition it would be a waste of money to buy smart suits and elegant gowns. But there were many other things to buy – including a three-quarter length fur coat. A fur coat in August? Yes: not to wear in the street, but to have; to keep for the autumn. At this time of the year, furthermore, good furs could be bought at a low price. She saw herself in December. The baby was born strong and healthy, and she was walking, slender in a tailor-made and gorgeous in a three-quarter length fur coat. But not a silver fox! Anything but a silver fox – marmot, catskin, rabbit, no fur at all rather than sickly-scented silver fox!

She kissed her sleeping husband lightly on the head and whispered: "There, you clever old darling! You wouldn't go and get yourself mixed up with horrible fat old ginger-heads, would you? . . . You and your silly old kites!"

Middleton slept peacefully until one o'clock, when he jumped out of bed with a joyous cry and forced Louisa to dance with him while he sang "Oh I Wonder What It Feels Like To Be Poor". "Stop it, you're making me giddy," she said. "What would you like to eat for lunch? I've got——"

" – Never mind what you've got. Give it to the cat. Get me a cup of tea and we'll go out. What would I like? I'd like another steak and chips, like last night. Don't argue, put on your hat!"

He wantonly threw away a razor blade less than half a week used, and shaved with a new blade – with such thoughtless vigour that he cut himself under the nose and bled for twenty minutes; so that it was nearly two o'clock before they arrived in a taxi at the French restaurant in Soho, where Middleton ordered cocktails, chicken à la King, steak, and half a bottle of wine. Partly in irony, but mainly in charity, nostalgically remembering a certain happy Sunday in Vienna in the summer of 1899, the restaurateur bowed low, danced attendance, and gave them of his best. The luncheon cost fifteen shillings; Middleton, who was beginning to get the hang of high life, worked out ten per cent of fifteen shillings with a fork on the tablecloth, and gave him one and sixpence for himself. The restaurateur, who recognised innocent happiness when he saw it, put the three sixpences in his wallet for good luck, and would be carrying them to this day if he had not been almost literally liquidated by a bomb in 1941, five years later.

But Middleton's cheque had already changed hands again, furtively, in the saloon bar of the "Silent Wife": a public-house in Mayfair, patronised almost exclusively by butlers and valets employed by the nobility and gentry of the great houses in the neighbourhood.

* * * * *

In this bar, if you kept your ears open, you might learn all kinds of out-of-the-way facts; for here the careful, sober, watchful manservants of the mighty relaxed as much as they dared, and compared notes. Here you might see prim, clipped, close-shaven, tight-lipped gentlemen's gentlemen in dark blue serge jackets buttoned up to the chin; and beautiful old shoes that must have cost every penny of ten guineas a few years before. (You can generally recognise a valet off duty by his shoes.) Portly, pedantic men of middle age, most of them with white bald heads and glossy purple faces, conversed in discreet undertones of things worth knowing that might be overheard if you waited long enough and listened hard. The landlord himself had been a butler and his wife had been housekeeper to an earl. The casual passer-by, slipping into the "Silent Wife" for a quick drink, felt that he had gone through a magic door into a strange family circle made up of one aunt, nine uncles, and twenty or thirty cousins, all dressed in dark clothes for the funeral of some unimaginable patriarch. Having drunk his beer the stranger went on his way and seldom if ever came back.

One of the most respected habitués of this public-house was a man named Groom who for thirty years had been valet of Colonel the Lord Ayrwick, one of the best-dressed men in the United Kingdom. The valet was darkly conspicuous in the lurid light of his master's strange glory. From time to time Lord Ayrwick blazed bright in the newspapers when he wrote some extraordinarily savage letter denouncing soft hats or open collars, or read bloody revolution in a gloveless hand in Hyde Park on Sunday: then Groom grew longer, narrower, and blacker. He had, indeed, the long-drawn-out two-dimensional look of a short, square man's shadow stretched out by a setting sun. He had refused to sit at the same table with another valet who was wearing brown shoes with a blue suit. When it was reported that Edward, Prince of Wales, had appeared in public wearing turned-up trousers with a morning coat there was hot argument in the "Silent Wife", until Groom shook his head; and then there was no more argument. Groom had shaken his head. Woe, therefore, to his Royal Highness! It was Groom's habit to keep himself to himself. He would briefly exchange the skimpiest of civilities with the landlord and landlady and then, unfolding the most infallible of newspapers, read while he drank a bottle of Worthington's ale.

So everyone was surprised one evening when a man came rolling into the bar, and creeping up behind Groom, whistled through his teeth so piercingly that the glasses behind the bar vibrated. Mr. Groom, instead of blasting the intruder with a look, offered him a double whisky-and-soda, invited him to sit down and make himself at home.

The new customer was an ugly one: five feet tall, three feet wide, and marked about the face with a variety of evil-looking scars, and dressed in a tight-fitting suit of dog-tooth black-and-green check. He said nothing until he had emptied his glass; when he made a noise in his nose that reminded someone of a hacksaw going through a piece of iron, and growled: *"Well?"*

Groom simply walked out of the bar, closely followed by the other man. It was conjectured that this man was Groom's son, or some near relation – a nephew, or something like that – who had gone to the dogs; there is at least one such in every family.

Later, the landlord, glancing at Groom's newspaper, observed that it was folded back at the sports page, and that a list of probable runners in the next day's races at Newmarket had been carefully marked, and that there were strange figures and hieroglyphics in the margin. He then came to the conclusion that Lord Ayrwick's gentleman was "indulging in a little harmless flutter on the turf". So when Mr. Groom came in next day, there being no one else in the bar at the time, the landlord asked in a husky whisper what Groom fancied for the first race. "I don't fancy anything for the first race," said Groom, coldly.

"I beg your pardon, Mr. Groom, but I couldn't help but observe that you had marked the list of Newmarket probables. Now young Lord Jones's young man was in yesterday, Mr. Groom, and he heard the owner tell Lord Willoughby to put his shirt on Bright Young Thing, and he assured me that it was definitely a stone ginger cert and unquestionably on the job. I occasionally indulge in a harmless flutter myself and propose to invest five shillings on Bright Young Thing. Labouring under the misapprehension that you were interested in the sport of kings, Mr. Groom, I thought the information might interest you. Pardon me."

"It's kind of you, I'm sure, Mr. Hibbs, but I seldom if ever bet. Once in a blue moon somebody tells me something and I put a shilling or two on it. If you're backing this horse, perhaps you'll be good enough to put half a crown each way on for me. I don't know any bookies, you see."

"I'll do that with pleasure, Mr. Groom. I do not hold with gambling, but a harmless flutter is quite another thing."

"Quite right, Mr. Hibbs, quite right. That paper you saw me reading was his Lordship's. I always take it when he's done with it. His Lordship still likes to keep in touch with the turf."

"Of course, perfectly natural, Mr. Groom. I'll put half a crown each way on Bright Young Thing for you, then."

"Thank you. Will you let me know if it wins? I don't take much interest in racing, and I can't make head or tail of all those lists and figures."

"Certainly, Mr. Groom, with pleasure. Would you prefer to

give me your five shillings now, or let it wait? It is all the same to me, I assure you."

"Now, if you please, Mr. Hibbs. A person in my position ought not to get into debt, I say," said Groom, putting down five shillings.

"Thank you, Mr. Groom. By the by, that was a . . . an interesting young fellow who came in to see you yesterday."

Unusually communicative, Mr. Groom said: "Ah, the less said the better about him, Mr. Hibbs. He's not a very edifying subject I'm afraid. I'd rather we didn't talk about him. But – a word to the wise, Mr. Hibbs, you understand – my youngest sister had a son."

"I quite understand, Mr. Groom, and sympathise. Mrs. Hibbs has a niece . . ."

Then Groom went away to a public call-box, telephoned his own bookie and put five pounds each way on Bright Young Thing. Later, in his room, he unlocked a drawer, took out *Sporting Life*, *Sporting Times*, the *Racing World*, and the *Racing Annual*, and settled down to study. Among other papers in his drawer there was a recently-dated bookmaker's bill.

For Mr. Groom was a secret gambler. Behind the soundproof walls of his tightly-closed face his soul howled, hopping mad, at the barrier, while the great gleaming horses passed in thunder. The disease had got hold of him suddenly in the early 1920s when Papyrus won the Derby; finding easy money in his hand Groom became mad. Before Papyrus's Derby he had had no vices. Now he had one; to conceal which, he had to acquire a second – he became a hypocrite. To preserve his hypocrisy unexposed, he was reduced, in due course, to stealing small articles of jewellery from Lord Ayrwick, who was half blind, and pathetically dependent on him. And that made three. So evil tends downwards. To be a hypocrite one must, of course, be a liar.

The scarred young man in the dog-tooth check suit was not Groom's nephew. His real name was known to the police; his friends called him Shiv, and he had achieved a kind of dirty glory in the bloody battle between the Sabini Gang and the Brummagem Mob. Shiv had been sentenced to a term of imprisonment and eighteen strokes of the cat for robbery with violence. After that, becoming respectable, he made a living as a collector of bookies' bills, on a commission basis. Boldly and shamelessly, he would push his way into the most private places, pull out the long narrow sheet of paper, and make his presence intolerable until the money was paid. Shiv was proud of his proficiency. Six bookmakers employed him. Feeling that he had a right to regard himself as one of the professional classes, Shiv called them his clients.

He had said to Mr. Groom: "Look. If you won you'd call my boss a welsher if he didn't pay, wouldn't you? Whenever you've won, my boss paid out, like a gentleman, didn't he? You was the first to collect when you was a winner, wasn't you? But now you've 'ad a couple of bad weeks, you don't want to lolly, do you? Want it all your own way, don't you? All take and no give, ain't you? You wouldn't stand for us if we done things like that, would you? Well, I'm gonna tell you something, Mr. Groom, for your own good. If – you – don't – pay – us – up – what – you – owe – us——"

"Give me time," said Mr. Groom.

"Don't interrupt. Where's your manners? I'll make it short and sweet, mister: if you don't pay us up what you owe us, may I fall down dead this minute, I'll come along to Lord Ayrwick's place, and I'll show you up till you never dare show your face again. I'll find you wherever you are. Because you are not a sportsman. You're a crook – you ain't honest, that's what you are. I'll give you one week. One week from to-day, to settle this little account. And after that . . . you wait and see, just you wait and see. Speaking for meself, I'd just as soon you didn't pay, because I'm only waiting for a chance to show you up; because if there's one thing that gets me down, it's an unsportsmanlike crook. So now you know. Find that money in a week. That's all."

Now Tishy had fallen a little short of the truth when he told Wild Rose that the old lord was dead. Lord Ayrwick was not quite dead; he was only moribund. His heirs had been expecting him to die any minute for the past seven years. Still he clung to life; paralysed with raging arthritis, but sound of mind; purblind but dangerously alert. Many years before, shortly after his first apoplectic stroke, he had called his servants together and told them that he had made his will, by which any servant still in his service at the time of his death would substantially benefit. The housekeeper, the butler, and Groom would receive £2,000 apiece. Since then, whenever the old gentleman (who also had bronchitis) made the house tremble with a most dreadfully-combined pent-up cough and howl of rage and pain, the servants nudged one another and exchanged looks full of meaning. Groom knew that at the first whisper of scandal, he would be sent packing with a quarter's salary, and so automatically cease to be a legatee of Lord Ayrwick, who, mysteriously, was acquainted with every little thing that went on in the house. His Lordship (may he die in his sleep, God bless him) could not possibly live very much longer. He could not move from his bed.

One fairly large room near his bedroom had been converted into a fabulous wardrobe, in which hung a hundred and thirty suits of clothes.

Quietly gliding about his business, always diligent, constantly on the look-out for stray specks of dust, Groom came and went with armfuls of clothes. Nobody observed that he carried upstairs less than he brought down; he carried so much at a time. He was dutifully putting the wardrobe in order "against your getting up, m'lord." So, in four days, Groom spirited away twenty-seven assorted suits, and fourteen pairs of boots and shoes.

Desperate diseases call for desperate remedies.

Lord Ayrwick's suits had cost, on the average, about fifteen pounds apiece in Savile Row. He never wore a suit more than half a dozen times, so that they were all as good as new. Groom calculated that he could get at least four pounds a suit, and a flat thirty shillings a pair for the boots and shoes. He went through the old lord's cupboards, winnowing and gleaning a shirt here, a pair of socks there – they could not possibly be missed. But when he thought of selling this loot, his heart sank again. How could Lord Ayrwick's valet offer for sale twenty-seven suits and fourteen pairs of boots and shoes – to say nothing of shirts and socks – without arousing suspicion?

His furtive connection with the sport of kings had thrown him into contact with many queer characters. So he had met

Tishy, who undertook to pay Groom fifty pounds for the lot.

Thus, meeting Shiv at the appointed place before half-past one that Sunday, Groom said:

"Look here. I haven't got the whole amount, I'm sorry to say. I've got thirty pounds here, and I can let you have the rest by this time next week, I swear."

"Well, let's see the colour of the thirty," said Shiv. " – Eh, what do you call *this*, eh? No kites."

"But it's all right, I tell you! It comes from Jack Duck."

"Who said so? The name I read here is Edward Middleton."

"It's all right, I tell you. As it happens, I know for a fact. Jack Duck cashed that cheque, and it's as good as gold."

Shiv reasoned that he had collected, at least, ten pounds on account. This little manservant was too badly frightened to try anything funny; he would pay, in the end; and if this cheque happened to bounce, why, then Shiv's grip on Groom would be all the more unbreakable. He would, in fact, have been contented for the time being with the ten pounds in cash on account. But he said, fiercely: "Well, I'll see what I can do. I'll talk to the boss. But I'll tell you something – if – this – here – kite – turns – out – to – be – rubber . . . may I drop dead, but I'll teach you a lesson that'll last you just about as long as you live, see? It better be good, I warn you."

Then Shiv put the cheque into a wallet stamped with someone else's initials, and went away.

Groom steadied himself with a glass of gin, and one of Lord Ayrwick's special cigarettes. Watching the smoke as it floated in the hot, heavy air, he prayed: "Oh . . . let it be all right! Lord, let that cheque be all right!"

The smoke thinned and disappeared, and Groom, fixing his little hard hat on his little hard head, walked sedately back to the house. It was possible – who knew? – the old gentleman might have died by now. But he hoped with all his heart that Edward Middleton, whoever he happened to be, was not one of those unscrupulous men that go about cashing worthless cheques.

* * * * *

Trew arrived one minute after half-past seven, for he believed in keeping people waiting. They went to the "Hero of Waterloo", on his suggestion. Jack Duck found time to take him aside and ask: "Everything all right?"

"More or less," said Trew, "but that girl friend of yours cost me every bean I had. Six pounds it cost me, before I could shake her off. And here I am, flat broke."

"Hang around, if you've got a few minutes, and I'll let you have the money back."

So they waited nearly an hour until Mrs. Duck went to the kitchen, when the old fighter crushed five pound notes into Trew's hands, saying: "I'm much obliged." After that they went to the French restaurant for dinner, and stayed there until nearly ten o'clock.

"I *had* thought of going to a night club," said Middleton, casually. "Eh, Louie dear?"

"That's a good idea," said Trew. "Which one?"

"I don't know anything about them," said Middleton. "Do you?"

"To tell you the truth, Middy, old man, I'm a bit out of touch just lately. I know what – let's ask a taxi-driver."

A taxi-driver, brooding over his wheel in a cab rank, said: "Well, if I was you, I'd go to the 'Mustard Pickle'. They treat you right there. I know the doorman. I dare say I could get you in there, if you like."

"Leave it to you, old man," said Trew. "Eh, Middy, old man?"

"Go ahead, old boy," said Middleton to the driver; and, since the driver assured him that there was nothing much doing before eleven o'clock at night, and offered to drive them round the park, they rode around and around. Trew told them funny stories. Middleton and Louisa, holding hands, looked at the stars. When, at last, the taxi stopped near a lurid yellow electric sign over a basement in a back street not far from Shaftesbury Avenue, the driver said: "Wait a minute in the cab and I'll go and see about it for you." He went to the doorman of the "Mustard Pickle" and whispered: "'Ere you are then – three good 'uns," and the doorman gave him half a crown; whereupon the driver opened the taxi door and said: "Yes, it'll be quite all right. I made it all right for you, and I only hope you'll make it worth my while. It's up to you."

Middleton paid him five shillings over and above the correct fare. He paid the doorman fifteen shillings for entrance fee at five shillings a head. Then they went down into the "Mustard Pickle". Middleton uttered a sharp exclamation as Louisa dug her nails into the softest part of his arm. Before he could ask her what she thought she was doing he saw what she had seen – a blond cigarette girl who, at first glance, appeared to be wearing nothing but a gold-frogged military tunic, high-heeled shoes, and black silk stockings.

"Oh crumbs!" said Middleton. But a very gentlemanly fellow in immaculate evening dress bowed to him and said: "Table for three, m'sieur? Yes m'sieur, with pleasure, m'sieur! – Hey, Tony! Table for three, the best we got, look sharp!"

"Oh yes, sure, certainly, of course! You bet!" said a waiter, and led them to an alcove hung with bamboo beads. The gentlemanly man clapped his hands like a pasha in an Arabian story, and four bored musicians snatched at their instruments, while something like a huge nosegay of rainbow-coloured artificial flowers burst and scattered as half a dozen hostesses came out of a scandalous conference and fluttered to their tables. Meanwhile the waiter, holding a wine list under Middleton's nose, smiled with all his teeth. "Champagne for madam? Whisky for m'sieur?"

"What do you fancy, Louie dear?"

"Champagne?" whispered Louisa.

The waiter said: "Heidsieck, Veuve Clicquot, Bollinger, Mumm, Irroy——"

" – Right you are," said Middleton.

"Irroy. Yes, sir. Thank you, sir. Irroy, Irroy, Irroy. Right!"

The musicians, screwing their faces into smiles, began to play a quickstep. Customers were coming in now. At the sight of two men in dinner jackets and two women in evening dress, Louisa pinched Middleton's arm again. He, deliberately looking away from the cigarette girl's legs, kicked Trew under the table. "Chocolates? Cigarettes? Cigars?"

Trew bought a packet of cigarettes for five times its market price; at which Middleton looked thoughtful. But then the waiter came running with a gold-capped bottle in a silver bucket. "In for a penny, in for a pound," said Middleton. " – Louie, dear, you're pinching my arm off!"

"Teddykins, I'm so *excited*!"

"Well, all right, no need to bruise a man from head to foot. I'm excited too; but you'll have to learn to behave as if you're used to all this kind of thing."

Before they had emptied their first glass five very loving couples were dancing on the little round floor. The waiter whispered to Trew: "If m'sieur would like to dance, there is a young lady who would very much like to dance with him." Trew shuffled his feet and looked foolish. A slender ash blond nodded and smiled.

"Well, to oblige a lady . . ." said Trew . . . and then he was half-walking, half-running up and down the dance floor in the arms of the ash blond, who was telling him that she was the granddaughter of a bishop. Louisa began to laugh: "Oh Ted, look – just look at him pretending to dance. With all his faults, I must say that you can't help laughing sometimes," she said. " – Ted! What is it? What's the matter?"

In the dim light, Middleton's face was dead-white like a peeled egg. In a thick, sick voice he said: "Look who's coming in."

"The elderly man with that skinny little thing in the white dress?"

"Ssh! Not so loud, Louie dear! That's Mr. Mawson, my boss," said Middleton.

PART IV

It could not be: yet it was. Here was indeed Mr. Mawson, the general manager, unconventionally dressed in a blue flannel suit, and accompanied by a tiny, thin girl, exotically painted about the mouth and eyelids. Middleton forgot everything but his hatred and fear of this man who had the power to kick him out of the office into the street. All in a moment he saw himself unemployed, dismissed at a second's notice, with one of Mr. Mawson's strictly honest references in his pocket saying that Edward Middleton had worked for Coulton Utilities for such-and-such a number of years during which time he had worked honestly, and diligently; but Mr. Mawson had been reluctantly compelled to dispense with Edward Middleton's services (he would combine honesty with Christian charity, like Lord Herring) for certain reasons, which he did not care to disclose, concerning Edward Middleton's personal habits.

Middleton could already feel that death sentence of a reference rustling in his breast pocket. And then he remembered that he had, in the same pocket, a document of vastly different significance, and the colour came back into his face. Touching the Pismire letter, he watched with narrowed eyes while the waiter bowed Mr. Mawson and the young lady into the adjacent alcove, and he distinctly heard the general manager say: "Well, Peach Blossom, name your poison" – in such an unfamiliar tone that Middleton began to wonder whether his eyes had deceived him. He drank some more wine and parted the bamboo curtain half an inch. The clothes were different. The voice was different; yet it was the voice of Mr. Mawson, curiously loosened. In any case there was no mistaking that peculiar bald head, the detestable double-crowned head that looked like a cottage loaf; and the parrot-face that had loomed, chattering *A minute's notice, a minute's notice, a minute's notice* in a dozen anxious dreams. There was no doubt about it: Mr. Mawson was sitting there three feet away from him, and only three inches away from a young woman who was certainly not his wife, in the "Mustard Pickle".

"Let us drink brandy, my pet," said Peach Blossom. If everything else were not scandalous enough, she spoke with a foreign accent.

Instead of giving her a heart-to-heart talk about the evils attendant on the drinking of fermented liquor, Mr. Mawson said: "Brandy, you say? Then brandy it shall be, Peach Blossom. Tony, bring us a bottle of Courvoisier and a syphon of soda."

The waiter brought the bottle, and Mr. Mawson clinked glasses with Peach Blossom and drank. Watching him, Middleton drank too. Then he took a cigarette out of Trew's packet on the table and, having asked Louisa to excuse him, walked boldly into the next alcove and said: "Pardon the intrusion, but could you oblige me with a light?"

Theatrically speaking, Middleton's timing could not have been better; Mr. Mawson achieved a perfect double-take. He said, genially: "With pleasure," and struck a match. Then his eyebrows went up, his chin went down, and he stared in unutterable dismay until the match flame burned his fingers, when he gasped, said *Uh?* dropped the burnt match into his brandy, and sucked his thumb.

"Fancy meeting *you* here!" said Middleton. "This *is* a surprise, Mr. Mawson."

"Mawson?" said Peach Blossom.

"This gentleman is labouring under a misapprehension," said Mr. Mawson, trying to strike a match, and breaking it. "My name is not Mawson, sir. My name is Wood."

"Accept my apologies," said Middleton. "I thought for the moment that you were a gentleman I know named Mawson. Ever so sorry. Thanks for the light." Then he went to wash his hands. Mr. Mawson followed him. Even in the rosy light under the tinted bulb in the men's room, the double-crowned head and the parrot-face appeared yellow, and the strong, high voice was thin and unsteady as he said: "Why, Middleton, I could scarcely believe the evidence of my eyes, seeing you in a place like this."

"No more could I," said Middleton, drying his hands.

Mr. Mawson said: "It is necessary, in certain circumstances, to . . . to investigate, you understand, to look into certain aspects of . . . of . . . to see for oneself what . . . what . . ."

"Yes, sir. As soon as I saw you I thought Lord Herring must have sent you to look around. I admit I was a bit startled, though. I suppose Miss Peach Blossom is a sort of friend of the family, showing you round, like a guide." Middleton carefully refolded a damp towel and was putting it back on the shelf when an attendant deftly took it away and threw it into a basket. He continued: "My wife and I came here to celebrate, sir. You see, I've had a stroke of luck."

"I'm delighted to hear it, Middleton, delighted!"

His hands clean and dry, Middleton took out the letter and let Mr. Mawson read it.

"God bless my heart and soul, Middleton! I congratulate you! Net personalty £76,000! That certainly justifies a little celebration,

I admit. Just for once, eh? And how *is* your wife? Well, I trust? Overjoyed by the good news, of course?"

"Definitely, sir. I hope Mrs. Mawson is quite well, sir."

"Thank you, yes, yes, Middleton, very well, thank you. By the way," said Mr. Mawson, in a whisper, "don't call me 'sir', Middleton – just call me Wood. It's necessary sometimes, to . . . to . . . Well, I must get back to – I had better get back. I congratulate you heartily, heartily, Middleton, with all my heart. We'll talk of this when we meet again, in private, on Tuesday. Meanwhile, I beg you to exercise discretion, complete discretion. I really must get back now. And don't be offended if I ask you again to address me by the name of Wood. Wood, John Wood."

"Yes, sir," said Middleton; and repeated to himself *Wood, Wood, Wood, Wood, Wood*. It was an order.

While he was fumbling for small change, Mr. Mawson said: "No, no, no, my dear Middleton, let me do this," and gave the cloakroom attendant two shillings.

Wood, Wood, Wood, Wood, Wood, said Middleton, as they walked back to their tables.

"My name is Wood and I'm a glass manufacturer – eh, Middleton?"

"That's all right, Wood."

Trew was saying to Louisa: "Her grandfather was a bishop. . . . Oh, Middy, old man, do you mind if I bring that young lady over to the table? She's a perfect lady, and her grandfather was a bishop. Make a foursome, eh?"

"Anything you say, eh Louie dear?" said Middleton, exuberantly. "It's all right, Louie dear, everything's all right."

"Oh Teddykins, I'm so glad!"

"Bring your lady friend by all means, Trewie, old boy. Foursome? Let's make it a six-some!" He knocked open the bamboo curtain, and said: "I say, Wood, would you and the lady care to join us in a glass of champagne?"

"Well, I don't know, Middleton," said Mr. Mawson, glancing at Peach Blossom.

She said: "But why not, my pet? I like this young man. He has an honest face. Introduce me . . . Yes, Mr. Middleton, we will make a party. You have champagne, we have brandy, and so we have champagne cocktails. Goody-goody!"

Trew appeared with the ash blond and said, proudly: "Meet Geraldine."

Middleton, flushed with excitement, was saying in a loud voice: "I say, Wood, haven't I got a pretty wife? Eh, Wood? Louie, dear, I'm sure you'll like Wood. Wood is one of the cleverest wood manufacturers ... pardon me, I mean glass manufacturers in the business, aren't you, Wood, old boy? He manufactures glass, Louie dear – don't you, Wood? Good old Wood!"

"I hope he didn't manufacture *this*," said Peach Blossom, holding up a wrist encircled by a narrow diamond bracelet; everyone laughed heartily – especially when Trew said: "He *would* if he could, I bet you."

The party broke up when Louisa said she was sleepy, at half-past one in the morning. Trew stayed in the "Mustard Pickle" to talk to Geraldine, who made him buy a bottle of champagne, and, having got two pounds for dancing with him and drinking his wine, sent him home, disconsolate, with only five shillings in small change in his pocket.

Louisa and Peach Blossom touched finger-tips while Mr. Mawson and Middleton shook hands.

Mawson said: "No thank you very much, my dear Middleton, don't trouble to give us a lift. I have to see this little lady safely home. Thank you for a very pleasant evening, and I'm overjoyed at your good fortune, Middleton, overjoyed! Let us have a chat together on Tuesday, eh?"

"Yes, Wood, by all means," said Middleton.

"We're men of the world, I take it, Middleton?"

"Don't worry, Wood. Good night, Wood, old boy."

"Good night, Middleton, my dear fellow."

Holding her husband's hand in the taxi, Louisa said: "Oh Ted, what a nice evening! It all seems like a dream, doesn't it?"

Kissing her, Middleton replied: "Louie dear, I can give you my word – I've never been so happy in my life."

"Ted – that funny little man with that horrible little girl; is *he* the one you kept on talking about?"

"Who, Wood?"

"I thought you said his name was Mawson."

"Of course, Louie, dear, so it is. Mawson? Yes, he's not so bad when you get to know him. You have to meet him outside the office. No need to worry about poor old Wood. *Oh-oh-oh!*" said Middleton, yawning, "I won't need any rocking to-night, Louie."

"Nor me, Ted. I'm half asleep already. What do you want to do to-morrow, Teddykins?"

"I'm going to sleep all the morning, Louie dear. Then you and I'll have something to eat in that French place, and d'you know what we're going to do then? We're going to Hampstead Heath."

"Just what I wanted you to say! Aren't you a clever Teddykins?"

The great Bank Holiday fair on Hampstead Heath is a kind of cockney *mardi gras* – a *mardi gras* turned inside out; for on this gay occasion the Londoner takes off the mask that he wears on working days before he lets himself go. Full-blood cockneys of the old school – may their breed never perish! – draw their savings for this uproarious day of reckless celebration. A diminishing few of the good-old-timers get out the traditional full-dress of the costermonger – the itinerant fruit-vendor, the proud aristocrat of the London gutters.

He wanted all the world to know him for what he was, neither more nor less. So he took to wearing, off duty, a black suit with preposterous trousers, tight along the thigh and belling out to the dimensions of skirts at the ankle; big, black boots, a black cap, and a white choker. His wife also wore black – a voluminous skirt; a long-skirted jacket, incredibly tight at her tight-laced waist, and a black hat as big as a cartwheel, draped with immense ostrich feathers.

To relieve this funereal blackness, or perhaps to make themselves more conspicuous, they went in for an extraordinary number of white pearl buttons. There was rivalry among the costers over the matter of buttons. It was not long before they were decorating their coats, caps and trousers, jackets, hats and skirts, with pounds of little buttons sewn on in bizarre designs. So they came to be called Pearly Kings and Pearly Queens. To this day they survive – I know one old lady who boasts that she has 2,800 pearl buttons on her coat alone. These are the intrepid people whose ear-splitting voices dominated the roaring of millions when they shouted: "Go it, old girl!" at Queen Victoria when she rode through London in the jubilee procession – at which that dry-eyed, weary, inflexible Queen of England shed affectionate tears.

The last surviving Pearly Kings and Pearly Queens still go for their ritual binge to Hampstead Heath on Bank Holiday; and half of London goes with them. Carnival men come rumbling in from every corner of England to meet them. For a week before Bank Holiday you see them coming in – another strange, exclusive breed; the carnival people; and always the dark whispering, sidelong-glancing, sidling gypsies – yet another Chosen People with a secret language to be spoken through the teeth. The attractions are screwed together. The steam organs honk and squeal while the spotted horses and smiling tigers and goggle-eyed ostriches go bounding round and round, and the Londoners find their voices. Women who make it a point of honour to laugh at two-thousand-pound bombs and lie quiet in childbirth scream themselves hoarse in cardboard caves of artificial darkness. Men who can suck chocolate when they peel off embattled squadrons in desperate power-dives through the high clouds shriek with the girls on the swings. . . . Housewives who count farthings throw pennies at the discs.

Buck navvies in their best clothes, anxious to forget that they are compelled to swing hammers in order to live, swarm about the apparatus that measures the power of your hammer-stroke; where they pay twopence for the privilege of lifting and swinging a great maul, to drive an indicator up toward a bell. If they ring the bell, they win no prizes – they have nothing to show for their money; they have swung a hammer until they are sore, as a matter of course, to get the money to pay for the privilege of swinging a hammer. The difference is that now their everyday skill is admirable.

Self-conscious fellows who never knew the feel of a heavy sledge smite with all their might and main, and send the indicator less than half-way toward the bell at the top.

"Go on, Lofty – 'ave a go!" says a young lady. Shy in his best clothes the navvy pays the twopence and picks up the maul, gets his balance, measures his distance, and without apparent effort lets fly such a blow that the bell rings. He may strike fifty such blows on a weekday to earn the twopence he had to pay for the privilege of striking that one. But he has struck a gasp out of a crowd, and refreshed his pride: it is money well-spent. The steak-fed football-player looks and shakes his head admiringly. "That's nothing," says the navvy, taking off his coat and spitting on his hands. He rings the bell six times more, bursting his collar at the last stroke; and this costs him a shilling, which he does not begrudge, for the audience cheers, and his girl feels his muscles while she leads him away to squander five shillings on the Wheel of Luck. There, if he comes away with a prize worth fourpence, he is satisfied.

With the late afternoon there comes a lull. Long-drawn screams have teased themselves into woolly wisps and fibres of sound. Children, exhausted with excitement, become fretful: listlessly tearing up red, white and blue paper trumpets which they have blown limp and dumb, they seem to become aware of the vanity of earthly pleasure, and they all begin to cry. They want to go home, or they do not want to go home; they want to do that which it is impossible to do, and are ready to cry themselves into convulsions rather than leave undone that which it is improper to do. All their expensively-won dolls disintegrate – noses fall off, eyes drop out, hands amputate themselves. Girls kick their fathers; boys bite their mothers. The joyous music of the calliope grows louder and more urgent as the crowds thin. One may hear, now, something that sounds like the killing of a thousand little pigs, as harassed parents smack their children. The fair-ground people bathe their sore throats in hot tea or cold beer; while around Jack Straw's Castle, and The Spaniards, fights break out. Misery comes back into the world.

Thus, a burly costermonger sat on the grass hugging his knees and saying: "Never again! Never again! Never again, not while I'm alive!"

His wife said: "Shut your jaw." She was holding a five-year-old girl, sticky with raspberry syrup, heavily asleep. Tightly gripped in the little girl's fingers was a rubber instrument which, if you blew into it, made an indecent noise: she had blown into this until she had become unconscious. Not far from the man sat a seven-year-old boy, quietly sullen, beating the grass with the remains of a doll that had been stuffed with sawdust, the crockery head of which he had broken on his father's chin; for which he had received a slap on the head.

"Just a minute," said the man, and he got up and accosted three people who were making their way to the road. There was a pretty young woman, arm-in-arm with a young man who might have passed as a city clerk if he had not looked so happy. His disengaged arm pressed to his bosom a large stamped tin tea-caddy, a Chinese-looking vase, and a glass flower-bowl. She was carrying a doll. Walking in step with them, a small, plump, humorous man was pretending to drop a pair of plaster buddhas painted to resemble ancient bronze.

"Wasn't it nice, Teddykins?" the lady was saying.

"Oi!" shouted the coster, catching Middleton by the lapels of his coat. "Samatter with *you*?"

"Grab hold of this stuff, will you, Trewie, old boy? Walk along with Trewie, will you, Louie dear?" said Middleton. "Trewie, take Louie along for a minute, can't you?"

Trew had already dragged Louisa ten yards along. "You coward!" she said. "You call yourself a friend? Leave go of my arm!"

"Take it easy," said Trew.

Middleton clenched his fists and said: "Well? Go on! What is it?"

The coster looked down at him, and frowned, red and exasperated. "Don't know me, now, is that it? Eh?" he said.

"Can't say I have the pleasure," said Middleton.

"Knew me on Saturday all right, though, eh? 'Ow'd the creases go down with that cue?"

"What?"

"I give you a bunch o' watercreases – remember? Last Saturday when you bought that cucumber?"

Then Middleton recognised the salad-seller and said: "I'm ever so sorry. Of course I remember. It was very nice watercress. We enjoyed it. But you look so smart, I didn't know you for the moment. I thought you were trying to pick a fight with me, you see."

"What, *me* – wiv *you*? Why, I wouldn't insult my own intelligence, picking a fight with *you*. Just wanted to know if you enjoyed them watercreases, to set my mind at rest."

"Very much indeed," said Middleton. "Have you had a good time?"

"Lovely. But me and the old ball-and-chain and the Gawd-ferbids over there done in every penny I 'ad and so we're getting ready to walk 'ome. That's 'ow it is, guv, 'ere to-day and gone to-morrow."

Now Middleton experienced a new sensation. He was going to reward somebody who was kind to him in the past when he was poor. Glowing with pleasure, he slid a pound note out of his pocket and pressed it into the coster's calloused palm, saying: "I wouldn't like to see you walking home. Better have this."

"Well!" said the coster, too surprised to swear. "Well, now, that's——"

" – That's quite all right."

"Next time you pass by my stall, I'll let you 'ave it back, if you make it late next week," said the coster; and such was the pressure of grateful emotion that the arteries in his neck became thick as ropes. "On my oath! Gawd bless you – good luck to you!"

"Say no more about it," said Middleton, and went to join Louisa and Trew.

"I was just getting the lady out of the way, and then I was coming back to give you a hand," said Trew.

"Quite unnecessary, old boy. I handled *him*," said Middleton.

"Oh Ted, I never knew you were so brave!" said Louisa.

"You certainly did stand up to him, old man," said Trew.

"More than some people would have done," said Louisa.

Trew was ashamed of his cowardice. He had had about enough of this Middleton, who was smiling smugly at the sky – this prig of a Middleton, who, not satisfied with seventy-six thousand pounds, had to push himself forward and blossom as a hero. *Well, let's wait and see his face to-morrow,* thought Trew, and smiled.

The coster went back to his wife and said: "There you are, you see! Do a good turn and get done one back. 'Arf the night you nagged me about them watercreases I give that clurk on Saturday. Better give 'em to some poor devil than chuck 'em in the dust-'ole, I said, them creases'r no good to us – blimey, do a good deed wiv 'em and chance it! Well, that was the geezer I give them creases to, and look at what 'e give me." He opened his hand dramatically; then continued: "Let's get back 'ome and put these bloody little miseries to bed, and you and me go to the rub-a-dub and 'ave a pig's-ear. What say?"

"Suits me."

So the coster and his old ball-and-chain took the God-forbids (or kids) to Uncle Ned (or bed); and went to the rub-a-dub (or pub) and drank pig's-ear (or beer), singing "Knees Up Mother Brown" until closing time. Then there was a bull-and-cow (or row), in the course of which the coster received a damaged mince-pie (or eye). Having won the battle and shaken hands with his defeated enemy, he was helped by his wife to climb the apples-and-pears (or stairs); and went to bo-peep . . . healthy, dreamless bo-peep.

Louisa, having put her prizes where she could see them when she awoke, slept deeply. Middleton twisted and turned until the small hours, thinking of to-morrow; but at last he too slept.

* * * * *

Pismire's managing clerk, a little brittle-looking half-transparent old man, opened the office punctually at nine o'clock in the morning. His name was Napking, and he was known and feared in legal circles; but admired as a "character". He was the worst-dressed man in the City of London. Strangers, seeing Napking in the tomb-like ante-rooms of the courts, thought of him as some poor, hopeless wretch of a creditor; or perhaps a palsied shorthand writer – one of the walking dead. His shoes were terribly run down. His coat had been black, his waistcoat had been blue; and his trousers, which had been striped black-and-grey, were of no colour at all. He wore a celluloid collar and cuffs, and a fivepenny readymade bow tie that clipped into a patent stud, and sometimes fell off. His hat was an antique billycock; it shone like a stove. In the cold weather he wrapped himself in a black ulster that had been the worse for wear when he had got it from the lawyer to whom he had been clerk when Edward VII was

King. But when he wanted to know the time Napking unbuttoned himself and took out a gold repeater worth two hundred pounds. It was said that Napking could lay his hands on a hundred thousand pounds.

Arriving at the office at one minute before nine o'clock on Tuesday morning, he paused on the landing to look at two young people who were standing nervously, hand-in-hand, close to the office door. Napking said nothing, but unlocked the door and went in.

"Ted, he went in," said Louisa.

"Yes I know, Louie dear. Take it easy. Everything's all right. I dare say he's the old man who opens the windows, and empties the wastepaper baskets, and all that."

"Wouldn't they have a woman to do that, Ted?"

"Not necessarily, Louie – not these old-established firms. Some of them won't even have a woman in the place, you know."

"Shall we ask him, Ted?"

"Ask him what?"

"I don't know . . . just ask him. Perhaps he could let us go in and sit down. It looks so silly, sort of standing."

Middleton knocked peremptorily at the door, pushed it open without waiting for a reply, and, feeling for a shilling (the poor old fellow might enjoy something hot for dinner) called: "I say!"

"What do you want?" replied Napking, in a tone that made Middleton jump, and put him out of countenance.

"Oh . . . I want to speak to Mr. Pismire."

"What's your business?"

"Private business with Mr. Pismire," said Middleton, sturdily.

"What's your name?"

"What business is that of yours?"

"I am Mr. Pismire's managing clerk. What is your business?"

"Oh," said Middleton, blushing, "I'm sorry. My name is Edward Middleton." He paused. The managing clerk said:

"Yes? Well?"

" – Mr. Pismire wrote me a letter asking me to come and see him about the estate of Mr. Joseph Hugh Middleton of Wagga-Wagga, Australia: net personalty £76,000," said Middleton.

"I know nothing about this. *Middleton*, did you say your name was? A *letter*? Where is it?"

Middleton said, indignantly: "Here it is. You don't mind if we sit down, I hope."

"Be seated, if you please. Middleton, eh? . . ." Mr. Napking glanced at the envelope and then looked at Middleton with suspicion in his washed-out eyes. Then he said: *"Express?* Hm!" He took out and unfolded the letter; read it and threw it on to a blotting pad. "That letter was never sent from this office, young man."

"What do you mean?" cried Middleton, while Louisa put her hand to her throat.

"No such letter as this was written in this office. This is not Mr. Charles Pismire's signature."

When the hangman pulls the hood over the eyes of a condemned man and the great heavy noose slides smoothly into position, the condemned man must see such a darkness and feel such inevitability of shameful doom as Middleton saw and felt then. He said: "You're wrong. You're mistaken. There's the letter to prove it. . . . You're not telling the truth!" he shouted, so that his voice beat up echoes in remote corners of the stony, quiet old building.

"Am I to call the police?" said Napking. But then Mr. Pismire came in, cheered and refreshed by his long week-end, and, with less than half a glance at Middleton and Louisa, said: "Good morning, Napking. What is it?"

"Good morning, sir," said Napking, handing Pismire the letter. "Look at this."

He read it, shook his head, and said gently: "Mr. Middleton – you are Mr. Middleton, are you?"

"Yes, sir. We . . . we . . ." Middleton gulped.

"Well, Mr. Middleton, I'm afraid you are the victim of a joke. This letter was never typed by one of our typewriters." Napking passed the envelope, and Mr. Pismire continued: "Our envelopes – show Mr. Middleton one of our envelopes, Napking – are of a very different quality. And this signature is not my signature . . . Napking, give me a scribbling pad. Here is my signature, Mr. Middleton. I hope, for your sake, that you have not built up too many hopes on this, because I can positively assure you that it is nothing but a hoax."

"But, Mr. Pismire, sir!" said Middleton, while Louisa fell heavily into a little green leather armchair. "I wouldn't have let myself in for what I have let myself in for without confirmation! I 'phoned your house. The gentleman who answered the 'phone said everything was quite in order."

"You must be mistaken, Mr. Middleton."

"Then do you mean to tell me that – that – that letter isn't worth the paper it's written on, sir?"

"Mr. Middleton, it is worth much *less* than the paper it is written on! The paper has a value; that which is written upon it has no value whatsoever."

"But what am I to do?" cried Middleton.

"I'm sure I don't know what you are to do. I cannot help you, I'm afraid. I would if I could. But let me tell you once and for all that I do not know either of the parties referred to in this letter. You would be well advised to put the matter out of your mind and go about your business as usual. Now you must excuse me, and so good day and good luck to you," said Mr. Pismire.

"Let's go and have a cup of coffee," said Louisa, when they were in the street.

"A cup of coffee," said Middleton. "Yes, let's have a cup of coffee!"

In the teashop they looked at each other across the marble-topped table for several minutes without speaking. Then Middleton's eyes filled and his voice thickened as he said: "Only about an hour or two ago I was thinking to myself that it'd make a nice change to go to the Savoy Hotel for lunch. . . . Never been inside the Savoy Hotel. I was going to take you shopping and buy up half Bond Street. Remember when we used to go for walks and look in the windows and pick out all the things we'd buy if we were rich? . . . I laid awake half last night thinking of all the things I was going to give you. Well, I can't give you anything . . . but love . . . and you won't get fat on that . . ."

"Dear, darling Ted! I don't want anything else. And I don't want to get fat. It's the thought that counts," said Louisa. "Don't be downhearted, Teddykins; it was all a dream. Just a dream."

Middleton said: "I wish it *was* all a dream, Louie. I wish to God it was. Don't you see that I'm sunk, absolutely finished? Don't you remember I cashed a cheque for twenty pounds? All right, I know, I know – you tried to stop me, and I wouldn't let you, and it's my fault, and I'm a damn fool, and I deserve everything I get. But why should *you* be the sufferer? Well, this is what's going to happen, Louie: my cheque'll come back, and the man in the pub'll go to the office, as sure as fate, and I'll be out in the street at a minute's notice. And then what are we going to do? We'll starve, that's all, Louie. I shall have to go on the dole. And what about the baby? What about *you*? What are we going to do? I don't know. Who could have played a trick like that on me? I can't see why."

"What about your friend, Dick Trew?"

"What, Trew? Oh no, not Trewie, Louie dear! He likes his little joke, but he wouldn't do a thing like that to me."

"Why wouldn't he?" asked Louisa. "Isn't he always sending people faked-up telegrams, and ringing people up in the middle of the night? Didn't you tell me once about how he rang up a doctor at three o'clock in the morning and said that he was to go at once to somebody-or-other's house on a matter of life and death? Well, I didn't think that was a bit funny. I thought it was a cruel, nasty trick. Anybody who'd do a thing like that would do anything, to anybody."

"But, Louie dear, how could it be Trew? I mean, he borrowed money off me on the strength of it. I spent pounds on him over the week-end. It'd be – why, it'd be getting money under false pretences – it'd be stealing!"

"Of course it would, Ted, but I dare say he'd think it was all the funnier for that. I know his kind."

Middleton, who had been toying nervously with his spoon, clenched his fist so violently that the spoon bent almost double. "I'll find out," he said, in a whisper, "and if Trew did that to me, I swear to God I'll murder the swine. I will, Louie – I will!" He was almost physically sick with anger and pain.

Louisa said: "The thing is, first of all, to make up our minds what we're going to do now."

"There isn't anything to do. We've got nothing to sell, nothing to pawn . . . Nothing!"

"Perhaps the bank would let you pay the money off."

"Some hopes. Even if they did, they'd make inquiries about me at the office, and I'd be out anyway. I haven't banked any money ever – I've only drawn out what there was after Mother died. No, I tell you, Louie dear, we're in the soup."

"There's one thing I could do," said Louisa. "That man Mr. Duck is a nice sort of man. I could go along to him and tell him the whole story, and promise faithfully that we'd pay him off at so much a week. You know, I think he might let us do that, Ted. I'll run along now and ask him not to pay that cheque in, and tell him the whole truth. Let's do that. I'll do it – it'll be better, coming from me. What do you say?"

"It might work," said Middleton, dubiously.

"Well, you run along to the office, and I'll go and talk to Mr. Duck, and we'll meet at one o'clock."

"The office!" said Middleton. "The office! The office! What the devil am I to say?"

"Don't say anything. Play for a bit of time. Say you're waiting for news, or something."

"There's nothing else for it," said Middleton, with a flash of that feverish cheerfulness which sometimes animates frightened men in condemned cells when they learn that the last appeal has been rejected, and catch the calculating eye of a grim man in dark clothes who is looking them over through the grille and calculating the length of the drop. "We'll meet at one o'clock sharp in Sweetings, and I'll be damned if we don't eat a steak. I've got over five pounds left. The last supper, eh?"

"I think you'd better give me the five pounds, Teddykins. I could give it to Mr. Duck. It would show willing."

"Oh. All right. I'll meet you just outside Sweetings, then, at one o'clock."

So they parted, and Middleton dragged himself to the office. He got there at half-past ten. He had been too excited to eat breakfast. The coffee squelched and gurgled in his nervous stomach as he pushed open the door and walked in. His desk was piled high with unopened letters. "Where do you think *you've* been?" asked the chief clerk of the mail order department.

"I'm a little late, I'm afraid," said Middleton.

"A *little* late! Do you realise it's twenty-three minutes to eleven?"

"Is it?"

"Yes, it is, Middleton. And the boss has been asking for you since half-past nine. He's asked for you three times. He said you were to go to his office the minute you came in," said the chief clerk, shaking his head.

"Oh. Tell me, was he . . . did he . . . how did he . . . ?"

"He's in a rotten temper, I can tell you, Middleton. He's been biting everybody's head off. He nearly gave young Oakley the sack for turning up in flannel trousers. I tell you, liver's twopence a pound this morning. Better think up something good by way of an excuse, I warn you, or I'm afraid you're in for it."

"Is my hair straight?"

"It'll do. But you've got rings under your eyes, you know; you look as if you've been having a pretty thick week-end. Well, better go in and get it over. I'll be sorry to lose you, Middleton – I'm not at all sure that Mr. Woolley can take over your job. It all falls on me. Let me know the worst."

Middleton's turbulent stomach reminded him, now, of those dry-cleaning machines in which a whirling glass drum tosses sodden rags up and down and around in some pungent, frothy liquid that grows darker and dirtier second by second. The secretary told him that he was to go in. The general manager was standing by the window.

"Good morning, Middleton," he said.

"Good morning, Wood," said Middleton.

Trying to still his noisy inside by brute force, he pressed his right hand over his breast-bone and struck himself in the small of the back with his left, so that he fell unconsciously into a Napoleonic attitude. Then the enormity of what he had said struck him with such force that he hiccupped loudly; and having hiccupped, tried to smile and said: "I'm sorry, I forgot; Mr. Mawson, sir . . . Only you did tell me to call you Wood on Sunday night."

Now Mr. Mawson saw in Middleton's attitude a badly overacted timidity; the ironically exaggerated diffidence of a man who can afford to be insolent if he chooses; and he was afraid: "Sit down, Middleton," he said, quietly. "I thought we had agreed, tacitly, that . . . in short, the office is the office, and, to put it in a nutshell, one's private affairs outside the office are, well, another thing."

"Slip of the tongue," said Middleton.

"Of course. Do sit down, Middleton. Ah . . . how is your charming wife?"

"Very well, thank you. How's yours?" said Middleton; it was all he could think of to say, and having said it his tongue went loosely stammering on: "A, a very nice lady, Mr. Mawson, sir. We met – I mean I saw Mrs. Mawson that day when I took the liberty of asking you if it would be convenient to . . ." Then he hiccupped again.

Then Mr. Mawson, getting hold of his courage, spoke with quiet desperation: "Look here, Middleton, I'm sure I can talk to you as man to man. I believe you understood me, the other evening, when – quite unnecessarily in your case, I'm sure – I mentioned the need for discretion."

"Oh yes," said Middleton.

"I feel I can speak to you as a friend; and equal. You are a man of the world, now, and I know that you'll understand. Rules are rules, of course, and must not be broken. I entirely approve of rules. It is quite impossible, to, to, ah, organise a great company without strict rules, my dear Middleton. If you reflect, you will see that this must be so. But circumstances alter cases and in your altered circumstances you'll understand that it is occasionally permissible for a person of proven integrity – for a man thoroughly tried in his various responsibilities, to, well, relax just a little, on exceptional occasions, in private. *Strictly* in private! I feel that you understand me, Middleton."

Middleton nodded. Mr. Mawson went on:

"Now there are all kinds of reasons why our little meeting should remain, as it were, a State secret. It was all perfectly innocent, of course. Still, as a married man you'll understand that the ladies, bless them, are quick to jump to conclusions."

He waited for a reply. Middleton came with a start out of a daze and said: "All right, Wood – I beg your pardon – I mean, yes, Mr. Mawson."

"You will have your little joke, I see," said Mr. Mawson,

with a sickly laugh. "I want you to understand, by the way, that my relations with that young lady are absolutely innocent, Middleton."

"Peach Blossom?"

"*Ssh!* Yes. I know that I can rely on you, Middleton. You always impressed me as thoroughly reliable. It is a little secret between us men, eh?"

"Why, yes, of course."

"Good. Now let us come to more important matters. I take it that you have spent the morning arranging your affairs, eh?"

"Well, in a way, yes."

"What a lucky young man you are, Middleton. Seventy-six thousand pounds was the sum you mentioned, I think?"

"Well, that's what it said in the letter," said Middleton.

"Everything in order?"

"Well . . . no, I wouldn't say in order," said Middleton, "no, not quite in order just yet."

"No, of course, these things take a little time. But I'm glad to see that you are keeping a level head and taking your good fortune so soberly. Nine hundred and ninety-nine men out of a thousand, finding themselves gentlemen of property overnight, would lose their balance completely, Middleton. This only serves to increase my already high regard for your character in general, Middleton. Ah . . . a little innocent celebration, of course, a little *discreet* celebration, is perfectly in order for men, ah, like ourselves who are in a position to afford it, and who can be relied upon to hold our peace in order not to set a bad example . . ."

Mr. Mawson went on and on, looking slyly out of the corners of his eyes. *Good Lord, the old hypocrite is frightened to death of me!* thought Middleton. *"Hold my peace," indeed! "Hold my peace"* . . . and then from out of some black cloud in his overcast mind there came a blinding flash of beautiful wit – a pun so perfect that Middleton had to give it voice, if the heavens fell. He said: "It's all right for a fellow to hold his *piece* in a night club, as long as he holds his *peace* in the City," and startled himself into a nervous giggle.

Now Mr. Mawson was convinced that this man was dangerous – an arrogant, jumped-up, newly-rich clerk who hated him and could – probably would – let fall certain words that might blast him. He said: "Ha-ha-ha – ha-ha-ha! – very neatly put. But tell me, what are your plans? It will hardly be worth your while to stay with us, now, surely?"

He said this hopefully, but Middleton replied: "I don't know, Mr. Mawson. I don't want to leave the firm. I'm not cut out to be a gentleman of leisure. I'd hoped . . . well, yes, I'd kind of hoped to go on as I was going on before I got that letter."

"A young man with a fortune could travel, and see the world."

"There's plenty of time," said Middleton.

"Yes, that's the right attitude, that's the right attitude! Well, Middleton, if you think of staying with us, I am pretty sure that I can put you in the way of something more suitable to your changed circumstances. You might think this over, Middleton. I have a letter here from Lord Herring, who has, I may say, a certain confidence in my judgment. We propose to establish an office in Sydney, Australia. Lord Herring has asked me to nominate a candidate for the post of manager of the Sydney branch. I instantly thought of you, Middleton, in that connection. I noticed, in the letter you were so good as to let me read, that your poor uncle was an Australian. It is a position of trust, of course, and of some responsibility, so that your being a man of substance would militate strongly in your favour. Your record in the office being what it is I have not the slightest doubt that if you were agreeable I could positively promise you our Sydney office. What do you think, Middleton?"

Middleton did not think: he uttered a curious exclamation – *Huk!* – and shook his head incredulously. Mr. Mawson continued: "The climate, I am told, is excellent. The city is bright and gay, Middleton, so that there is no lack of . . . of discreet enjoyment. The salary starts at £650 a year, plus bonuses. The business would be exclusively mail order, to begin with. It seems to me that this position is cut and dried for you, Middleton. There is a career in it. We must expand, expand, Middleton. In two years, three years, five years, the manager of the Sydney office, if he is attentive to his business – which I know you are – he should draw fifteen hundred pounds a year, or more. Would you like to try it? If so, I can definitely promise it, for Lord Herring wants a London man out there (our Australian cousins speak in a sort of London accent, as you must know) and has entrusted me with the selection. What do you say?"

"Well ... Why, thank you very much, sir ... yes!" said Middleton.

Mr. Mawson shook him by the hand, and said: "Excellent! I'll write a letter to Manchester this very minute. I dare say you'll have many matters to attend to. Take any time you need. Have you any suggestions as to who might be eligible to fill your place in the office here?"

"Mr. Woolley?" said Middleton, at random.

"An excellent idea. Now I'll write to his Lordship, and you run along. Ah, what opportunities open themselves before you, Middleton!"

"I shall do my best," said Middleton, "and I'm very grateful."

"Not at all, not at all. Let us arrange to have a bite to eat together soon, eh?"

Middleton went blindly back to his desk, cursing his fate. He had always thought of Australia as a sun-baked land soaked in the exotic. If Louisa failed to keep back the cheque he had given to Jack Duck, he was out in the dusty street. He had forgotten what it felt like to be rich: he wanted nothing but the Australian office. Seeing his face the chief clerk said: "Sorry, old fellow. Got the boot?"

"Not yet," said Middleton. He wanted to say that he was the new manager of the Sydney office at a salary of £650 a year plus bonuses and etceteras; but he said nothing more. He could not work, so he went out to drink tea, and everybody said: "Poor old Middleton has got the bullet ... poor old Middleton has got the sack ... poor old Middleton, it's a pity ..."

In a teashop near Cheapside, Middleton prayed: *Oh God, let Louie dear hold Mr. Duck off just for a month!* He thought, vaguely, of going to the bank and pleading with the manager; but he had no more strength or courage, so he sat and waited for Louisa. A miserable silence seemed to have fallen on the City. Time flowed muddy and slow. Middleton waited, not daring to hope.

* * * * *

As soon as she left Middleton, Louisa hurried to the "Hero of Waterloo".

"Not open till eleven-thirty," said an old woman who was polishing the scratched mahogany bar.

"I don't want to come in," said Louisa, "I want to speak to Mr. Duck."

"'E's out. I mean, 'e's not in. 'E went out. Won't be back till twelve."

"Any idea where I could find him?"

"That I don't know. I mean, I couldn't say. Monday morning Mr. Duck goes to the bank."

"D'you know what bank?"

"No. The bank. 'E'll be back by twelve, though, dear."

Poor old Ted, him and his dreams about kites, the poor old darling, Louisa thought, sitting in their little flat and listening to the urgent tinny ticking of the alarm-clock. *My poor old Ted. What wouldn't I do to take this off his poor old mind!* She remembered a story she had read about a woman who sold her hair and her teeth to get money for her child. But Louisa's hair was ordinary brown hair cut short; and her teeth, although they were even and white, were commonplace teeth. *I'd gladly sell them if anybody would buy them, though,* she said, running a thumb over the smooth, clean white incisors. At a quarter to twelve she rubbed off her lipstick with a handkerchief because she wanted to appear pathetic, and went back to the "Hero of Waterloo".

Mrs. Duck was behind the bar. Her husband, she said, with a suspicious glance, had gone to the bank, and there was no telling when Jack Duck would get home on Monday when he went to the bank.

"Could I have a lemonade?" said Louisa.

Then a man said: "Looking for me, I suppose, eh, Mrs. Middleton?" and she turned and saw the bookmaker, Joe Gutkes, accompanied by a stocky, scarred man tightly buttoned into a green-and-black dog-tooth check suit.

"Oh my goodness, yes!" said Louisa, remembering Middleton's mad bet.

"Luck o' the game, luck 'o the game," said Joe Gutkes to the scarred man. "Lady's hubby put ten quid on Little Sneeze. What do you think of that, Shiv?"

Shiv laughed and said: "Better luck next time, eh, Joe?"

"I gave him fifties," said Gutkes, "fifty to one."

Louisa was going to say that Middleton would pay sometime, when Gutkes said: "You know me, lady – Joe Gutkes – straight as a ruler, straight as a gun. Gutkes never owes. When Joe Gutkes wins, Joe Gutkes expects to be paid. When Gutkes loses Gutkes pays. My name is Joe Gutkes. Ever heard of it? I owe your old man five hundred smackers. You was here in this bar when he laid that bet. You come to collect? Joe Gutkes pays on the nail. I'll write you the kite on the spot," said the bookmaker, taking out a cheque book and a thick green fountain-pen. "Wait a minute – here's a funny thing. Look – I'll show you something. See this? Shiv just brought it in from one of my clients. Cash cheque for twenty pounds, signed by Edward Middleton. That'll be your husband's cheque, Mrs. Middleton, unless my eyes deceive me. Shiv just got it off of one of my clients. Well, there's life for you, ain't it? To-day to me to-morrow to thee; to-day to thee to-morrow to me. Marvellous! Your husband cashes a cheque with Jack Duck for twenty pounds. Jolly old Jack Duck pays some other party with this cheque for twenty pounds. This other party gives it over again to a third party to pay for some goods. This third party gives it to me to pay off twenty pounds worth of debt. And I give it over to you, to pay twenty pounds off of *my* debt to you. That makes you the fifth party, so catch hold. It's your husband's cheque so you needn't be afraid of it. That makes £480 I've got to give you."

"I don't understand," said Louisa, faintly.

"Here you are then, here you are – tell your mother and dear old pa – Joe Gutkes pays on the nail! The old firm, straight-as-a-die Joe Gutkes, the old firm!" said Gutkes, in his race-course bark. "Here you are then, £480 payable to Mr. Edward Middleton. And my cheque is as good as gold. Grab hold of it, lady, it won't bite and it won't bounce. . . . What's the matter?"

"I felt a little faint."

"It's the heat," said Joe Gutkes. "Have a glass of brandy. . . .

Go on, drink it up, it won't hurt you – Gutkes buys the best and nothing but the best . . ."

When she was gone he said to Shiv: "There you are, luck of the game. I don't mind telling you when that geezer put a tenner on Little Sneeze I thought the money was as good as in my pocket."

"You've got nothing to cry about, Joe, with all the money in the world on the favourite and the second favourite disqualified. You must have cleared two thousand on that race, so what's an odd monkey? Now! What about my commission?"

"How'll you have it, Shiv, cash or credit?"

"Credit," said Shiv, taking a folded pink newspaper out of his pocket. For Shiv, the collector, invariably gambled away his earnings, and was always in debt to his employers; and the more he was in debt, the more eloquent his indignation with unsportsmanlike debtors who gambled on credit.

So runs the world away.

Louisa met Middleton outside Sweetings.

"What happened?" he asked, frightened by the pallor of her face and the strange shining of her eyes.

"Oh Ted – that horse, that horse – the horse you went and put ten pounds on, on Saturday!"

"Oh my God! As if I didn't have enough without that! I'd forgotten all about it. It seems like a hundred years ago. Ten pounds on a horse!" cried Middleton, "ten *pounds* – on a *horse!*"

"I met Mr. Joe Gutkes———"

"Don't tell me. I know. He won't sue me, but he'll send somebody up to the office to talk to me. I know."

"No you don't, because look!" said Louisa, and showed him Joe Gutkes's cheque. "It won at fifty to one, and we've got five hundred pounds!"

*   *   *   *   *

They walked to St. Paul's and back, before Middleton was calm enough to talk coherently. Then he said: "We'd better bank this money at once, to meet that cheque."

"I forgot," said Louisa, opening her purse, "look, Ted – here it is."

"Come on in here and let's have something decent to eat,

Louie dear," said Middleton, leading her into Sweetings, "because all of a sudden I feel hollow."

"Me too, Teddykins. I feel I could eat a horse."

After Louisa had eaten one of her lamb cutlets, and Middleton had taken the fine edge off his hunger with the better half of a fillet steak, he put down his knife and fork suddenly and said: "I don't understand this. You say that Gutkes said this cheque changed hands five times. Now look. I gave Jack Duck this cheque and got twenty pounds in cash. Then Duck pays this cheque to number two. Number two pays it to number three, who pays it again to number four – who pays it back to me, number five. And here I am, Louie, with this bit of paper in my hand. I've had twenty pounds in cash, and five people have been paid twenty pounds apiece out of this bit of paper. Now look, Louie: I'm going to tear this cheque up."

Middleton tore the cheque into tiny pieces and mixed them in the ash-tray. Then he continued: "Now look, there's nothing. Well look here, Louie dear. How do you make this out? I've had twenty pounds in money. Parties number one, two, three, four and five, have been paid twenty pounds each. Five twenties are a hundred, and twenty makes one hundred-and-twenty. So it means to say that my cheque, which was nothing but a valueless bit of paper, has paid six people £120. It has paid me twenty pounds twice over! How would you work that out?"

"Oh, but it can't be, surely!"

"That's what I'd have thought. But it *must* be. It *is* so, Louie dear! My cheque was worth nothing, you'll admit that."

"I should say so!"

"For a cheque worth nothing I got twenty pounds. Paid into my hand. This cheque goes from hand to hand, five people get twenty pounds or twenty pounds worth each, the cheque comes back to me, and I tear it up, having had forty pounds out of it! Now where did all that money come from?"

"And there's £480 on top of it," said Louisa.

"Yes," said Middleton, nibbling a pencil and describing figures in the air with a forefinger, "yes, but what gets me is: *how did a hundred-and-twenty pounds in money or money's worth come out of nothing?*"

"There must be a catch in it somewhere," said Louisa. "Don't let's worry about it now. We've got enough to tide us over."

" – And that reminds me! You'll never guess what happened this morning. You can imagine what a state I was in when I got to the office. I don't mind telling you I'd half a mind not to go back at all. And then, when Mawson tells me to come along, well, my heart was . . ."

A quarter of an hour later Louisa said, with a great sigh: "Oh, Teddykins, Teddykins, you clever darling! *Australia!*"

"Have a glass of port," said Middleton.

"Well, Ted, just this once. But promise me – no more bottles of wine and no more gambling. Promise?"

"Promise, Louie dear. Look, it's just on two o'clock. Walk back with me to the office. I don't want it to look as though I was imposing on them."

On the way they met Trew, who, having eaten a cheese-and-tomato sandwich and a plate of tomato soup in a milk bar, was wretchedly hungry. Trew had been very humorous. With tremendous gusto, he told three junior clerks how he had telephoned an old lady in the middle of the night and asked: "Are you the woman who washes?" Shivering with cold and indignation the lady replied: "Certainly not!" Then Trew said: "Oh, you dirty old woman!" But when he tried to borrow five shillings until Friday the junior clerks looked at their watches and said that they had to be getting along; so that Trew had three-and-sixpence to see him through the week.

Louisa felt her husband's arm growing tense. She pinched it and whispered: "Don't do anything silly, Teddykins. Leave it to me, please!" She saw that Trew was trying to pretend that he had not seen them. "Hullo!" she cried.

"Oh – hullo. Didn't see you," said Trew. "Seen the lawyer?"

"We spent half the morning with him," said Louisa.

"Everything all right, Middy, old man?"

Louisa pinched Middleton's arm again and he, understanding, said: "Yes, Trewie, old boy, couldn't be better. Everything's in order. We talked to Mr. Charles Pismire."

"You did?"

"Yes. And another thing, over and above that," said Louisa.

"Do you remember Ted picking a horse and putting ten pounds on it? Little Sneeze – remember? Well, it came home at fifty to one. . . . Show him the cheque, Teddykins."

Taking Joe Gutkes's cheque out of his wallet, Middleton said: "Good luck never comes singly, Trewie, old boy, does it? What do you think of this – I've just been made manager of the new Australian office at £650 a year plus bonuses and expenses for a start."

"Eh?"

" – So it looks as though we won't have the pleasure of your company much longer," said Louisa. Then she jogged Middleton's arm, urging him forward, and they walked on, leaving Trew standing, stunned.

Louisa whispered: "He wrote that letter all right, Teddykins, but how are you going to prove it? And how is he going to find out that what we just said isn't the truth? He'll eat his heart up, don't you see? It'll just about kill him."

* * * * *

Trew did not die, as men who are mourned die. He faded, curdled, and grew silent. He will never make more than five pounds a week. But Middleton went with Louisa to Australia, where their son was born. One of the news magazines has printed a story about Edward Middleton of Coulton Utilities – the diligent, early-rising man; non-smoker, teetotaller, implacable enemy of gamblers, and inveterate Puritan. He is supposed to have a large private fortune, which he never touches. But whatever may be written, this is the true story behind the story.

THE END

RECENT AND FORTHCOMING TITLES FROM VALANCOURT BOOKS

Michael Arlen	Hell! said the Duchess
R. C. Ashby	He Arrived at Dusk
Frank Baker	The Birds
Charles Beaumont	The Hunger and Other Stories
	The Intruder
	A Touch of the Creature
Charles Birkin	The Smell of Evil
John Blackburn	A Scent of New-Mown Hay
	A Ring of Roses
	Children of the Night
	Nothing but the Night
	Bury Him Darkly
	Our Lady of Pain
Michael Blumlein	The Brains of Rats
Jack Cady	The Well
David Case	Among the Wolves
	Fengriffen
R. Chetwynd-Hayes	The Monster Club
	Looking for Something to Suck
Basil Copper	The Great White Space
	Necropolis
	The House of the Wolf
Frank De Felitta	The Entity
	Golgotha Falls
Lord Dunsany	The Curse of the Wise Woman
A. E. Ellis	The Rack
Barry England	Figures in a Landscape
Ronald Fraser	Flower Phantoms
Stephen Gilbert	Ratman's Notebooks
F. L. Green	Odd Man Out
Stephen Gregory	The Cormorant
	The Blood of Angels
Alex Hamilton	Beam of Malice
Thomas Hinde	The Day the Call Came
Claude Houghton	Neighbours
	I Am Jonathan Scrivener
Fred Hoyle	The Black Cloud
James Kennaway	The Mind Benders
Gerald Kersh	Nightshade and Damnations
Hilda Lewis	The Witch and the Priest

John Lodwick	Brother Death
Robert Marasco	Burnt Offerings
Gabriel Marlowe	I Am Your Brother
Michael McDowell	The Amulet
	Cold Moon Over Babylon
	The Elementals
John Metcalfe	The Feasting Dead
Oliver Onions	The Hand of Kornelius Voyt
Dennis Parry	The Survivor
Christopher Priest	The Affirmation
J.B. Priestley	Benighted
	The Magicians
Forrest Reid	Uncle Stephen
	Denis Bracknel
Philip Ridley	In the Eyes of Mr Fury
Andrew Sinclair	The Raker
	Gog
	The Facts in the Case of E. A. Poe
Colin Spencer	Panic
David Storey	Radcliffe
	Pasmore
	Saville
Michael Talbot	The Delicate Dependency
	The Bog
	Night Things
Bernard Taylor	The Godsend
	Sweetheart, Sweetheart
	The Moorstone Sickness
Russell Thorndike	The Slype
	The Master of the Macabre
John Trevena	Sleeping Waters
Hugh Walpole	The Killer and the Slain
Keith Waterhouse	There is a Happy Land
	Billy Liar
	Jubb
	Billy Liar on the Moon
Robert Westall	Antique Dust
Colin Wilson	Ritual in the Dark
	Man Without a Shadow
	The World of Violence
	Necessary Doubt
	The Glass Cage
	The Philosopher's Stone
	The God of the Labyrinth

WHAT CRITICS ARE SAYING ABOUT VALANCOURT BOOKS

"Valancourt are doing a magnificent job in making these books not only available but – in many cases – known at all . . . these reprints are well chosen and well designed (often using the original dust jackets), and have excellent introductions."

Times Literary Supplement (London)

"Valancourt Books champions neglected but important works of fantastic, occult, decadent and gay literature. The press's Web site not only lists scores of titles but also explains why these often obscure books are still worth reading. . . . So if you're a real reader, one who looks beyond the bestseller list and the touted books of the moment, Valancourt's publications may be just what you're searching for."

MICHAEL DIRDA, *Washington Post*

"Valancourt Books are fast becoming my favourite publisher. They have made it their business, with considerable taste and integrity, to put back into print a considerable amount of work which has been in serious need of republication. If you ever felt there were gaps in your reading experience or are simply frustrated that you can't find enough good, substantial fiction in the shops or even online, then this is the publisher for you."

MICHAEL MOORCOCK

"The best resurrectionists since Burke and Hare!"

ANDREW SINCLAIR

TO LEARN MORE AND TO SEE A COMPLETE LIST OF AVAILABLE TITLES, VISIT US AT VALANCOURTBOOKS.COM

Lightning Source UK Ltd.
Milton Keynes UK
UKHW012216271220
375841UK00003B/498